**W9-AOA-608**

# Mary,
# Mary

# Mary, Mary

A NOVEL BY

## James Patterson

LITTLE, BROWN AND COMPANY

NEW YORK    BOSTON

Little, Brown and Company
Time Warner Book Group
1271 Avenue of the Americas, New York, NY 10020
Visit our Web site at www.twbookmark.com

First Edition: November 2005

The characters and events in this book are fictitious. Any similarity to
real persons, living or dead, is coincidental and not intended by the
author.

Information on locations included in the book provided by
aolcityguide.com.

Library of Congress Cataloging-in-Publication Data

Patterson, James.
  Mary, Mary : a novel / by James Patterson. — 1st ed.
    p. cm.
  ISBN 0-316-15976-X
  1. Cross, Alex (Fictitious character) — Fiction.  2. African American psychologists —
Fiction.  3. Actresses — Crimes against — Fiction.  4. Government investigators —
Fiction.  5. Los Angeles (Calif.) — Fiction.  6. Serial murders — Fiction.  I. Title.
PS3566.A822M37  2005                                    2005005736
813'.54 — dc22

10 9 8 7 6 5 4 3 2 1

QFF

Printed in the United States of America

*This one is for my buds — Johnny, Frankie, Ned, Jim and Jim, Steve, Mike, Tom and Tom, Merrill, David, Peter, B.J., Del, Hal, Ron, Mickey and Bobby, Joe, Art.*

*And it's for Mary Jordan, who makes it all work somehow, and who couldn't be more different from the notorious Mary, Mary.*

## Prologue

# THE STORYTELLER

# Chapter 1

*ACT ONE, SCENE ONE,* the Storyteller thought to himself, and couldn't hold back a dizzying rush of anticipation. The truth was that ordinary people committed perfect crimes and perfect murders all the time. But you didn't hear about it for the simple reason that the killers never got caught.

And neither would he, of course. That was a given in the story he was about to tell.

Which didn't mean that today wasn't nerve-racking. Actually, this was the most intense moment in the past couple of insane years for him. He was ready to kill somebody, a complete stranger, and he had figured out that New York City was the right place for his first.

It *almost* happened just outside a basement restroom in Bloomingdale's, but he didn't feel right about the location.

Too crowded, even at half past ten in the morning.

Too noisy, and yet not noisy enough to provide the proper distraction.

Plus, he didn't like the idea of trying to escape out onto the unfamiliar territory of Lexington Avenue, or especially down into the claustrophobic IRT subway tunnels. When it felt right, he'd know it, and act accordingly.

So the Storyteller moved on and decided to catch a flick at the Sutton Theater on East 57th Street, a funky, run-down place that had obviously seen better days.

Maybe *this* was a good place for a murder. He liked the irony, even if he was the only one who got it. Yes, maybe this was going to work out great, he thought as he sat in one of the two small auditoriums inside.

He began to watch *Kill Bill Volume 2* with seven other Tarantino aficionados.

Which one of these unsuspecting people would be his victim? You? You? You there? The Storyteller spun the tale inside his head.

There were two loudmouths in identical New York Yankees baseball caps, worn backward, of course. The irritating morons didn't shut up once through the interminable ads and trailers. They both deserved to die.

So did an atrociously dressed elderly couple, who didn't talk to each other at all, not once in fifteen minutes before the houselights went down. Killing them would be a good deed, almost a public service.

A fragile-looking woman, early forties, seemed to be having the shakes two rows in front of the moldy oldies. Bothering no one — except him.

And then a big black dude with his sneakered feet up on the seat in front of him. Rude, inconsiderate bastard in his old-school Converses that must have been at least size fourteens.

Next, a black-bearded movie nerd who probably had seen the movie a dozen times already and worshipped Quentin Tarantino, of course.

Turned out, it was the bearded wonder who got up about halfway through the movie, just after Uma Thurman was buried alive. Jesus, who could walk out on that classic scene?

Duty-bound, he followed, a couple of seconds behind. Out into the dingy hall, then into the men's room, which was located near theater two.

He was actually shaking now. Was this it? His moment? His first murder? The beginning of everything he'd dreamed about for months? Make that *years*.

He was pretty much on autopilot, trying not to think about anything except doing this right, then getting in and out of the movie theater without anybody noticing his face or too much else about him.

The bearded guy was standing at the urinal, which was kind of good news, actually. The shot was nicely framed and art-directed.

Wrinkled, grungy black T-shirt that said NYU FILM SCHOOL with a clapsticks logo on the back. Reminded him of a character out of a Daniel Clowes comic book, and that graphic shit was *hot* right now.

"And . . . *action!*" he said.

Then he shot the poor bearded loser in the back of the head, watched him drop like a heavy sack to the bathroom floor. Lie there — nothing moving. The blast roared through his head in the tiled room, louder than he'd dreamed it would be.

"Hey — what the? What happened? *Hey!*" he heard, and the Storyteller whirled around as if there was an audience watching him in the men's room.

Two guys from the Sutton Theater crew had entered behind him. They must have been curious about the noise. And how much had they seen?

"Heart attack," he said, blurted it out, tried to sound convincing. "Man just fell over at the urinal. Help me get him up. Poor guy. He's bleeding!"

No panic, no affect, no second thoughts whatsoever. Everything was pure instinct now, right, wrong, or indifferent.

He raised his gun and shot both theater workers as they stood walleyed and dorky at the door. He shot them again when they were down on the floor. Just to be careful. Professional.

And now he was really shaking, legs like J-E-L-L-O, but trying to walk very calmly out of the men's room.

Then out of the Sutton Theater onto 57th, heading east on foot. Everything outside feeling completely unreal and otherworldly, everything so *bright* and *brassy*.

He'd done it. He'd killed three people instead of just one. His first *three* murders. It was just practice, but he'd done it, and you know what? He could do it again.

"Practice makes perfect," the Storyteller whispered under his breath as he hurried toward his car — his getaway car, right? God, this was the best feeling of his life. Of course, that didn't say much for his life up to now, did it?

But watch out from here on, just watch out.

*For Mary, Mary, quite contrary.*

Of course, he was the only one who got *that*. So far, anyway.

# Chapter 2

*YOU THINK YOU CAN KILL again in cold blood?* he asked himself many times after the New York murders.

*You think you can stop this now that you've started? You think?*

The Storyteller waited — almost five months of self-torture, also known as discipline, or professionalism, or maybe cowardice — until it was his time.

Then, he arrived in the kill zone again, and this time it wasn't going to be practice. This was the real deal, and it wasn't a stranger who was going to die.

He was just a face in the crowd at the 3:10 showing of *The Village* at the Westwood Village Theater in Los Angeles. There were a number of patrons, which was good news for him and, he supposed, for the film's star director, M. Night Shyamalan. What kind of name was that? M. Night? Self-conscious phony.

Apparently Patrice Bennett was among the last people in town to see the horror film. Also, Patrice actually deigned to sit in a real movie theater, with real ticket-buyers, for her movie fix. How quaint was that? Well, she was famous for it, wasn't she? It was Patrice's shtick. She'd even bought her ticket ahead of time, which was how he knew she'd be there.

So this wasn't target practice anymore, and everything had to be just right, and it would be. Never a doubt. The story was already written in his head.

For one thing, he couldn't be spotted by anyone in the theater. So he went to the twelve-o'clock; then, when the show let out, he waited around in a bathroom stall until the 3:10. Nail-biting, nerve-thwacking ordeal, but not that bad really. Especially since if he was spotted, he'd simply abort the mission.

But the Storyteller wasn't seen — at least he didn't think so — and he didn't see anyone he knew.

Now, the theater had more than a hundred viewers, or rather, *suspects,* right? At least a dozen of them were perfect for his purposes.

Most important — his gun had a silencer now. Something he'd learned from the thrill-packed run-through in New York City.

Patrice sat in the balcony. *Works for me, Patsy,* he thought. *You're being way too thoughtful, especially for you, you über-bitch.*

He was watching her from across the aisle and a few rows behind. This was so delicious — he wanted the luxurious anticipation of revenge to go on and on. Except that he also wanted to pull the trigger and get the hell out of the

Westwood theater before something went wrong. But what could go wrong, right?

When Joaquin Phoenix got stabbed by Adrien Brody, he calmly rose from his seat and went directly to Patrice's aisle. He never hesitated for an instant.

"Excuse me. Sorry," he said, and started to make his way past her, actually *over* her bare, skinny legs, which weren't very impressive for such an important woman in Hollywood.

"Jesus Christ, will you watch it," she complained, which was just like her, so unnecessarily nasty and imperial-sounding.

"Not exactly who *you* can expect to see next. Not *Jesus*," he quipped, and wondered if Patrice got his little joke. Probably not. Studio heads didn't get subtlety.

He shot her twice — once in the heart and once right between her totally shocked, blown-away eyes. There was no such thing as too dead when it came to this kind of power-mad psycho. Patrice could probably come back at you from the grave, like that reverse trapdoor ending in the original *Carrie,* Stephen King's first story to reach the silver screen.

Then he made his perfect escape.

*Just like in the movies, hey.*

The story had begun.

## Part One

# THE "MARY SMITH" MURDERS

# Chapter 3

To: agriner@latimes.com
From: Mary Smith

Arnold Griner squeezed his small, squinty eyes shut, put his hands over his practically hairless skull, and scrubbed his scalp hard. *Oh, God save me, not another one,* he was thinking. *Life is too short for this shit. I can't take it. I really can't take this Mary Smith deal.*

The *L.A. Times* newsroom buzzed around him as if it were any other morning: phones jangling; people coming and going like indoor race walkers; someone nearby pontificating about the new fall TV lineup — as if anybody cared about the TV lineup these days.

How could Griner feel so vulnerable sitting at his own desk, in his cubicle office, in the middle of all *this*? But he did.

The Xanax he'd been popping since the first Mary Smith e-mail a week ago did absolutely nothing to hold back the spike of panic that shot through him like the needle used in a spinal tap.

Panic — but also morbid curiosity.

Maybe he was "just" an entertainment columnist, but Arnold Griner knew a huge news story when he saw one. A blockbuster that would dominate the front page for weeks. *Someone rich and famous had just been murdered in L.A.* He didn't even have to read the e-mail to know that much. "Mary Smith" had already proved herself to be one sick lady and true to her word.

The questions attacking his brain were who had been killed this time? and what the hell was he, Griner, doing in the middle of this awful mess?

*Why me of all people? There has to be a good reason, and if I knew it, then I'd really be freaking, wouldn't I?*

As he dialed 911 with a badly shaking hand, he clicked open Mary Smith's message with the other. *Please, God, no one I know. No one I like.*

He began to read, even though everything inside told him not to. He really couldn't help himself. *Oh, God! Antonia Schifman! Oh, poor Antonia. Oh no, why her? Antonia was one of the good people, and there weren't too many of those.*

To: Antonia Schifman:

I guess you could call this anti-fan mail, although I *used* to be a fan.

Anyhow, 4:30 in the morning is awfully early

for a brilliant, three-time Academy Award winner
and mother of four to leave the house and her
children, don't you think? I suppose it's the
price we pay for being who we are. Or at least
it's one of them.

I was there this morning to show you *another*
downside of fame and fortune in Beverly Hills.

It was pitch-black dark when the driver came
to take you to "the set." There's a sacrifice you
make that your fans don't begin to appreciate.

I walked right in the front gates behind the
car and followed him up the driveway.

Suddenly, I had the feeling that your driver
had to die if I wanted to get to you, but still,
there wasn't any pleasure in killing him. I was
too nervous for that, shaking like a sapling in
a fierce storm.

The gun was actually trembling in my hand
when I knocked on his window. I kept it hidden
behind my back and told him you'd be down in a
few minutes.

"No problem," he said. And you know what? He
barely even looked at me. Why should he? You are
the star of stars, fifteen million a picture
I've read. I was just the maid as far as he was
concerned.

It felt like I was playing a bit part in one
of your movies, but trust me, I was planning to
steal this scene.

I knew I had to do something pretty dramatic soon. He was going to wonder why I was still standing there. I didn't know if I'd be too scared to do it if he actually looked at me. But then he did — and everything just happened.

I shoved the gun into his face and pulled the trigger. Such a tiny action, almost a reflex. A second later, he was dead, just blown away. I could do pretty much whatever I wanted to now.

So I walked around to the passenger side, climbed inside the car, and waited for you. Nice, nice car. So plush and comfortable, with leather, soft lighting, a bar and small refrigerator stocked with all your favorites. *Twix bars, Antonia? Shame, shame.*

In a way, it was too bad you came out of the house so soon. I liked being in your limo. The quiet time, the luxury. In those few minutes, I could see why you would want to be who you are. Or at least, who you were.

My heart is beating faster just writing this, remembering the moment.

You stood outside the car for a second before you opened the door for yourself. Dressed down, without makeup, yet still breathtaking. You couldn't see me or the dead driver through the one-way glass. But I could see you. That's how it's been all week, Antonia. I've been right there and you've never noticed me.

What an incredible moment this was for me!

Me, inside your car. You, outside, in a tweed jacket that made you look very Irish and down-to-earth.

When you got in, I immediately locked the doors and put down the partition. You got this amazing look on your face the second you saw me. I'd seen that same look before — *in your movies, when you pretended to be afraid.*

What you probably didn't realize was that I was just as scared as you. My whole body was quivering. My teeth were hitting together. That's why I shot you before either of us could say anything.

The moment went by way too fast, but I had planned on that. That's what the knife was for. I just hope it isn't your children who find you. I wouldn't want them to see you that way. All they need to know is that Mommy is gone, and she's not coming back.

Those poor children — Andi, Tia, Petra, Elizabeth.

They're the ones I feel so sorry for. Poor, poor babies without their mommy. Could anything be sadder?

I know something that is — but that's *my* secret, and no one will ever know.

# Chapter 4

MARY SMITH'S ALARM CLOCK went off at 5:30 A.M., but she was already awake. Wide awake, thinking about, of all things, how to make a porcupine costume for her daughter Ashley's school play. *What would she possibly use for porcupine needles?*

It had been quite a late night, but she never seemed to be able to shut off the mental ticker tape that was her "to do" list.

They needed more peanut butter, Kid's Crest, Zyrtec syrup, and one of those little bulbs for the bathroom nightlight. Brendan had soccer practice at three, which started at the same time as — and fifteen miles away from — Ashley's tap class. Figure that one out. Adam's sniffles could have gone either way in the night, and Mary *could not* afford another sick day. Speaking of which, she needed to put in for some second shifts at her job.

And this was the *quiet* part of the day. It wasn't long before she was at the stove, calling out orders and fielding the usual spate of morning-time needs.

"Brendan, help your sister tie her shoes, please. Brendan, I'm talking to you."

"Mommy, my socks feel weird."

"Turn them inside out."

"Can I take Cleo to school? Can I please? Please, Mommy? Oh, please?"

"Yes, but you'll have to get her out of the dryer. Brendan, what did I ask you to do?"

Mary expertly flipped a portion of perfectly fluffed scrambled eggs onto each of their plates just as the bread in the four-slice toaster popped up.

*"Breakfast!"*

While the two older ones dug in, she took Adam to his room and dressed him in his red overalls and a sailor shirt. She cooed to him as she carried him back out to his high chair.

"Who's the handsomest sailor in town? Who's my little man?" she asked, and tickled him under his chinny-chin-chin.

*"I'm* your little man," Brendan said with a smile. "I am, Mommy!"

"You're my *big* little man," Mary returned, chucking him lightly under the chin. She squeezed his shoulders. "And getting bigger every day."

"That's 'cause I clean my plate," he said, chasing the last bit of egg onto a fork with the flat of his thumb.

"You're a good cook, Mommy," Ashley said.

"Thank you, sweetheart. Now come on, let's go. B.B.W.W."

While she cleared the dishes, Brendan and Ashley marched back down the hallway in a singsong chant. "Brush, brush, wash, wash. Teeth and hair, hands and face. Brush, brush, wash, wash . . ."

While the older two washed up, she put the dishes into the sink for later; gave Adam's face a quick once-over with a wet paper towel; took the kids' lunches, packed the night before, out of the fridge; and dropped each one into the appropriate knapsack.

"I'm going to put Adam into his car seat," she called out. "Last one outside is a googly worm."

Mary hated the rotten-egg thing, but she knew the value of a little innocent competition for keeping the kids in gear. She could hear them squealing in their rooms, half laughing, half scared they'd be the last one out the door and into her old jalopy. *Gawd, who said* jalopy *anymore? Only Mary, Mary. And who said* Gawd?

As she strapped Adam in, she tried to remember what it was that had kept her up so late the night before. The days — and now the nights as well — seemed to blur all together in a jumble of cooking, cleaning, driving, list-making, nose-wiping, and more driving. L.A. definitely had its major-league disadvantages. It seemed as if they spent half their lives in the car, stalled in traffic.

She should really get something more fuel efficient than the big old Suburban she had brought west.

She looked at her watch. Somehow, ten minutes had gone

by. Ten precious minutes. How did that always happen? How did she seem to *lose* time?

She ran back to the front door and ushered Brendan and Ashley outside. "What is taking you two so long? We're going to be late again. Jeezum crow, just look at the time," said Mary Smith.

# Chapter 5

HERE WE WERE, smack in the middle of an age of angry and cynical myth-busting, and suddenly I was being called "America's Sherlock Holmes" in one of the country's more influential, or at least best-read, magazines. What a complete crock that was, and it was still bugging me that morning. An investigative journalist named James Truscott had decided to follow me around and report on the murder cases I was working on. I'd fooled him, though. I'd gone on vacation with the family.

"I'm going to Disneyland!" I told Truscott and laughed the last time I'd seen him in D.C. The writer had only smirked in response.

For anyone else, maybe a vacation was an ordinary thing. Happened all the time, twice a year sometimes. For the Cross family, it was a major event, a new beginning.

Appropriately, "A Whole New World" was playing in the hotel lobby as we passed through.

"Come on, you pokes!" Jannie urged us as she ran ahead. Damon, newly minted teenager, was somewhat more reserved. He stuck close and held the door for Nana as we passed from air-conditioned comfort out into bright Southern California sunshine.

Actually, it was a full-out attack on the senses from the moment we left the hotel. Scents of cinnamon, fried dough, and some kind of zingy Mexican food reached our noses all at the same time. I could also hear the distant roar of a freight train, or so it seemed, along with screams of terror — the good kind, the "don't stop" kind. I'd heard enough of the other kind to appreciate the difference.

Against all odds, I had put in for vacation, been approved, and actually gotten out of town before FBI Director Burns or his people came up with a half-dozen reasons why I couldn't go away at this time. The kids' first choice had been Disneyworld and Epcot Village in Florida. For my own reasons, and also since it was hurricane season down South, I steered us to Disneyland and their newest park, Disney's California Adventure.

"California, indeed." Nana Mama shaded her eyes from the sun glare. "I haven't seen a naturally occurring thing since we arrived here, Alex. Have you?"

She pursed her lips and pulled down the corners of her mouth, but then she couldn't help laughing, putting herself in stitches. That's Nana. She almost never laughs at other people — she laughs with them.

"You can't fool me, old woman. You just love to see us all together. Anywhere, anyhow, anytime. We could be in Siberia for all you'd care."

She brightened. "Now, *Siberia*. That's somewhere I *would* like to see. A trip on the Trans-Siberian Railroad, the Sayany Mountains, Lake Baikal. You know, it wouldn't kill American children to take a vacation once in a while where they actually learned something about another culture."

I rolled my eyes in Damon and Jannie's direction. "Once a teacher . . ."

"Always a teacher," Jannie said.

"Always a tee-cha," repeated Little Alex. He was three years old, and our own little myna bird. We got to see him too infrequently, and I was partially amazed by everything he did. His mother had taken him back to Seattle more than a year ago. The painful custody struggles between Christine and me were still dragging on.

Nana's voice cut through my thoughts. "Where do we go fir —"

"Soarin' Over California!" Jannie had it out before Nana was even finished asking the question.

Damon chimed in. "Okay, but then we're hitting California Screamin'."

Jannie stuck her tongue out convivially at her brother, and he gently hip-checked her in return. It was like Christmas morning for these two — even the disagreements were mostly in fun.

"Sounds like a plan," I said. "And then we'll hit *It's Tough to Be a Bug!* for your little brother."

I scooped up Alex Junior in my arms and held him close, kissed both of his cheeks. He looked back at me with his peaceable little smile.

Life was good again.

# Chapter 6

THAT WAS WHEN I SAW James Truscott approaching, all six foot five of him, with waves of red hair hanging down over the shoulders of a black leather jacket.

Somehow, some way, Truscott had gotten his editors in New York to agree to do a continuing series on me, based on my track record for getting involved with high-profile murder cases on a fairly regular basis. Maybe it was because the last one, involving the Russian Mafiya, had been the worst case of my career and also very high-profile. I had taken the liberty of doing some research on Truscott. He was only thirty, educated at Boston University. His specialty was true crime, and he'd published two nonfiction books on the mafia. A phrase I'd heard about him stuck in my head: He plays dirty.

"Alex," he said, smiling and extending his hand as if we were old friends meeting by chance. Reluctantly, I shook hands with Truscott. It wasn't that I disliked him, or objected to his right to write whatever stories he wanted to, but he had already intruded into my life in ways that I felt were inappropriate — like writing daily e-mails and arriving at crime scenes, and even at our house in D.C. Now, here he was, showing up on our family vacation.

"Mr. Truscott," I said in a quiet voice, "you know I've declined to cooperate with these articles."

"No problem." He grinned. "I'm cool with that."

"I'm not," I said. "I'm officially off the clock. This is family time. Can you give us some space? We're at Disneyland."

Truscott nodded as though he understood completely, but then he said, "Your vacation will be interesting to our readers. The calm-before-the-storm kind of thing. This is great! Disneyland is perfect. You have to understand that, right?"

"I don't!" Nana said, and stepped toward Truscott. "Your right to stick out your arm ends at the other person's nose. You ever hear that wise bit of advice, young man? Well, you should have. You know, you have some kind of nerve being here."

Just then, though, I caught something even more disturbing out of the corner of my eye — a movement that didn't fit the circumstances: a woman in black, slowly circling to our left.

She had a digital camera and was already taking pictures of us — of my family. Of Nana confronting Truscott.

I shielded the kids as best I could, and then I really lit into James Truscott. "Don't you dare photograph my kids!" I said. "Now you and your girlfriend get out of here. Please, go."

Truscott raised his hands over his head, smiled cockily,

and then backed away. "I have rights, just like you, Dr. Cross. And she's not my fucking girlfriend. She's a colleague. This is all business. It's a story."

"Right," I said. "Well, just get out of here. This little boy is three years old. I don't want my family's story in a magazine. Not now, not ever."

# Chapter 7

WE ALL TRIED TO FORGET about James Truscott and his photographer for a while after that. Did pretty good, too. After umpteen different rides, a live show starring Mickey Mouse, two snacks, and countless carnival games, I dared to suggest that we head back to the hotel.

"For the pool?" Damon asked, grinning. We had glimpsed the five-thousand-square-foot Never Land Pool on our way to breakfast early that morning.

When I got to the front desk, there was a message waiting, one that I was expecting. Inspector Jamilla Hughes of the San Francisco Police Department was in town and needed a meeting with me. *ASAP, if not sooner,* said the note. *That means move it, buster.*

I gave my smiling regrets to the pool sharks and took my leave of them. After all, I was on vacation, too.

"Go get 'em, Daddy," Jannie ribbed me. "It's Jamilla, right?" Damon gave a thumbs-up and a smile from behind the fogged lens of a snorkel mask.

I crossed the grounds from the Disneyland Hotel to the Grand Californian, where I had booked another room. This place was an entirely American Arts and Crafts affair, much more sedate than our own hotel.

I passed through stained-glass doors into a soaring lobby. Redwood beams rose six floors overhead, and Tiffany lamps dotted the lower level, which centered on an enormous field-stone fireplace.

I barely noticed any of it, though. I was already thinking about Inspector Hughes up in room 456.

Amazing — I was on vacation.

# Chapter 8

JAMILLA GREETED ME at the door, lips first, a delicious kiss that warmed me from head to toe. I didn't get to see much of her wraparound baby-blue blouse and black pencil skirt until we pulled apart. Black sling-back heels put her at just about the right height for me. She sure didn't look like a homicide cop today.

"I just got in," she said.

"Just in time," I murmured, reaching for her again. Jamilla's kisses were always like coming home. I started to wonder where all this was going, but then I stopped myself. *Just let it be, Alex.*

"Thanks for the flowers," she whispered against my ear. "*All* of the flowers. They're absolutely beautiful. I know, I know, not as beautiful as me."

I laughed out loud. "That's true."

I could see over her shoulder that the hotel's concierge,

Harold Larsen, had done a good job for me. Rose petals were scattered in a swath of red, peach, and white. I knew there were a dozen long-stems on the bedside table, a bottle of Sauvignon Blanc in the minifridge, and a couple of carefully chosen CDs in the stereo — best of Al Green, Luther Ingram, Tuck and Patti's *Tears of Joy*, some early Alberta Hunter.

"I guess you really did miss me," Jamilla said.

Suddenly, the two of us were like one body, my mouth exploring hers, my hands holding her up from the rear. She already had my shirt half unbuttoned, and then I was reaching down her side for the zipper on her skirt. We kissed again, and her mouth was so fresh and sweet, like it always was.

" 'If lovin' you is wrong, I don't want to be right,' " I sang in a half-whisper.

"Loving me isn't wrong." Jamilla smiled.

I danced her backward toward the bedroom.

"How do you do this in heels?" I asked along the way.

"You're right," she said, and kicked off her shoes even as her skirt slid to the floor.

"We should light these candles," I said. "You want me to light them?"

"Shhh, Alex. It's already warm enough in here."

"Yeah, it is."

There wasn't a whole lot of talking for a while after that. Jamilla and I always seemed to know what the other was thinking anyway — no conversation required at certain times. And I had missed her, even more than I thought I would.

We pressed hard against each other, chest to chest, breathing in a nice rhythm. I rose and hardened against her

31

leg, and I could feel moistness on my thigh. Then I reached up and held Jam's lovely face in both of my hands.

I felt as though she could hear my thoughts. She smiled, drinking in what I hadn't even said. "Is that so?" she finally whispered, then winked. We had shared the mind-reading joke before.

We kissed some more, and Jamilla breathed deeply as I slowly worked my lips over her neck, her breasts, and her stomach. Everywhere I stopped, I wanted to stay, but just as badly, I couldn't wait to move on. She wrapped her arms around my back and rolled us both over on the bed.

"How can you be so hard and so soft?" I asked.

"It's a woman thing. Just enjoy it. But I could say the same about you. Hard and soft?"

A moment later, I was inside Jamilla. She sat bolt upright, her head thrown back, her lower lip clenched tightly between her teeth. Sunlight reached through the bedroom window and slowly crossed her face. Absolutely gorgeous, all of it.

We climaxed together — one of those ideals that everyone says is just an ideal, but it's not, not always, anyway.

She lay lightly down on top of me, the air slowly escaping from her lungs, our bodies melding as they always did.

"You're going to be too tired for the rides tomorrow," she finally said and smiled.

"Speaking of rides . . . ," I said.

She started to laugh. "Promises, promises."

"But I always keep mine."

# Chapter 9

I DON'T REMEMBER when Jamilla and I eventually drifted off to sleep that afternoon, but I was woken up by my pager. My brand-new pager. The one I got especially for this trip so only a few people would have the number — John Sampson, Director Burns's assistant, Tony Woods, that's about it. Two people too many? So what now?

I groaned. "Sorry, sorry, Jam. I didn't expect this. I don't have to answer it." The last part I said halfheartedly. We both knew better.

Jamilla shook her head. "I'll tell you a little secret: I've got mine here in the nightstand. Go ahead, Alex, answer the call." *Yeah, answer the call.*

Sure enough, it was the director's office reaching out from D.C. I picked up the bedside phone and dialed the number while lying there flat on my back. I finally looked at my watch — 4:00 P.M. The day had flown, which was a good thing, sort of. Until now, anyway.

"Ron Burns," I mouthed to Jamilla while I was on hold. "This can't be good." This has to be bad.

She nodded. A call from the top of the pyramid had to mean some kind of serious business that couldn't wait. Whatever it was, I didn't want to hear about it right now.

Ron Burns himself came on the line. This was getting worse by the second. "Alex? Is that you?"

"Yes, sir." I sighed. Just Jamilla, and me, and you.

"I appreciate your taking this call. I'm sorry to be bothering you. I know it's been a while since your last real vacation."

He didn't know the half of it, but I kept quiet and listened to what the director had to say.

"Alex, there's kind of a sticky case in L.A. I probably would have wanted to send you out on this one anyway. The fact that you're in California is a lucky coincidence. Lucky, of course, being a relative concept."

I shook my head back and forth. This was sounding really bad.

"What's the case? This lucky coincidence that I'm out here?"

"You ever heard of Antonia Schifman?"

That got my attention a little. "The actress? Sure."

"She was murdered this morning, along with her limo driver. It happened outside her home. Her family was inside sleeping."

"The rest of the family — they're okay?" I asked.

"No one else was hurt, Alex. Just the actress and her driver."

I was a little confused. "Why is the Bureau on this? LAPD request a consult?"

"Not exactly." Burns paused. "If you wouldn't mind keeping this between the two of us, Antonia Schifman was friends with the president. And a close friend of his wife. The president has asked for our help on the murder investigation."

"Oh." I saw that Ron Burns wasn't quite as immune to Washington pressure as I had thought. Even so, he was the best thing that had happened to the FBI in a long time. And he'd already done me more than one favor in my short tenure. Of course, I had done him a few good turns, too.

"Alex, just do a quick in-and-out on this one. I'd really appreciate it. We'll have you back with your family for dinner. A late dinner, anyway. Just check out the murder scene for me. I want to hear your take on what happened. I took the liberty — they're waiting for you to get there."

I finished the call and cast a look at Jamilla. "Well, the good news is, I don't have to fly anywhere. It's something in L.A. The actress Antonia Schifman was murdered today."

She pushed up next to me in bed. "Oh, that's terrible, Alex. I liked her movies. She always seemed nice. That's really a shame. Well, at least I'll get to dish with Nana and the kids while you're out of earshot."

"I'll meet you all back here for dinner. Might be a little late."

"My flight's not until eleven, Alex. But I have to be on the late flight out."

I kissed her, just a little sheepishly, ashamed that I'd given in to Burns. But what choice did I have?

"Go make California safe — safer," she said. "I'll keep an eye on Mickey and Donald to make sure they don't go postal."

What a thought.

# Chapter 10

THE STORYTELLER DROVE right by the Schifman murder scene, *right by the crime scene.* He knew he shouldn't have come out here again, but he couldn't help himself. In a way, he thought this might even be a good idea. So he stopped his car and got out to look around.

What an incredible rush it turned out to be. He knew the house, knew the ritzy neighborhood in Beverly Hills really well — Miller Place. Suddenly, he almost couldn't catch his breath, and he loved the feeling of danger, of "anything can happen now!" And it definitely could. He *was* the Storyteller, after all.

The press was everywhere, along with the LAPD, of course, and even some police brass, and he'd had to park about a quarter of a mile away. That was fine with him — safer, smarter. A minute or so later, he joined in with fans and other lookyloos making the pilgrimage to the shrine where poor Antonia had checked out of the rat race this morning.

"I can't believe she's dead," a young couple was saying as they walked arm in arm, heads bowed as if they'd lost a real loved one. What was with some people? Could anybody be this nuts?

*I can believe she's dead,* he wanted to tell them. *First, I put one in her head; then I hacked her face until her own mother wouldn't recognize her. Believe it or not, there's even a method to my madness. There is a grand plan, and it's a beauty.*

But he didn't speak to the creepy bereaved, just made his way to the pearly gates of the Schifman house. He stood there respectfully with the others — probably a couple of hundred mourners. The Beverly Hills sideshow was just getting started, just getting warmed-up.

Man, this was some huge story, and guess what? Not one of these reporters had the *real* story. Not about Antonia — and not about her murder.

Only he did — he was the only person in L.A. who knew what had happened, where it was going, and it felt pretty good to be in the know.

"Hey, howya doin'?" he heard. The Storyteller froze, then turned slowly to see who was talking to him.

He recognized the guy's face but not exactly who the hell it was. *Where do I know this jerk from?*

"Jeez, I was just passin' by. Heard what had happened on the radio. So I stopped to pay my respects, or whatever this is. What a shame, some tragedy, huh? This crazy world out here, you just never know," said the Storyteller, realizing he was babbling a little bit.

38

The other guy said, "No, you never do. Who the hell would want to kill Antonia Schifman? What kind of maniac? What kind of complete lunatic?"

"Out here in L.A.," said the Storyteller, "it could be anybody, right?"

# Chapter 11

FIFTEEN MINUTES AFTER the call from D.C., a black Grand Marquis was waiting for me outside the Disneyland Hotel. I shook my head in disappointment, but also in anger — this sucked in a way that broke new territory.

The FBI agent standing next to the car wore a pair of neatly pressed khakis and a pale-blue polo shirt. He looked ready for a round of golf at the Los Angeles Country Club. His handshake was vigorous, and a little too eager.

"Special Agent Karl Page. I'm really glad to meet you, Dr. Cross. I've read your book," he said. "Couple of times."

He couldn't have been long out of the Academy at Quantico from the look of him. The California tan and nearly white blond flattop suggested that he was a local boy. Probably in his midtwenties. An eager beaver for sure.

"Thank you," I said. "Exactly where are we headed, Agent Page?"

# Chapter 12

HERE WE GO AGAIN. . . . The president has asked for our help. . . . I want to hear your take on what happened. My take? That was a laugh. My take was that I was being used and I didn't like it. Also, I hated it when I whined like this.

We took the Santa Ana Freeway into downtown Los Angeles and then the Hollywood Freeway back out again. Agent Page drove with a kind of automatic aggressiveness, passing cars closely and frequently. One cell-phone-using business-man took his other hand off the wheel long enough to give us the finger.

Page seemed oblivious to all of this as he sped north-ward and told me what else he knew about the grisly double murder.

Both Antonia Schifman and her driver, Bruno Capaletti, had been shot somewhere between 4:00 and 5:30 in the morning. A gardener had discovered the bodies around 7:15.

Schifman's beautiful face had also been slashed with a sharp blade of some kind.

Apparently no money or other valuables had been taken. Bruno Capaletti was found with almost two hundred dollars in his pocket, and Schifman's handbag was still in the limo next to her body. It held credit cards, diamond earrings, and more cash.

"Any prior connection between the two of them?" I asked. "Schifman and the limo driver? What do we know about the two of them?"

"The only other movie of hers Capaletti worked on was *Banner Season,* but he drove for Jeff Bridges on that one. We're still checking the driver out, though. You ever see *Banner Season*?"

"No, I didn't. How hot is the crime scene? Our people, LAPD, the media? Anything else I should know before we arrive?"

"I haven't actually been there yet," Page admitted. "But it's probably going to be off the charts. I mean, it's Antonia Schifman, you know? She was a really good actress. Supposed to be a nice lady."

"Yes, she was. It's a shame."

"She had kids, too. Four little girls: Andi, Elizabeth, Tia, and Petra," said Page, who clearly liked to show off.

Minutes later, we were off the highway and driving west on Sunset. I watched as the cityscape changed from the cliché-defying urban grittiness of downtown Hollywood to the lush green — and cliché — residential avenues of Beverly Hills. Rows of palm trees looked at us from above, as if down their noses.

We turned off Sunset and drove up Miller Place, a winding canyon drive, with stunning views of the city behind us. Finally, Page parked on a side street.

Television and radio vans were everywhere. Their satellite towers extended into the air like huge sculptures. As we got closer, I spotted CNN, KTLA, KYSR Star 98.7, *Entertainment Tonight*. Some of the reporters stood facing cameras with their backs to the estate, presumably reporting live on the L.A. and network shows. What a circus. So why do I have to be here, too? I'm supposed to be at Disneyland, a kinder, gentler circus.

None of the media people recognized me, a refreshing change from D.C. Agent Page and I politely made our way through the crowd to where two uniformed police officers stood guard. They looked carefully at our creds.

"This is Dr. Alex Cross," said Page.

"So?" said the uniform.

I didn't say a word. "So?" seemed like an appropriate response to me.

The uniform finally let us pass, but not before I noticed something that made me a little sick to my stomach. James Truscott, with his cascading red hair, was standing there in the crowd of reporters. So was his cameraperson — the same woman, dressed all in black. Truscott saw me, too, and nodded my way. A smile may have even crossed his lips.

He was taking notes.

She was taking photographs — of me.

# Chapter 13

I WAS CURSING SOFTLY as Page and I followed a long, circular white-pebbled driveway up to the main house. *Mansion* was definitely a better word for this place, a two-story, Spanish-style construction. Dense foliage on all sides blocked my view past the facade, but the main house had to be at least twenty thousand square feet, probably even more. Who needed this much space to live? Our house in D.C. was under three thousand, and that was plenty of room for us.

A series of balconies rimmed the second floor. Some of them looked down onto the driveway, where a black limo was cordoned off with yellow crime-scene tape.

This was where Antonia Schifman and Bruno Capaletti had died.

The area around the limo was blocked off in a wide circle, with only one way in and out. Two more LAPD officers took names as people came and went.

Techs in white bunny suits were going over the car with a handheld USB microscope and evidence vacuums. A few others were snapping Polaroids as well as regular photographs.

Another whole squad was already fanned out, taking exemplars from the surrounding area. It was all fairly impressive, as well as depressing. The best forensic police department in the world is supposed to be Tokyo's. Domestically, though, Los Angeles and New York were the only departments that could rival the FBI's resources.

"We're in luck, I guess," Page said. "Looks like the ME's just finishing up." He pointed toward the medical examiner, a heavyset, gray-haired woman standing next to the limo and speaking into a handheld recorder.

That meant the bodies hadn't been removed. I was surprised, but it was good news for me. The less disturbed the crime scene, the more information I could get for Burns. And the president. And his wife. I supposed that was why the bodies hadn't been moved: The dead were waiting on me.

I turned back to Page. "Tell whoever's in charge from the LAPD not to move anything yet. I want to get a clean look.

"And try to clear some of these people out of here. Necessary personnel only. Fibers, printing, but that's it. Everyone else is on break."

For the first time that morning, Page paused before he responded. This was an all-business side of me he hadn't seen. Not that I'm big on throwing my weight around, but right now I had to use it. There was no way I could do a proper job in the middle of all this chaos and confusion.

"Oh, and one other thing you should tell whoever's in charge," I said.

Page turned back. "Yeah?"

"Tell them as long as I'm here, *I'm* in charge."

# Chapter 14

I COULD STILL HEAR Director Burns's voice in my head. *I want to hear your take on what happened. . . . We'll have you back with your family for dinner.*

But would I want to eat after this?

With two dead bodies still inside, the limousine was absolutely fetid. One of the best tricks I'd learned was to gut it out for about three minutes, until the olfactory nerves were numb. Then I would be fine. I just had to get through those three minutes that told me I was back in the homicide business.

I focused, and took in the grisly details one by one.

First came a shocker that I wasn't ready for, even though I partly knew it was coming.

Antonia Schifman's face was almost completely unrecognizable. A portion of the left side was gone altogether where she had been shot, probably at close range. What flesh remained — mostly the right eye, cheek, and her mouth — had been slashed several times. The killer, Mary Smith, had been in a frenzy — but only against Antonia Schifman, not the driver, or so it seemed.

The actress's clothing appeared to be intact. No indication of any kind of sexual assault. And no sign of blood froth from the nostrils or mouth, which meant she'd died and stopped breathing almost immediately. Who would make this kind of violent attack? Why Antonia Schifman? She'd seemed like a nice person, got good press. And everybody liked her, according to, well, *everybody*. So what could explain this massacre? This desecration at her home?

Agent Page appeared and leaned in over my shoulder. "What do you think the cutting is about? Some kind of reference to plastic surgery maybe?"

The young agent had shaken off every subtle and not-so-subtle clue I had dropped that I needed to be alone right now, but I didn't have the heart to dress him down.

"I don't think so," I said. "But I don't want to speculate yet. We'll know more once she's checked in and cleaned up." *Now, please let me work, Page.*

A dull-brown wash of dried blood covered the actress's ruined face. What a terrible waste. And what exactly was I supposed to relay to the president about what I'd seen here, about what had happened to his friend?

The driver, Bruno Capaletti, was still propped up at the steering wheel. A single bullet had entered his left temple before it destroyed most of his head. The blood on the empty seat next to him was smeared, possibly by his own body but more likely by the killer, who had apparently shot

Antonia Schifman from the front seat. A small amount of co-caine had been found in the driver's jacket pocket. Did it mean anything? Probably not, but I couldn't rule out any-thing yet.

I finally stepped out and away from the limousine and took a breath of fresh air. "There's a strange disconnect going on here," I said, more to myself than to anyone else.

"Neat *and* sloppy?" Page asked. "Controlled, yet out of control."

I looked at him, and my mouth twisted into something re-sembling a smile. The insight surprised me a little. "Yes. Ex-actly." The bodies had been arranged, just so, inside the car. But the shooting and, in particular, the cuts on Schifman's face had an angry, haphazard quality to them.

There was a calling card, too. A row of children's stickers was affixed to the car door: glittery, bright-colored pictures of unicorns and rainbows. The same kind had apparently been left at the scene of the previous week's murder.

Each of the stickers was marked with a capital letter, two with an *A*, one with a *B*. What was that all about?

Page had already briefed me on the companion case to this one. Another woman in the movie business, Patsy Ben-nett, a successful production head, had been shot dead in a movie theater in Westwood six days prior. There were no witnesses. Bennett was the only victim that day, and there had been no knife work. But the stickers at that scene had also been marked with capital *A*'s and a *B*.

Whoever was doing this certainly wanted to take credit for the murders. The murders weren't improvisatory, but the killer's methods were dynamic. And evolving, of course.

"What are you thinking?" Page asked. "Do you mind if I ask? Or am I getting in the way?"

Before I could tell him, another agent interrupted the two of us. If it was possible, she was tanner and maybe even blonder than Agent Page. I wondered if maybe they'd been put together at the same factory.

"We've got another e-mail at the *L.A. Times*," she said. "Same editor, Arnold Griner, and the same Mary Smith."

"Has the paper reported on the e-mails yet?" I asked. Both agents shook their head. "Good. Let's try to keep it that way. And keep a cap on these kids' stickers, too. If we can. And the A's and B's."

I checked my watch. Already 5:30. I needed at least another hour at the Schifman property; then I wanted to speak with Arnold Griner at the *Times*. And I would definitely have to meet with the LAPD before the day was over. James Truscott was probably still prowling around outside, too. At home in D.C., I missed meals as often as not. Nana and the kids were used to it, and Jamilla would probably understand, but none of that was an excuse. This had been as good a time as any to break one of my very worst habits in life: missing dinner with my family.

But it wasn't going to happen, was it? I called Nana at the hotel first, and then I called Jamilla. Then I thought about the poor Schifman and Bennett families, and I went back to work.

## Part Two

# I LOVE L.A.

# Chapter 15

"WHY ME, OF ALL PEOPLE? Why do you think she's writing these awful missives to *me?* It doesn't make any sense. Does it? Have you found out anything that makes some sense of this? The mothers being slaughtered? Hollywood's about to go totally insane over these murders, trust me. Mary's dirty little secret will get out."

Arnold Griner had already asked me the same questions a couple of times during the interview. Our meeting was taking place in an L-shaped glass fishbowl of an office at the heart of the *L.A. Times* newsroom. The rest of the floor was a wide expanse of desks and cubicles.

From time to time, someone would pop his or her head over a cubicle wall, steal a quick glance our way, and duck back down. *Prairie-dogging,* Griner called it, chuckling to himself.

He sat on a brown leather couch, clutching and unclutching the knees of his wrinkled gray Dockers. Occasionally, he scribbled something on a legal pad on his lap.

The conversation so far had focused on Griner's background: Yale, followed by an internship at *Variety*, where he proofed copy and ran coffee for entertainment reporters. He had earned a staff position quickly, and famously, when he managed to interview Tom Cruise on the record at an industry party. Two years ago, the *L.A. Times* had wooed him away with an offer for his own column, "Behind the Screens." His reputation in the business, he told me, was for "insider" Hollywood stories and "edgy" reviews. He obviously had a very high opinion of himself.

I hadn't found any further links, between Griner and either of the murders outside of the movie-industry connection. Still, I wasn't prepared to believe that he'd been randomly selected to receive Mary Smith's e-mails.

Griner didn't seem inclined to believe it either. His focus was all over the place, though, and he'd been peppering me with questions since we started.

I finally sat down close to him. "Mr. Griner — will you relax? Please."

"Pretty easy for you to say," he shot back, and then almost immediately said, "Sorry. Sorry." He put two fingers to his forehead and rubbed between his eyes. "I'm high-strung to begin with. Ever since I was a kid growing up in Greenwich."

I'd seen this kind of reaction — a mix of paranoia and anger that comes from getting blindsided the way Arnold Griner had been. When I spoke again, I kept my voice just low enough that he'd have to concentrate to hear me.

"I know you've already gone over this, but can you think of any reason you might be receiving these messages? Let's start with any prior contact you've had with Patsy Bennett, Antonia Schifman, or even the limo driver, Bruno Capaletti."

He shrugged, rolled his eyes, tried desperately to catch his breath. "We might have been at some of the same parties, at least the two women. I've certainly reviewed their movies. The last was one of Antonia's, *Canterbury Road,* which I hated, I'm sorry to say, but I loved her in it and said so in the piece.

"Do you think that could be the connection? Maybe the killer reads my stuff. I mean, she must, right? This is so incredibly bizarre. How could I possibly fit into an insane murder scheme?"

Before I could say anything at all, he threw out another of his rapid-fire questions.

"Do you think Antonia's driver was incidental? In the e-mail it seems like he was just . . . *in the way.*"

Griner was obviously hungry for information, both personally and professionally. He was a reporter, after all, and already reasonably powerful in Hollywood circles. So I gave him my stock reporter's response.

"It's too early to say. What about Patsy Bennett?" I asked. "Do you remember the last time you wrote about one of her films? Something she produced? She still produced films occasionally, right?"

Griner nodded; then he sighed loudly, almost theatrically. "Do you think I should discontinue my column for now? I should, shouldn't I? Maybe I better."

The interview was like a Ping-Pong match against a kid with ADD. I eventually managed to get through all my questions, but it took almost twice as long as I thought it would when I had arrived at the *Times*. Griner constantly needed reassurance, and I tried to give it to him without being completely dishonest. He *was* in danger, after all.

"One last thing," Griner said just before I left him. "Do you think I should write a book about this? Is that a little sick?"

I didn't bother to answer either question. He went to Yale — he should be able to figure it out.

# Chapter 16

AFTER THE INTERVIEW, I slouched out to Arnold Griner's desk to touch base with Paul Lebleau, the LAPD tech in charge of tracing Mary Smith's e-mails.

He tapped away on the keyboard of Griner's computer while he spoke to me in a rapid-fire patter. "Two e-mails came through two different proxy servers. First one originated from a cybercafe in Santa Monica. That means Mary Smith could be one of a few hundred people. She's got *two* different addresses. So far. Both just generic Hotmail accounts, which tells us nothing really, except we do know that she signed up for the first one from the library at USC. Day before the first message."

I had to concentrate just to follow Lebleau. Did everybody out here have ADD? "What about the second e-mail?" I asked him.

"Transmission didn't originate in the same place as the first one. That much I can tell you."

"Did it come from the L.A. area? Can you tell me that?"

"Don't know yet."

"When will you know?"

"Probably end of the day, not that it's going to be much help." He leaned forward and squinted at several lines of code on the screen. "Mary Smith knows what she's doing."

There it was again — *she*. I understood why everyone was using the pronoun. I was doing it, too — but only for the sake of convenience.

That didn't mean I was convinced the killer was a woman, though. Not yet, anyway. The letters to Griner could represent some kind of persona. But *whose?*

# Chapter 17

*HOW DO YOU LIKE YOUR VACATION so far, Alex? Having a lot of fun?*

I took copies of both bizarre e-mails and headed out for a meeting with the LAPD. The detective bureau on North Los Angeles Street was only a quarter mile from the *Times* offices — a Los Angeles miracle, given the cliché that it takes forty-five minutes to get anywhere in the city.

*Oh, the vacation's great. I'm seeing all the sights. The kids are loving it, too. Nana is over the moon.*

I walked slowly, rereading the two e-mails on my way to LAPD. Even if the writing was persona-based, it had come from the mind of the killer.

I started with the first one, which described the last moments of Patsy Bennett's life. It was definitely chilling, this diary of a psychopath.

To: agriner@latimes.com

From: Mary Smith

To: Patrice Bennett:

*I am the one who killed you.*

Isn't that some sentence? I think so. Here's another one that I like quite a lot.

Somebody, a total stranger, will find your body in the balcony at the Westwood Village Theater. *You,* Patrice Bennett.

Because that's where you died today, watching your last movie, and not a very good one at that. *The Village*? What were you thinking? What could have brought you to the theater on this day, the day of your death, to see *The Village*?

You should have been home, Patsy. With your darling little children. That's where a good mom belongs. Don't you think so? Even if you spend much of your home time reading scripts and on the phone playing studio politics.

It took me a long time to get so close to you. You are a Big Somebody at your Studio, and I am just one of the nobodies who watches movies on video and *Entertainment Tonight* and *Access Hollywood*. I couldn't even get inside the big arched entrance at your Studio. No sirree.

All I could do was watch your dark-blue Aston Martin going in and out, day after day. But I'm a really patient person. I've learned how to wait for what I want.

Speaking of waiting, that incredible house of

yours is hard to see from the street. I did spot
your lovely children — a couple of times, actually. And I know with some time I could have
found a way into the house. But then today, you
changed everything.

You went to a movie, in the middle of the
afternoon, just like you say you do in some of
your interviews. Maybe you missed the smell of
popcorn. Do you ever take your little girls to
the movies, Patsy? You should have, you know. As
they say, it all goes by in a blink.

It didn't make sense to me at first. You're
such a busy little Big Shot. But then I figured
it out. Movies are what you do. You must see
them all the time, but you also have a family
waiting for you every night. You're supposed to
be home for dinner with little Lynne and Laurie.
How old are they now? Twelve and thirteen? They
want you there, and you want to be there. That's
good, I suppose. Except that tonight, dinner is
going to come and go without you. Kind of sad
when you think about it, which is what I'm doing
right now.

Anyway, you sat in the balcony in the ninth
row. I sat in the twelfth. I waited, and watched
the back of your head, your brunette-from-a-
bottle hair. That's where the bullet was going
to go. Or so I fantasized. Isn't that what one
is supposed to do at the movies? Escape? Get
away from it all? Except that most movies are so

dismal these days — dismally dumb or dismally dreary.

I didn't actually pull out my gun until after the film started. I didn't like how scared I felt. That was how scared *you* were supposed to be, Big Shot. But you didn't know what was happening, not even that I was there. You were out of the loop.

I sat like that, holding the gun in my lap, pointing it at you for the longest time. Then I decided I wanted to be closer — right on top of you.

I needed to look in your eyes after you knew you'd been shot, knew that you would never see Lynne and Laurie again, never see another movie either, never green-light one, never again be a Big Shot.

But then seeing you wide-eyed and dead was a surprise. A shock to my nervous system, actually. What happened to that famed aristocratic bearing of yours? That's why I had to leave the theater so quickly, and why I had to leave you *undone*.

Not that you really care anymore. How's the weather where you are now, Patsy? Hot, I hope. Hot as Hades — isn't that an expression?

Do you miss your children terribly? Have some regrets? I'll bet you do. I would if I were you. But I'm no Big Shot, just one of the little people.

# Chapter 18

NINE O'CLOCK, and all was not well, to put it mildly.

LAPD detective Jeanne Galletta's handshake was surprisingly soft. She looked as though she could give out bone-crushers if she wanted to. Her orange short-sleeved turtleneck showed off her biceps. She was slim, though, with a strikingly angular face and the kind of piercing brown eyes that could make you stare.

I caught myself midstare, and glanced away.

"Agent Cross. Have I kept you waiting?" she asked.

"Not very long," I told her. I'd been in Galletta's position before. When you're a lead investigator on a high-profile case, everyone wants a piece of your time. Besides, my day was almost over. Detective Galletta would probably be up all night. This case warranted it.

The mess had landed in her lap about twelve hours ago. It had originated at the West Bureau, in Hollywood, but serial cases were automatically transferred downtown, to the Special Homicide Unit. Technically, "Mary Smith" couldn't be classified as a serial killer until there were at least four attributed murders, but LAPD had decided to err on the side of caution. I agreed with the decision, not that anyone had asked me for an opinion.

The media coverage on this one, and the subsequent pressure on the department, was already intense. It could go from intense to insane soon, if the e-mails to the *Times* got out.

Detective Galletta led me upstairs to a small conference room turned crisis room. It acted as a makeshift clearinghouse for all information related to the murders.

One entire wall was already covered with police reports, a map of the city, sketches of the two crime scenes, and dozens of photographs of the dead.

A wastebasket in the corner overflowed with empty cups and greasy restaurant takeout bags. Wendy's seemed to be winning the battle of the burgers at this precinct.

Two detectives in shirtsleeves sat at a large wooden table, both of them bent over separate piles of paperwork. Familiar, depressing.

"We need this space," Galletta said to the detectives. There was nothing overly aggressive about it. She had the kind of unassuming confidence that made bullying unnecessary. The two men cleared out without a word.

"Where do you want to start?" I asked her.

Galletta jumped right in. "What do you make of the sticker thing?" She pointed to an 8½ x 11 black-and-white photo of the back of a movie seat. It had the same brand of kiddie stickers on it as the ones left on Antonia Schifman's limo. Each sticker was marked either *A* or *B*.

One of the stickers showed a wide-eyed pony, and the other two a teddy bear on a swing. What was with the killer and children? And mothers?

"It feels awfully heavy-handed to me," I told her. "Just like everything else so far. The overwrought e-mails. The shootings at close range. The knife work. Hell, the celebrities. Whoever's doing this wants to go big. Very high-profile."

"Yeah, definitely. But what about the kiddie stickers themselves? I mean, why stickers? Why that kind? What's with the *A*'s and *B*'s? Must mean something."

"She's mentioned the victim's kids both times. In the e-mails. Kids are a part of this puzzle, a piece. To be honest, I've never come across anything even remotely like it."

Galletta bit her lip and looked at the floor. I waited to see what she would say next.

"We've got two threads here. It's all film industry, Hollywood, at least so far. But there's the mother thing. The kids. Never mentions the husbands in either e-mail." She spoke slowly, mulling it over, the way I often did. "She's either a mother herself or has a thing for mothers. Mommies."

"You're assuming Mary Smith is a woman?" I asked.

# Chapter 19

DETECTIVE GALLETTA ROCKED back on the heels of her Nikes, and then she looked at me quizzically. "You don't know about the hair? Who's been briefing you, anyway?"

I felt a pang of frustration about my own time being wasted again. I sighed, then asked Galletta, "What hair?"

She went on to tell me LAPD had found a human hair under one of the stickers at the movie theater in Westwood. Testing indicated it was Caucasian female, and it was *not* Patrice Bennett's. The fact that it was trapped on a smooth, vertical surface under the sticker gave it some pretty good weight as evidence, though certainly not ironclad.

I juggled this new information with what I already knew as I gave Galletta my own take on Mary Smith. It included my gut feeling that we shouldn't rule out either sex just yet.

"But you should take everything I tell you with a grain of salt. I'm not an all-science kind of guy."

She smirked, though the effect was pleasant enough. "I'll take that into account, Agent Cross. Now, what else?"

"Do you have a media plan?"

I wanted to emphasize it as her plan, completely her show, which it was, of course. This was going to be my first and last day on the Mary Smith case. If I played it right, I wouldn't even have to say that out loud. I would just walk away.

"*Here's* my media plan."

Jeanne Galletta reached up and flipped on a wall-mounted television. She punched through several channels, stopping wherever there was coverage of the two murders.

"The shocking double murder of actress Antonia Schifman and her driver . . ."

"We're taking you live now to Beverly Hills . . ."

"Patrice Bennett's former assistant on the line . . ."

Many of them were national broadcasts, everything from CNN to E! Entertainment Television.

Galletta pushed a button that muted the sound.

"This is the kind of crap that some reporters live for. I've got a twenty-four-hour detail on both crime scenes just to keep these assholes away, plus the damn paparazzi. It's totally out of control, and it's going to get much worse. You've been through it. You have any suggestions?"

Did I ever. We had all learned a few painful lessons about the double-edged sword of media coverage with the D.C. sniper case a few years back.

"Here's my take on it — for what it's worth, and I hope it's something. Don't try to control the coverage, because you never will," I told her. "The only thing you can control is what crime-scene information gets out there. Put a gag order on everyone connected to the case. No interviews without specific permission from the department. And this might sound a little crazy, but get a couple of people onto a phone detail. Call every retired officer you can find. Tell them not to make any comments to the press, nothing at all. Retired cops can be one of your biggest problems. Some of them just love making up theories for the camera."

She gave me another sly smile. "Not that you have an opinion about all this or anything."

I shrugged. "Believe me, most of it was learned the hard way."

While I spoke, Detective Galletta paced slowly in front of the big wall board. Absorbing the evidence. That's the way to do it. Let the details gather in the corners of your mind, where they'll be when you need them. I could already tell that she had good instincts. Healthy cynicism for sure, but she was also a listener. It was easy to see how she'd come into her position so young. Now, could she survive *this*?

I said, "Just one more thought. Mary Smith is probably going to be watching what you do. My suggestion is, don't disparage her or her work publicly, at least not yet. She's already playing it as a media game. Right?"

"Yeah, that's true. I think so."

Detective Galletta stopped and looked up at the silent TV images. "She's probably eating this all up with a spoon."

My thought, too. And this monster needed to be fed very, very carefully.

This *lady* monster?

# Chapter 20

IT WAS JUST AFTER MIDNIGHT when I finally got back to the hotel at Disney and received some more bad news. It wasn't just that Jamilla had flown back to San Francisco. I already knew that much and figured I was in the doghouse again with Jam.

When I entered the hotel room, I saw that Nana Mama was fast asleep on the sofa. A cluster of pale-blue crocheting was still wrapped around her fingers. She slept peacefully, like a child.

I didn't want to disturb the poor girl, but she came awake on her own. It had always been that way with Nana. When I was little, all I had to do was stand next to her bed if I was sick or had a nightmare. She always said that she watched over me, even while she was sleeping. Had she been watching over me tonight?

I stared at the old woman for a quiet moment. I don't know how most people feel about their grandparents, but I loved her so much it hurt sometimes. Nana raised me from the age of nine. I finally leaned down and kissed her on the cheek.

"Did you get my voice mail?" I asked.

Nana glanced absently at the hotel phone, with its flashing red message light.

"I guess not," I said with a shrug.

She put a hand on my forearm. "Oh, Alex. Christine was here at the hotel. She came, and she took Little Alex back to Seattle. He's gone."

My brain had a quick does-not-compute moment. Christine wasn't due to pick Alex up for another two days. She currently had custody of our son, but the trip to Disneyland had been talked out and agreed to. She even said it was a good idea.

I sat down hard on the edge of the couch. "I don't understand. What do you mean, she took Alex home? What's going on? Tell me everything."

Nana shoved her crocheting into a tapestry bag at her side. "I was so mad, I could've spit. She didn't seem like herself at all. She was shouting, Alex. She shouted at me, even at Janelle."

"What was she doing here, anyway? She wasn't supposed to —"

"She came down early. That's the worst part. Alex, I think she was coming to spend some quality time with you and Little Alex. With all of us. And then when she found out you were working, she completely changed. Turned into an angry hornet just like that. There was nothing I could say to her. I never saw anyone so angry, so changed."

It was all coming too fast, and I struggled with a barrage of feelings. Most of all, I realized, I hadn't even gotten to say good-bye to my son, and now he was gone again.

"What about Alex? How was he?"

"He was confused, and seemed sad, the poor little boy. He asked for you when his mother took him away. He said you promised him this would be a vacation. He'd so looked forward to it. We all did. You know that, Alex."

My heart clenched, and I saw Alex's face in my mind. It felt as though he was getting farther and farther from me, as if a piece of my life was slipping away.

"How were Jannie and Damon about it?" I asked then.

Nana sighed heavily. "They were brave soldiers, but Jannie cried herself to sleep tonight. I think Damon did, too. He hides it better. Poor things, they just moped around most of the night."

We sat together on the sofa for a long, silent moment. I didn't know what to say.

"I'm sorry I wasn't here today," I finally told Nana. "I know that doesn't mean much."

She took my chin in her hand and stared into my eyes. *Here it comes. Batten down the hatches.*

"You're a good man, Alex. And you're a good father. Don't you forget that, especially now. You just . . . you have a very difficult job."

A few minutes later, I slipped into the room where Jannie and Damon were sleeping. The way they lay on the covers, they looked like little kids again. I liked the visual effect, and

I stood there, just watching them. Nothing ever healed me the way these two did. *My babies, no matter how old you are.*

Jannie slept at the edge of her bed with the comforter in a wad off to the side. I went over and covered her up.

*"Dad?"* Damon's whisper from behind caught me off guard. "That you?"

"What's up, Day?" I sat down on the edge of his bed and rubbed his back. I'd been doing it since he was an infant, and wouldn't stop until he made me.

"You have to work tomorrow?" he asked. "Is it tomorrow already?"

There was no malice in his voice. He was too good a person for that. If I was a pretty good father, Damon was a great son.

"No," I told him. "Not tomorrow. We're on vacation, remember?"

# Chapter 21

FOR THE SECOND day in a row, I got a disturbing wake-up call.

This one was from Fred Van Allsburg, the assistant director in charge of the FBI's Los Angeles office. I had seen the name on organizational charts, but we'd never actually met or even spoken. Still, he treated me with a kind of instant familiarity over the phone.

"Alex! How are you enjoying the vacation?" he asked within seconds of saying hello.

Did everyone know my business? "Fine, thanks," I answered. "What can I do for you?"

"Listen, thanks very much for making yourself available on Mary Smith yesterday. We've got a good jump on this case, and what feels like a relatively functional relationship with LAPD.

"Listen, I'll cut right to the chase. We'd like you to represent us for the rest of the investigation out here. It's big, and
it's important to us. And, obviously, to the director. This case
is going to be huge, unfortunately."

I thought of a line from *The Godfather: Part III* — *"just
when I thought I was out, they pull me back in."*

Not this time, though. I hadn't slept much, but I did wake
with a clear sense of what this day was going to be about —
and it had absolutely nothing to do with Mary Smith, or any
other heinous murder investigation.

"I'm going to have to give my regrets on this one. I've got
family commitments that I cannot turn my back on."

"Yes, I understand," he said, too quickly to have meant it.
"But maybe we could pry you away for just a while. A few
hours in the day."

"I'm sorry, you can't. Not right now."

Van Allsburg sighed heavily on the other end of the line.
When he spoke again, his tone was more measured. I don't
know if I was reading him right, but I got a hint of conde-
scension, too. "Do you know what we're dealing with here?
Alex, have you seen the news this morning?"

"I'm trying to stay away from the news for a few days. Remember, I'm on vacation. I *need* a vacation. I just came off the
Wolf."

"Alex, listen, we both know this isn't over. People are
dying here. Important people."

*Important people?* What the hell was that supposed to
mean? Also, I'm not sure if he was conscious of it, but he
seemed to start every other sentence with my name. I sort of

understood the position he was in, the pressure, but I was going to hold firm this time.

"I'm sorry," I told him. "The answer is *no*."

"Alex, I'd prefer to keep this between you and me. There's no reason to go up to Ron Burns, is there?"

"No, there isn't," I told Van Allsburg.

"Good —," he started in, but I cut him off.

"Because I'm turning off my pager right now."

# Chapter 22

I'LL ADMIT, when I hung up the phone, my pulse was racing a little, but I felt relieved as well. I thought that Ron Burns would probably back me up on this, but you know what? I didn't even care.

An hour later I was dressed and ready to go be a tourist. "Who wants to have breakfast with Goofy?" I called out.

The hotel offered "character breakfasts," and it seemed like a good way to channel our energies right back into vacation mode. A little corny for sure, but sometimes corny is good, real good, keeps everything in perspective.

Jannie and Damon came into the suite's living room, both of them looking a little wary. I held out two fists, fingers up.

"Each of you pick a hand," I said.

"Daddy, we're not babies anymore," Jannie said. "I'm eleven. Have you noticed?"

I put on a shocked expression. *"You're not?"* It brought out the kind of laughter I was looking for.

"This is serious business," I told them. "I'm not kidding. Now, pick a hand. Please."

"What is it?" Damon asked.

But I kept mute.

Jannie finally tapped my left hand, and then Damon shrugged and pointed to the right.

"Good choice." I turned it over and unclenched my fingers. Both kids leaned in for a closer look.

"Your *pager?*" Damon asked.

"I just turned it off. Now Nana and I are going to wait out in the hall, and I want you two to hide it somewhere. Hide it good. I don't want to see that thing again, not until we're back in D.C."

Both Jannie and Damon began to whistle and cheer. Even Nana let out a whoop. We were finally on vacation.

# Chapter 23

MAYBE THERE WAS a silver lining in all of this misery and desolation. Not likely, but maybe. Arnold Griner knew he had exclusive rights to his own story when this terrible mess was all over. And you know what else? He wouldn't settle for just a TV movie. He was going to try to serialize the whole thing in his column, and then sell it as a prestige project at one of the studios. *Hollywood Under Siege? The War Against the Stars?* Bad titles. That was the concept, anyway.

He shook his head and refocused on the San Diego Freeway. The Xanax he'd taken was making him a little loopy. He'd kept the caffeine going, too, just to maintain some kind of balance through the day. Actually, the morning commute was the hardest time of his day. It was a daily transition from not worrying as much to worrying a lot and feeling sick to his stomach. The closer he got to his office, his desk, his computer, the more anxious he felt.

If he knew for certain that another creepy e-mail was coming, it would almost be easier. It was the not-knowing part that made it hell.

Would Mary be back? Would it happen today? But, most important, why was she writing to him?

All too soon, he arrived at Times Mirror Square. Griner worked in the older part of the complex, a 1930s-era building that he had a certain affection for, under normal circumstances, anyway.

The main doors were large bronze affairs, flanked with imposing twin eagle sculptures. He walked right by them this morning, around to the back entrance, and took the stairs to the third floor. One couldn't be too careful, could one?

A reporter named Jennie Bloom fell into step with him the second he hit the newsroom floor. Among all the staff who had shown a sudden interest in his well-being, she was by far the most obvious about it. Or was that odious?

"Hey, Arnold, how's it going? You doing okay, man? What are you covering today?"

Griner didn't miss a beat. "Jen, if that's your idea of a pickup line, you must be the most unlaid woman in L.A."

Jennie Bloom merely grinned and kept on coming on. "Spoken like someone with experience in matters of the heart. All right then, let's skip the foreplay. You get any more e-mails? You need help on this, right? I'm here for you. You need a woman's point of view."

"Seriously, I just need some space. Okay? I'll let you know if I get anything else." He turned abruptly and walked away from her.

"No you won't," she called after him.

"No I won't," he said, and kept walking.

In some ways, even the annoying distractions were a relief. As soon as he turned away from Bloom, his mind went back into the disturbing loop it had been on before.

*Why me? Why did Crazy Mary pick me out? Why not Jennie Bloom?*

*Would it happen again today? Another high-profile murder?* And then it did.

# Chapter 24

A CALM, MEASURED FEMALE voice said, "Nine-one-one, what is your emergency?"

"This is Arnold Griner at the *Los Angeles Times*. I'm supposed to call a Detective Jeanne Galletta, but I don't . . . I can't find her number on my desk. I'm sorry. I'm a little rattled right now. I can't even find my Rolodex."

"Sir, is this an emergency call? Do you need assistance?"

"Yes, it's definitely an emergency. Someone may have been murdered. I don't know how long ago this happened, or even if it did for sure. Has anyone called about someone named Marti Lowenstein-Bell?"

"Sir, I can't give out that kind of information."

"It doesn't matter. Just send someone to the Lowenstein-Bell residence. I think she's been killed. I'm almost sure of it."

"How can you be sure?"

"I just am. Okay? I'm almost positive there's been a murder."

"What is the address?"

"The address? Oh, Jesus, I don't know the address. The body is supposed to be in the swimming pool."

"Are you at the residence now?"

"No. No. Listen, this is a . . . I don't know how to make this clear to you. It's the Mary Smith murder case. The Hollywood celebrity killings. Do you know what I'm talking about?"

"All right, sir, I think I understand. What was the name again?"

"Lowenstein-Bell. Marti. I know her husband's name is Michael Bell. You might find it under that. I don't know for certain if she's dead. I just got this awful message. I'm a reporter at the *L.A. Times*. My name is Arnold Griner. Detective Galletta knows who I am."

"Sir, I have the information now. I'm going to put you on hold for just a minute."

"*No, don't —*"

# Chapter 25

LAPD DISPATCH PUT OUT A CALL at 8:42 A.M., sending officers, backup, and emergency medical personnel to the Lowenstein-Bell address in Bel Air.

Two separate 911 calls on the same incident had come within a few minutes of each other. The first one was from the *Los Angeles Times*. The second came from the Lowenstein-Bell residence itself.

Officers Jeff Campbell and Patrick Beneke were first at the scene. Campbell suspected before they arrived that this was another celebrity murder. The address alone was unusual for this kind of call, but dispatch had mentioned a single adult female victim. And possible knife wounds. The couple who owned the house were both Hollywood types. It added up to trouble no matter what.

A short, dark-haired woman in a gray-and-white maid's uniform was waiting in the driveway. She was wringing some kind of towel. As the patrolmen got closer, they could see that the woman was sobbing, and walking in circles.

"Great," Beneke said. "Just what we need, some Carmelita who doesn't even speak English, bawling her eyes out and acting *muy loco.*"

Campbell responded the way he always did to the younger officer's tiresome, racist cynicism. "Shut the hell up, Beneke. I don't want to hear it. She's terrified."

As soon as they were out of the car, the maid went hysterical. *"Aquí, aquí, aquí!"* she screeched, motioning them toward the front door. *"Aquí! Aquí!"*

The residence was an ultramodern stone-and-glass structure high in the Santa Monica Mountains. As he approached, Officer Campbell could see straight through the green-glass entryway to the back patio and the sweeping coastal view beyond.

*What was that on the front-door glass?* It looked totally out of place. A label or a sticker of some kind. A kiddie decal? With a large *A* on it.

He had to practically pry the maid's grip from his forearm. "Ma'am, just please be calm. *Uno momento, por favor. Como te llamas?*"

The woman may or may not have heard him. Her Spanish came much too quickly for him to understand. She pointed toward the house several more times.

"Let's just get in there," Beneke insisted. "We're wasting time with her. She's living the *vida loca.*"

Two more cruisers and an ambulance pulled up. One of the paramedics spoke quickly, and more efficiently, with the maid.

"In the pool in the back," he reported. "No one else is here — as far as she knows."

"She don't know shit," said Beneke.

"We'll go around," Campbell said. He and Beneke took the north side of the house, their weapons drawn. The other teams went to the south, straight through a set of hedges.

Campbell felt the old rush of adrenaline as they worked their way through a dense cluster of hydrangea. Homicide calls used to be almost exhilarating. Now they just made him feel light-headed and weak in the legs.

He squinted through the thick brush as best he could. From what he knew of the Hollywood murders, there was no way the killer would still be around.

"You see anything?" he whispered to his partner, who was twenty-nine, a California cowboy, and a total asshole most of the time.

"Yeah, a bunch of flowers," Beneke answered. "We were the first ones here. Why'd you let them go ahead of us like that?"

Campbell stifled his first response. "Just keep your eyes open," he said. "The killer could still be here."

"That's my hope, *podjo.*"

They emerged onto a sweeping black-slate patio in the back. It was dominated by an enormous dark-bottomed infinity pool. The water seemed to flow right up to and over the edge of the terrace.

"There she is." Campbell groaned.

A woman's stark-white body floated facedown, arms perpendicular to the torso. She wore a lime-green one-piece. Her long blond hair was splayed gently over the surface of the water.

One of the paramedics jumped into the pool and with some difficulty turned her over. He put a finger to her throat, but it was already obvious to Campbell there would be no pulse.

"Holy shit!" Campbell grimaced and looked away, then back again. He held his breath to keep everything down. Who the hell could do something like this? The poor woman was practically erased from the neck up. Her face was a tangle of cut flesh. The pool's water was tinted bright pink all around the body.

Beneke walked over to get a closer look. "Same killer. I'll bet you anything. Same crazy killer did this." He leaned over to help pull the woman out.

"Wait," Campbell barked. He pointed to the paramedic who was still in the water. "You. Get out of the pool. Get out of the pool right now."

Stone-faced, they all looked at Campbell, but they knew he was right. Even Beneke didn't say a word. There was no sense putting any more of their stamp on the murder scene until an investigative team got there. They would have to leave the victim where she was.

*"Hey! Hey, guys!"*

Campbell looked up to see another officer, Jerry Tounley, calling down from an open window upstairs. "Office is completely trashed up here. There's broken pictures, stuff everywhere, glass. And get this — the computer's still on and open to a mail program! Looks like someone was sending an e-mail before they left."

# Chapter 26

To: agriner@latimes.com

From: Mary Smith

To: Marti Lowenstein-Bell:

I watched you having dinner last night. You and your fine family of five. Very cozy and nice. "Mother Knows Best." With those immaculately clean glass walls of yours, it couldn't have been easier to watch. I enjoyed seeing you with your kids at your last supper.

I could actually see the delicious-looking food on your plates, prepared by your cook and nanny, of course. You were having a swell time, and that's fine with me. I wanted you to enjoy yourself on your last night. I especially wanted your kids to have a lasting memory. Now I have a memory of them, too.

I'll never forget their sweet faces. Never, ever forget your kids, Marti. Trust me on it.

What a beautiful, beautiful house you have, Marti, as befits such an important writer and film director. Is that the right order, by the way? I think so.

I didn't come inside until later, when you were putting the girls to bed. You left the patio doors open again, and this time I used them.

I couldn't resist. I wanted to see things just the way you see them, from the inside looking out.

But I still don't understand why all you rich people feel so safe in your houses. Those big castles can't protect you if you aren't paying close attention. *And you weren't. You weren't paying attention at all. Too busy being a mom — or too busy being a star?*

I listened to you upstairs, doing bedtime with the girls. It was kind of touching, and I mean that. You probably thought you would be the last one to tuck them in, but you weren't.

Later, when everyone was asleep, I watched each of those girls in her bed, breathing so peacefully. They were like little angels with no cares in the world.

I didn't have to tell them they had nothing to worry about, because they already knew. It was just the opposite for you. I decided to wait until the morning, so that I could be with you alone, Madam Director.

I'm really glad I waited, too. Your husband, Michael, took the girls to school today. His turn, I guess. That was lucky for everyone, but especially for him. He got to live, and you didn't have to watch him die. And I got you the way I wanted, just the way I had imagined it for such a long time.

Here's what happened next, Marti.

Your last morning started like any other. You did your precious Pilates and then went for laps in the pool. Fifty laps, just like always. It must be nice to have such a big swimming pool. Heated, too. I stood and watched you gliding back and forth in the sparkling blue water. Even there, so close, it took you forever to see me.

When you finally looked up, you must have been good and tired. Too tired to scream I suppose. All you did was turn away, but it didn't stop me from shooting you. Or then cutting your pretty face to ribbons and shreds.

Tell you what, Marti, that was the best part of all. I'm starting to really like defacement.

Now, let me ask one final question—*do you know why you had to die? Do you know what you did to deserve this? Do you know, Marti, do you know?*

Somehow, I doubt it.

# Chapter 27

BUT THAT WASN'T EXACTLY the way it happened, the Storyteller knew.

Of course, he wasn't going to tell the *L.A. Times* and the police everything, only what he needed them to know, only what was in the story he wanted them to help authenticate.

It was such a good story, a helluva story if he didn't say so himself. Mary Smith! Jesus. A classic horror tale if ever there was one.

Speaking of stories, he'd heard a good one the other day — the "psychopath's test." It was supposed to tell you if you had the mind of a psycho. If you got it right, you did. The story went like this. At her mother's funeral, a woman met this guy and fell instantly in love. But she never got his name, number, or anything about him. A few days later, the woman killed her sister.

Now . . . the test! Why did she kill the sister? If you answer correctly, then you think like a psychopath.

The Storyteller did, of course. He figured it out immediately. This woman killed her sister . . . because she was hoping the guy she liked would appear at the funeral.

Anyway, after he killed Marti Lowenstein-Bell, he was high as a kite, but he knew he had to stay in control, more or less anyway. He had to keep up appearances.

So he hustled on back to work.

He roamed the halls of the office building in Pasadena and talked to half a dozen coworkers about things that bored the living shit out of him, especially today. He wanted to tell every one of them what had just happened — about his secret life, about how none of them *got* him at all, about how smart and clever he was, and about what an incredible planner, schemer, and killer he was.

Jesus, how they loved to toss that word around — so and so was a *killer,* this one had a *killer* smile, a *killer* act, but it was all such incredible bullshit.

All of these people were wimps. They didn't know what real killing was all about. But he sure did.

And he knew something else — he liked it a lot, even more than he thought he would. And he was good at it.

He had this sudden urge to pull his gun at the office and start shooting everything that moved, squeaked, or squealed.

But hell, that was just a fantasy, a little harmless daydreaming. It would never measure up to the real story, his story, *Mary's* story, which was so much better.

# Chapter 28

"ALEX, YOUR OFFICE AT THE FBI called so many times, I had to stop answering the phone. Good Lord, what is *wrong* with those people?" My great aunt Tia was holding forth at the kitchen table at home, admiring the colorful scarf we had brought her as thanks for house-sitting while we were in California. Nana sat next to Tia, sorting through a thick stack of mail.

Our cat, Rosie, was in the kitchen, and looked a bit heavier if I wasn't mistaken. She rubbed hard up against my legs, as if to say, *I'm mad you left, but I'm glad you're back. Tia sure is a fine cook.*

I was glad to be back, too. I think we all were. Christine's taking Alex away to Seattle had more or less ended our vacation, at least the joy in it. My one conversation with her had been tense and also sad. She and I were both so controlled, so intent on not losing our temper, that we ended up with almost nothing to say.

But Christine worried me — the ups and downs, the inconsistencies I saw all the time these days. I wondered what she was like with Little Alex when I wasn't around the two of them. Alex never complained, but kids usually won't.

Now I was back in my kitchen in D.C., feeling almost as if I hadn't had any time off at all. Today was Thursday. I had until Monday morning to not think about work — a resolution that lasted a whole five minutes.

Almost by habit, I wandered up to my office in the attic. I threw my fat pile of mail on the desk and, without thinking about it, pressed Play on the answering machine.

Big mistake. Nearly fatal.

Nine new messages were waiting for me.

The first was from Tony Woods at the Bureau.

"Hello, Alex. I've tried paging you a few more times but haven't had any luck. Please call me at Director Burns's office as soon as you can. And please apologize to your house sitter for me. I suspect she thinks I'm stalking you. Possibly because I am. Call me."

I smiled thinly at Tony's dry humor and delivery as a *second* message from him began.

"Alex, Tony Woods again. Please call in as soon as you can. There's been another incident with the murder case in California. Things are most definitely running out of control there. There's a lot of hysteria in L.A. The *L.A. Times* has finally broken the story about Mary Smith's e-mails. Call me. It's important, Alex."

Tony knew enough not to leave too many specific details on my home phone. He may also have been hoping to hook my curiosity with his vagueness.

He did.

# Chapter 29

I WAS FAIRLY CERTAIN the latest victim would have to be another Hollywood mother, but I couldn't help wondering if Mary Smith's methods had continued to evolve. And how about the e-mails to the *Times*? The TV news and the Web would only give me half the story, at best.

If I wanted to know more, I would have to call in.

No, I reminded myself. No work until Monday. No murder cases. No Mary Smith.

The machine beeped again, and Ron Burns came on. He was brief and to the point, as he almost always is.

"Alex, I've been in touch with Fred Van Allsburg in L.A. Don't worry about him, but I do need to ask you a few questions. It's important. And welcome back to Washington, welcome home."

And then another call from Ron Burns, his voice still carefully modulated.

"Alex, we've got a phone conference next week, and I don't want you coming in cold. Call me at home over the weekend if you have to. I'd also like you to speak with Detective Galletta in L.A. She knows something you need to hear. If you don't have her phone numbers, Tony can get them for you."

The implication was clear already. Ron Burns wasn't asking me to stay on this case. *He was telling me.* God, I was tired of this — the murders, the horrific cases, one after another. According to estimates at the Bureau, there were more than three hundred pattern killers currently operating in the United States. Hell, was I supposed to catch all of them?

I clicked Pause on the machine to take a second and decide how I felt about what was going on here. My thoughts went straight back to Mary Smith. I had let her into my head again. She'd caught my interest, my curiosity, probably my ego. A female serial killer — could it be? Killing other women? Mothers?

But why? Would a woman do that? I didn't think so. I just couldn't imagine it happening, which didn't mean that it hadn't.

I also wondered if there had been another e-mail to Arnold Griner. What part did Griner, or the *L.A. Times,* play in all this? Did Mary Smith already have the *next* victim in her sights? What was her motivation?

That was the line of thought that finally got to me. Some unsuspecting woman, a mother, was going to lose her life in L.A. soon. A husband, and probably children, would be left behind. It hit too close to home for me, and I think Burns knew that when he called. Of course he did.

Several years before, my own wife, Maria, had been gunned down in a drive-by shooting. Maria had died in my arms. No one was ever convicted, or even arrested. My biggest case, and I'd failed on it. It was all so unspeakably senseless. And now this terrible case in L.A. I didn't need my PhD in psych to know that Mary Smith was pushing all my buttons, both personally and professionally.

Maybe I would just check in, I thought. Besides, Burns was right — I didn't want to show up behind the ball on Monday morning.

*Damn it, Alex, you're weakening.*

When I picked up the phone, though, I was surprised to hear Damon's voice already on the line.

"Yeah, I missed you, too. I was thinking about you. I swear I was, all the time."

Then an adolescent girl's laughter. "Did you bring me anything from California, Day? Mouse ears? Somethin', somethin'?"

I forced myself to hang up, quietly.

*Yeah, I missed you, too?* Who was this girl? And since when was Day keeping secrets? I had fooled myself into thinking that if a girlfriend came along, he'd want to tell me about it. That suddenly seemed like a silly delusion on my part. I'd been thirteen before, too. What was I thinking?

One teenage moment down. About two million to go. I'd give him five minutes and then tell him it was time to hang up. Meanwhile, I went back to the answering machine — where another message was waiting.

A real mindblower.

# Chapter 30

"ALEX, IT'S BEN ABAJIAN calling on Thursday, one-thirty my time in Seattle. Listen, I have bad news I'm afraid.

"It seems that Christine's attorney has filed a motion to move up the final custody hearing date out here. I'm not sure I'll be able to block it, or even that we should. There's more, but I'd rather not go into it until we speak. Please give me a call as soon as possible."

My heart picked up its pace. Ben Abajian was my lawyer in Seattle. I had hired him soon after Christine brought Little Alex to live there. We'd talked a couple dozen times since then — on my dime, of course.

He was an excellent attorney, a good guy, too, but his message was a bad sign. My guess was that Christine had taken her own interpretation of what had happened in California and run with it, straight to her counsel.

With the time difference out west, I was able to catch Ben Abajian still in the office. He tried to emphasize the positive for me, but his tone was all bad.

"Alex, this is only temporary, but they've also filed an ex parte motion asking for sole physical custody of Alex Junior until the final hearing is over. The judge went for it. I'm sorry to have to tell you that."

I squeezed the phone tight in my hand. It was hard to respond, or even take in what Ben was telling me. Christine had never gotten this aggressive before. Now she seemed to be trying to keep me from even seeing Little Alex. In fact, she'd just succeeded, at least temporarily.

"Alex, are you there?"

"Yeah, Ben, I'm here. Sorry. Just give me a second."

I put down the phone and took a deep breath. It would do me no good to spiral down right now. Or to blow up over the phone. None of this was Ben's fault.

I put the phone back to my ear. "What was the basis for the claim?" I asked. Not that I didn't already know, or at least suspect.

"Concern for Alex's safety. The motion cited the dangerous police work you were doing while you were in California with him. The fact that you supposedly abused your privileges while he was in your care at Disneyland."

"Ben, that's bullshit. It's a complete rearrangement of the facts. I consulted on a case with LAPD."

"I'm assuming as much," he told me. "Anne Billingsley's her attorney. It's not beyond her to do a little grandstanding, even at this phase. Don't let it get to you, okay?"

Ben went on, "Besides, there's some good news here, believe it or not. An earlier trial date means they have less time for Christine to establish a status quo under the new arrangement. The judge isn't supposed to take these temporary orders into account, but it's like unringing a bell. So the sooner the better, really. We were actually lucky to get on the calendar this early."

"Great," I said. "Lucky us."

Ben told me to write an account of exactly what happened in California. I had been keeping a diary on his advice ever since I'd hired him. It included time spent with Alex, things I noticed about his development, family photos, and, maybe most important, any concerns I had about Christine. The fact that she had whisked our son away from me two days early certainly qualified. Those ups and downs of hers were a concern, deeply troubling. Was this latest development one of them?

"There's one other thing," Ben told me. "You might not like it a whole lot."

"Listen, you find something for me to like about all this and I'll double your fee."

"Well, one of your strongest arguments is going to be Alex's relationship to his siblings."

"Jannie and Damon aren't going on the witness stand," I said flatly. "That's a no, Ben; I won't allow it."

How many times had I seen capable adult witnesses eviscerated in a courtroom? Too many to even consider putting my kids up there.

"No, no, no," Ben assured me. "Definitely not. But it would have a positive impact if they could be present for the hearing. You want Alex back, don't you? That's our goal, right? If I'm wrong about that, then I don't want to spend time on your case."

I looked around my office, as if for some kind of magic answer. "I'm going to have to think about it," I finally said. "I'll get back to you."

"Remember the big picture, Alex. This isn't going to be pleasant, far from it, but it will be worth it in the long run. We can win this thing. We will win."

He was so calm and collected. Not that I expected him to get emotional — I just wasn't in the mood for a rational conversation with my attorney.

"Can we talk first thing tomorrow?" I asked.

"Sure. But listen, you can't give up hope. When we get in front of a judge, you need to know in your heart that you're the best parent for your son. That doesn't mean we have to trash Christine Johnson, but you can't come in looking, seeming, or even feeling defeated. Okay?"

"I'm not defeated. Not even close to it. I can't lose my son, Ben. I won't lose Alex."

"I'll do everything I can to make sure that doesn't happen. I'll talk to you tomorrow. Call me at work or at home. You have my cell?"

"I have it."

I don't know if I said good-bye to Ben or even hung up before I threw the phone across the room.

# Chapter 31

"WHAT'S GOING ON UP THERE?" Nana called from below. "Alex? Are you okay? What happened?"

I looked at the smashed phone on the floor and felt unhinged. "It's all right," I called back. "I just dropped something. Everything's fine."

Even the little lie didn't sit well with me, but I couldn't face anyone right now. Not even Nana Mama. I pushed back from my desk and put my head down between my knees. Goddamn Christine. What was wrong with her? It just wasn't right, and she had to know that.

She couldn't have chosen a worse way of going about this, either. She was the one who decided to leave, who said she was unfit to be Alex's mom. She told me that. She used the word — unfit. And she was the one who kept changing her mind. Nothing had ever changed for me. I wanted Alex from the moment I set eyes on him, and I wanted him even more now.

I could see his face, his shy little smile, a cute wink he'd developed lately. I could hear his voice inside my head. I wanted to give him a big hug that wouldn't stop.

It felt so unfair, so completely wrongheaded. All I had in me was anger and even a little hatred for Christine, which only made me feel worse. I'd give her a fight if that's what she wanted, but it was insane that she did.

*Breathe,* I told myself.

I was supposed to be good at staying calm in a bad situation. But I couldn't help feeling that I was being punished for doing my job, for being a cop.

I don't know how long I sat up there, but when I finally left the attic, the house was dark and still. Jannie and Damon were asleep in their rooms. I went in and kissed them good night anyway. I took Jannie's mouse ears off and put them on the bedside table.

Then I went out to the back porch. I flipped the lid on the piano and sat down to play. Therapy for one.

Usually, the music took hold of me, helped me work through or forget whatever was bothering me.

Tonight, the blues just came out angry and all wrong. I switched to Brahms, something more soothing, but it didn't help in the least. My pianissimo sounded forte, and my arpeggios were like boots clomping up and down stairs.

I finally stopped midphrase, hands over the keys.

In the silence, I heard the sharp intake of my own breath, an involuntary gulp of air.

*What if I lose Little Alex?*

# Chapter 32

NOTHING COULD BE WORSE than this, nothing I could imagine.

A few days later, we all flew out to Seattle for Alex's custody hearing. The whole Cross family went west again. No vacation this time, though, not even a short one.

The morning after we arrived, Jannie, Damon, and Nana sat quietly behind me on the courtroom benches as we waited for things to get started. Our conversation had dropped off to a tense silence, but having them there meant even more than I would have thought.

I straightened the papers in front of me for about the tenth time. I'm sure I looked fine to everyone, but I was a wreck inside, all hollowed out.

Ben Abajian and I were seated at the respondent's table on the left side of the room. It was a warmly appointed but impersonal space, with honey-colored wood veneer on the walls and standard-issue contemporary furniture.

There were no windows, not that it mattered. Seattle was showing off its dark, rainy side that morning.

When Christine came in, she looked very fresh and put together. I'm not sure what I expected, maybe some outward indication that this was as hard for her as it was for me. Her hair looked longer, pulled back in a French braid. Her navy suit and gray high-collared silk blouse were more conservative than I was used to with her — and more imposing. She looked as if she could be another lawyer in the room. It was perfect.

Our eyes met briefly. She nodded my way, without showing any emotion. For a second, I flashed onto a memory of her looking at me across the table at Kinkead's, our old favorite dinner spot in D.C. It was hard to believe these were the same eyes meeting mine in this courtroom, or that she was the same person.

She said a brief hello to Jannie, Damon, and Nana. The kids were reserved and polite, which I appreciated.

Nana was the only one to be somewhat hostile. She stared at Christine all the way to the petitioner's table.

"So disappointing," she muttered. "Oh, Christine, Christine, who are you? You know better than this. You know better than to cause harm to a child."

Then Christine turned back and looked at Nana, and she seemed *afraid,* something I'd never seen in her before.

What was she afraid of?

# Chapter 33

MS. BILLINGSLEY SAT on Christine's left, and Ben was on my right, blocking our view of each other. That was probably a good thing. I didn't want to see her right now. I couldn't remember ever being so mad at anyone before, especially not someone I had cared for. *What are you doing, Christine? Who are you?*

My mind whirred as the hearing began and Anne Billingsley went into her slickly rehearsed opening statement.

It wasn't until I heard the phrase "born in captivity" that my focus really snapped into place. She was talking about the circumstances of Little Alex's birth, after Christine had been kidnapped while we were on vacation in Jamaica, the beginning of the end for us.

I began to see that Billingsley was every bit the viper Ben had made her out to be. Her wrinkled face and cropped silver hair belied a certain lawyerly showmanship. She hit all her key words hard and with perfect enunciation.

"Your Honor, we will discuss the *many dangers* encountered by Ms. Johnson's son and also by Ms. Johnson herself, during a *brief, tumultuous* relationship with Mr. Cross, who has a long history of involvement with the most extreme homicide cases. And a long history of putting those around him in jeopardy."

It went on and on from there, one loaded statement after another.

I glanced briefly in Christine's direction, but she just stared straight ahead. Was this really what she wanted? How she wanted it to go? I couldn't interpret her flat expression, no matter how I tried.

When Ms. Billingsley was through assassinating my character, she stopped her manic pacing and sat down.

Ben stood up immediately, but he stayed right next to me throughout his opening speech.

"Your Honor, I needn't take up a lot of the court's time at this point. You've seen the trial brief, and you know the key factors in this case. You already know that the first seeds of this arbitration were planted on the day that Ms. Johnson abandoned her newborn son.

"You also know that Doctor Cross provided Alex Junior with the kind of loving home any child would want during the first year and a half of his life. And you know that the longest bond, as they call it, the one we share with our siblings, exists for Little Alex at home in Washington, D.C., with the only family he knew up until last year.

"Finally, we all know that structure and opportunity for success are key issues in determining what is best for a child in the unfortunate circumstance of separated parents. I will say right now, and I believe you will agree, that a home with a father, great-grandmother, brother, sister, and numerous cousins and aunts nearby would provide a more thoroughly supportive experience for a child than to be raised by a mother who lives three thousand miles from what little family she does have, and who thus far has changed her mind twice about her own commitment to the child in question.

"Having said that much, I am not here to malign Ms. Johnson. She is, by all accounts, a perfectly decent parent when she chooses to be one. What I am here to do is illuminate the common-sense conclusion that my client's son, and any child, is better off with a parent whose commitment has never wavered, and shows no sign of doing so in the future."

In our pretrial meetings, Ben and I had agreed to keep everything civil, if we could. I knew ahead of time what he was going to say, but here in the courtroom, and in front of Christine, it sounded different to my ears. It now seemed depressingly combative, not unlike what Anne Billingsley had just done to me in her opening.

I felt a little guilty. No matter what kind of mud Christine's lawyer wanted to fling, at the end of the day I was still responsible for my own actions, and even my lawyer's. That was something Nana had hardwired into me a long time ago.

One thing hadn't changed, though. My resolve was still strong; I was here to bring my youngest son back home to Washington. But listening to Ben Abajian's statement, I had the feeling that this case would have no winners. It was only a matter of who lost less.

Hopefully, it wouldn't be Little Alex who lost.

# Chapter 34

"MS. JOHNSON, can you please tell us in your own words why you are here today?"

I wondered if anyone else could see how nervous Christine was on the stand. She grasped the fingers of one hand with the other, stopping all but the tiniest bit of shaking. I couldn't help grimacing, and my stomach was tightening up. I hated to see her like this, even now, under the circumstances that she had created for herself.

When Christine answered Anne Billingsley's questions, her voice was steady, though, and she seemed perfectly at ease.

"It's time for my son to have a permanent arrangement and stability in his homelife. I want to ensure him the kind of consistency I know he should have. And most of all, I want him to be safe."

Billingsley stayed in her chair, feigning — or maybe

feeling — supreme confidence. "Could you please tell us about the events leading up to your separation from Mr. Cross?"

Christine looked down and took a moment to gather herself. I couldn't imagine that she was acting right now. Her integrity had been one of the reasons I fell in love with her, in that previous lifetime of ours.

"Just after I became pregnant, I was kidnapped and held hostage for ten months," she said, looking up again. "The people who kidnapped me were out to hurt Alex. When that terrible time was all over, I found it impossible to return to a normal life with him. I wanted to, but I just couldn't."

"And just for the record, by Alex you mean Mr. Cross?"

Not Agent or Doctor Cross, but Mister Cross. Any little dig the lawyer could get in.

Even Christine winced, but then she said, "That's right."

"Thank you, Christine. Now, I want to go back just a little bit. Your son was born in Jamaica, while you were being held hostage. Is that correct?"

"Yes."

"Was he born in a hospital in Jamaica, or under any medical supervision?"

"No. It was in a small shack in the woods, the jungle. They brought a midwife of some kind, but she didn't speak English, at least not to me, and there was no prenatal care at all. I was extremely thankful that Alex Junior was born healthy, and stayed that way. Essentially, we lived in a prison cell for those months."

Ms. Billingsley got up, crossed the room, and handed Christine a tissue. "Ms. Johnson, was this abduction the first time that your involvement with Mr. Cross brought violence into your life?"

"Objection!" Ben was on his feet right away.

"I'll rephrase, Your Honor." Billingsley turned her solicitous smile back to Christine. "Were there any other violent incidents, prior to or after your son's birth, related to Mr. Cross's line of work that directly affected you?"

"There were several," Christine said without hesitation.

"The first time was just after we met. My husband at the time was shot and killed by someone Alex was looking for in another terrible homicide case. And then later, after our son was born, and when he was living in Washington with his father, I know that at least once Alex Junior was taken out of the house in the middle of the night, for safety's sake. Actually, all of the Cross children were taken out of the house. A serial killer was coming after Alex."

Billingsley stood at the petitioner's table, waiting. Finally, she pulled a stack of photographs from a manila folder.

"Your Honor, I would like to submit these as evidence. They clearly show Mister Cross's home on the night of one such emergency evacuation. You will see my client's son here being carried out by a non-family member in the midst of the confusion that was apparently taking place."

I wanted to yell out my own objection to this so-called evidence. I knew for a fact that it was John Sampson and not some nameless police officer who carried Little Alex out that night, the night Christine had a photographer — *a private investigator!* — outside my house. No one had been in danger because we had acted judiciously and quickly. But the photos were allowed to speak for themselves, at least for the time being.

It got worse from there.

Anne Billingsley walked Christine through a series of misleading events related to my job, virtually putting words in her mouth. The charade concluded with the trip to Disneyland, which the lawyer dressed up as some horrible minefield of dangers for Little Alex, whom I "abandoned" to go searching through Southern California for a psychopath who could terrorize my family again.

# Chapter 35

THEN IT WAS MY TURN.

The time Ben spent interviewing me on the witness stand was the hardest and trickiest ordeal I'd ever faced, with the most at stake. He had coached me not to address the judge directly, but it was hard not to. My little boy's future was in her hands, wasn't it?

Judge June Mayfield. She looked to be about sixty, with a stiff beauty-shop kind of hairdo that was more middle-America 1950s than new-millennium Seattle. Even her name sounded old fashioned to me. As I sat in the witness chair, I wondered if Judge Mayfield had children. Was she divorced? Had she been through anything like this herself?

"I'm not here to say negative things about anyone," I said slowly. Ben had just asked me if I had any concerns about Christine as a parent. "I just want to talk about what's best for Alex. Nothing else matters."

His nod and the pursing of his lips told me that was the right answer — or was the look merely for the judge's benefit?

"Yes, absolutely," he said. "So could you just please explain to the court how Alex Junior came to live with you for the first year and a half of his life?"

Sitting there on the stand, I had a direct sight line with Christine. That was good, I thought. I didn't want to say anything here that I wasn't willing to say to her face.

I explained as straightforwardly as I could that Christine hadn't felt prepared to be with me or raise a child after what had happened in Jamaica. I didn't need to dress it up. She had chosen not to stick around, period. She'd told me that she was "unfit" to bring up Alex. Christine had used that word, and I would never forget it. How could I?

"And how long would you say it was between Ms. Johnson's abandonment —"

"Objection, Your Honor. He's putting words into his client's mouth."

"Overruled," said Judge Mayfield.

I tried not to invest too much in her response, but it felt good to hear the overrule anyway.

Ben went on with his questions. "How long would you say it was between that abandonment and the next time Ms. Johnson actually laid eyes on her son?"

I didn't have to think about it. "Seven months," I said. "It was seven months."

"Yes, seven months without seeing her son. How did you feel about that?"

"I guess I was surprised to hear from Christine more than anything else. I had begun to think that she wasn't coming back. So had Little Alex." That was the truth, but it was hard to say out loud in the courtroom. "Our whole family was surprised, by both her absence and then her sudden return."

"And when was the *next* time you heard from her?"

"When she said she wanted Little Alex to come live in Seattle. By that time, she had already hired a lawyer in D.C."

"How much time had passed this time?" Ben asked.

"Another six months had gone by."

"That's it? She abandons her son, sees him seven months later, goes away again, and comes back wanting to be a mother? Is that how it happened?"

I sighed. "Something like that."

"Dr. Cross, can you tell us now, from the heart, why you are asking for custody of your son?"

The words just poured out.

"I love him tremendously; I adore Little Alex. I want him to grow up with his brother and sister, and his grandmother, who raised me from the time I was nine. I think Jannie and Damon are my track record. I've shown that whatever faults I have, I'm more than capable of raising happy and, if I may say so, pretty amazing kids."

I looked over at Jannie, Damon, and Nana. They smiled my way, but then Jannie started to cry. I had to look back at Ben, or I thought I might lose it, too.

I noticed that even Judge Mayfield had looked over at the kids, and that she seemed concerned.

"I love my children more than anything in the world," I said. "But our family isn't complete without Little Alex, or Ali, as he likes to be called. He's part of us. We all love him dearly. We couldn't leave him for six months, or six minutes."

Out of the corner of my eye, I saw Nana nodding, and she looked infinitely wiser than Judge Mayfield in her high chair and black robes, especially when it came to raising kids.

"Please go on, Alex," Ben said quietly. "You're doing very well. Go on."

"If I had my wish, Christine never would have left Washington. Ali deserves to have us both around. But if he can't have that, then he should be with as much of his family as possible. I don't think he's bad off here in Seattle, but this is supposed to be about what's best for him. And as I said, I don't know what this is worth, but I love him so much. He's my buddy. He has my heart." And then I did tear up, and definitely not for effect or the benefit of the judge.

Testimony continued through the afternoon and for much of the next morning, and it was brutal at times. After closing arguments from the lawyers, we waited out in the courthouse hallway while Judge Mayfield considered her next move.

"You were great, Daddy." Jannie held my forearm and nuzzled my shoulder with her head. "You *are* great. We're going to get Alex back. I can feel it."

I put my free arm around her shoulder. "I'm sorry for this. But I'm glad you guys are here."

Just then, a court clerk came out to call us back inside. His blank face showed nothing, of course.

Ben spoke quietly to me on the way in. "This will just be a formality. She's probably going to take it under consideration, and we'll hear back anywhere from two to six weeks. I'll motion for a revised temporary visitation agreement in the meantime. I'm sure that won't be a problem. You were great on the stand, Alex. No worries there. You can just relax for now."

# Chapter 36

AS SOON AS WE WERE gathered back in the courtroom, Judge Mayfield came in and sat at the bench. She fiddled with her skirt, and then didn't waste any time.

"I've considered all the testimony and the evidence put before me, and I've reached my decision. Based on everything I've heard, it all seems very clear."

Ben looked reflexively at me, but I wasn't sure what the look meant. *"Ben?"* I whispered.

"Court rules for the petitioner. Residential parentage will remain with Ms. Johnson, upon whose counsel I will lay the burden of facilitating a mutually agreed-upon visitation schedule. I'm going to require mediation for any disputes regarding this agreement before I'll consent to seeing you back here in this courtroom."

The judge took off her glasses and rubbed her eyes, as if ruining a life was a tiresome part of her day. She then continued, "Given the geographic disparity, I am, however, encouraging creative solutions, and I am ruling that Dr. Cross will be entitled to the equivalent of at least forty-five days visitation per year. That's all."

And just like that, she rose and left the room.

Ben put a hand on my shoulder. "Alex, I don't know what to say. I'm stunned. I haven't seen a ruling from the bench in five years. I'm so sorry."

I barely heard him, and I was hardly conscious of my family swarming around me. I looked up to see Christine and Anne Billingsley squeezing past to leave.

"What happened to you?" I asked, the words just coming. It was as if every muscle of control I had been exercising for the past couple of days gave out at once. "Is this what you wanted? To punish me? To punish my family? Why, Christine?"

Then Nana Mama spoke. "You're cruel, and you're selfish, Christine. I feel sorry for you."

Christine turned from us and started to walk away very quickly, without saying a word. When she reached the courtroom doors, her shoulders hunched forward. Suddenly, she put a hand to her mouth. I couldn't tell for sure, but I thought that she began to sob. Ms. Billingsley took her by the arm and ushered her out into the hallway.

I didn't understand. Christine had just won, but she was weeping as if she had lost. Had she? Was that it? What had just happened inside her head?

A moment later I entered the hallway in a daze. Nana was holding one of my hands, Jannie the other. Christine was already gone, but someone else I didn't want to see was waiting there.

James Truscott had somehow gotten inside the court-house. And his photographer, too. What the hell was with him? Coming here. Now. What kind of story was he writing?

"Tough day in court, Dr. Cross," he called up the corridor. "Care to comment on the ruling?"

I pushed past him with my family, but the photographer snapped off several invasive pictures, including single shots of Damon and Jannie.

"Don't print a single picture of my family." I turned to Truscott.

"Or what?" he asked, standing defiantly with his hands on his hips.

"Do not put my family's pictures in your magazine. *Do not.*"

Then I yanked away the photographer's camera and took it with me.

# Chapter 37

LATE THAT SAME DAY, the Storyteller was driving north on the 405, the San Diego Freeway, which was moving okay at about forty or so, and he was working over his "hate list" in his mind. Who did he want to do next, or if not next, before this thing wound down and he had to stop killing or be caught?

*Stop! Just as suddenly as it had begun. The end. Finished. Story over.*

He made a scribbly note in a small pad he always carried in the front-door pocket. It was difficult to write as he drove, and his car edged a little out of its lane.

Suddenly some moke to the right sat on his horn, and stayed on it for several seconds.

He glanced over at a black Lexus convertible, and there was this total moron screaming at him — "Fuck you, asshole, fuck you, fuck you" — and giving him the finger.

The Storyteller couldn't help himself — he just laughed at the red-faced idiot in the other car.

The jerk was so out of it. If he only knew who he was going postal at. This was hilarious! He even leaned over toward the window on the passenger side. And his laughter apparently made the nutcase even angrier. "You think it's funny, asshole? You think it's funny?" the guy screamed.

So the Storyteller just kept laughing, ignoring the irate bastard as if he didn't exist and wasn't worth coyote piss if he did. But this guy did exist, and actually, he'd gotten under the Storyteller's skin, which really wasn't advisable, was it?

Eventually, he drifted behind the Lexus, as if chastened and remorseful, and then he followed. The moke's black convertible got off two exits later. So did he.

And this wasn't in the story. He was improvising now.

He continued to trail the convertible's taillights up into the Hollywood Hills, onto a side road, and then up another steep hill.

He wondered if the driver of the Lexus had spotted him by now. Just to be sure he did, he started honking and didn't stop for the next half mile or so. Figured the other guy might be getting a little spooked by now. He sure would if it were him, especially if he knew *who* he had hassled down on the freeway.

Then he pulled out and started to pass the convertible. This was the coolest goddamn scene yet — he had all the windows open in his car, wind whipping through.

The driver of the Lexus stared over at him, and he wasn't cursing or flipping him the bird anymore. Now who was showing a little remorse? A little r-e-s-p-e-c-t.

The Storyteller's right hand came up, aimed, and he fired four times into the other driver's face, and then he watched the convertible veer into the rocky wall on the side of the road, carom off, swerve back onto the road, then hit the rocks again.

Then nothing — the annoying bastard was dead, wasn't he? Deserved it, too, the asshole. The shame of it, the pity, was that sooner or later this killing had to stop. At least that was the grand plan, that was the story.

# Chapter 38

DETECTIVE JEANNE GALLETTA floored her two-year-old Thunderbird. She had driven faster than this before but never on L.A. city streets. The storefronts on Van Nuys blurred past while her siren droned a steady rhythm overhead.

Two black-and-whites were parked in front of the café when she got there. An unruly crowd had already begun to clot the sidewalk across the street. She was sure that TV cameras wouldn't be far behind, and news helicopters, too.

"What's the situation?" she barked at the first officer she saw, who was halfheartedly doing crowd control.

"All contained," he said. "We did a silent approach, front and back. There's a few of our guys up on the roof, too. You've got about two-dozen customers and staff inside. If she was here when we pulled up, then she's still in there."

That was a big *if*, but it was something to go on, Galletta thought to herself. *Mary Smith might still be inside. This thing could end right here. Please, dear God.*

"All right, two more units inside as soon as you can get them here, two more on crowd control, and keep that guard front, back, and top."

"Ma'am, this isn't my crew —"

"I don't care whose crew it is. Just get it done." She stopped and stared into the officer's eyes. "Am I clear? Do you follow?"

"Perfectly, ma'am."

Galletta headed inside. The café was one big rectangle, with a coffee bar in front and rows of computer carrels in the back. Each electronic terminal was its own little booth, with shoulder-high privacy walls.

Everyone in the place had been corralled at the mismatched tables, chairs, and couches. Galletta quickly surveyed their faces.

Students, Yuppies, senior citizens, and a few Venice Beach hippie-freak types. An officer reported to her that they had all been searched and no weapons were found. Not that it meant anything. For now, they were all suspects by default.

The manager was a very nervous young guy in horn-rims who didn't look old enough to drink, and who had the worst case of acne Galletta had seen since her high school days in the Valley. A mini CD-ROM pinned to his chest said BRETT in red Magic Marker. He showed Galletta to one of the computer carrels near the back.

"This is where we found it," he said.

"Is there an exit that way?" Galletta asked, pointing down a narrow hallway to her left.

The manager nodded. "The police are already back there. They sealed it off."

"And do you keep some record of who uses the machines?"

He pointed to a credit-card swiping device. "They had to use that. I don't really know how to get the info out, but I can find out for you."

"We'll take care of it," Galletta told him. "Here's what I want you to do, though. Keep everyone in here as comfortable as you can. To be honest, it's going to be a while. And if anyone wants anything, make it a *decaf*."

She gave him a wink and a grin that she didn't feel, but it seemed to calm the poor guy down some.

"And ask Officer Hatfield over there to come see me." She had met Officer Bobby Hatfield briefly once before, and she always remembered his name because it was the same as one of the Righteous Brothers.

She sat at the computer and pulled on a pair of latex gloves. "What do you know so far?" she asked when Hatfield came over.

"Same kind of message, written to the same guy at the *Times*. Arnold Griner. It's possible someone got hold of those other e-mails, but this feels like her to me. You've heard of Carmen D'Abruzzi, right?"

"The chef? Of course. She's got her own show. I watch it occasionally; I just don't cook."

Trattoria D'Abruzzi was a flavor-of-the-month restaurant in Hollywood, an A-list dinner and after-hours place. More important, Galletta knew, Carmen D'Abruzzi had a very popular syndicated show in which she cooked for her beautiful husband and her two perfect children. Everything was a little *too* perfect for Galletta's taste, but she did watch the show sometimes.

Galletta shook her head. "Goddammit. D'Abruzzi's just this killer's type. Have you found her yet?"

"That's the kicker," Hatfield told her. "She's fine, no problem. A little freaked out maybe, but okay. Same with her family. We've got a unit at her house already. Check it out — whoever wrote that e-mail never sent it or even finished it."

Jeanne Galletta's head bobbed again. "What the hell? She didn't send it?"

"Maybe she got spooked for whatever reason, wasn't thinking clearly, and just left. Maybe she didn't like the coffee here. I sure don't."

Galletta stood up and looked over the assembled customers and staff again. "Or maybe she's still here."

"You really think so?"

"Actually, no fucking way. She's not dumb. Still, I want to talk to every one of these dinks. This place is a closed box until further notice. Do some initial screening, but no one leaves without going through me personally. Understand? No one. Not for any reason. Not even if they have a note from their mom."

"Yeah, yeah, okay," Hatfield answered. "I got it."

As Hatfield walked away, Jeanne Galletta heard him mutter something like "calm down" under his breath. Typical. Male cops tended to respond one way to a man's orders and another to a woman's. She shrugged it off and turned her attention to the half-finished e-mail on the screen.

*Half-finished? What the hell was that all about?*

# Chapter 39

To: agriner@latimes.com

From: Mary Smith

To: Carmen D'Abruzzi:

You worked at your restaurant until three in the morning last night, didn't you? Busy, busy girl! Then you walked two long blocks by yourself to your car. That's what you thought, isn't it? That you were all alone?

But you weren't, Carmen. I was right there on the sidewalk with you. I didn't even try to be careful. You made it easy for me. Not too bright. So into yourself. *Me, me, me, me.*

Maybe you don't watch the news. Or maybe you just ignore it. Maybe you don't care that someone is out there looking for people just like you. It was almost like you wanted me to kill you. Which is good, I guess. Because that's what I wanted, too.

Watching you, trying to *be* you, I had to wonder if you ever told your two darling children to look both ways when they cross the street. You sure didn't set a good example for Anthony and Martina last night. You never looked around, not once.

Which is too bad for all of you, the whole damn pretty-as-a-picture family as seen on your cooking show.

There's no telling when your children might end up alone on the curb without you, is there? Now they'll have to learn that important safety lesson from someone else.

After you got

# Chapter 40

IT ENDED JUST LIKE THAT — in midsentence.

Even if it hadn't, this was a whole new wrinkle in the case. Carmen D'Abruzzi wasn't dead, and they had the death-threat note. That was something positive, right?

Jeanne Galletta squeezed her eyes shut, trying to process the new information quickly and correctly. Maybe Mary Smith drafted her messages ahead of time and then finalized them posthomicide.

But why leave this one here? Would she do it on purpose? Was this even her at all? Might not be.

Jesus Christ, the questions never ended on this one. So where the hell were the answers? How about just one answer for starters?

She thought about Alex Cross — something he'd said in that book of his. "Keep asking until you find the *keystone*, the one question at the heart of it all. Then you can start working your way back out again. That's when you start finding answers."

The one question. The keystone. What the hell was it?

Well, six hours later it was still a mystery for Galletta. Just after dark, she finally let the last of the morning's customers go home. Five people had given five different eyewitness accounts about who was sitting at the computer in question; the rest of them had no clue.

No one Detective Galletta spoke to struck her as remotely suspicious, but all twenty-six would require follow-up. The paperwork alone was more than she wanted to think about, now or ever.

To no one's surprise, Mary Smith's credit card turned out to be hot. It belonged to an eighty-year-old woman in Sherman Oaks who didn't even realize it was gone, a Mrs. Debbie Green. Nothing else had been charged on the card; there was no paper trail, no anything. *She's careful, and she's organized — for such an obvious nutcase.*

Galletta asked Brett the manager for a full-strength espresso. From here, it was back to the office, where she would sort through the day's events while they were fresh in her memory. Her neighbor said he'd let the dog out. The Chinese place along the way to her office said twenty minutes for pickup. Life was good, no? *No!*

She wondered if she'd be home before midnight and, even then, if she'd be able to sleep.

Probably not — on both counts.

So what was the one question she needed to ask? Where was that *keystone?*

Or was Alex Cross just full of shit?

# Chapter 41

"SHE NEVER KNEW what she wanted, Sugar, and maybe she still doesn't. I liked Christine, but she was never the same after what happened in Jamaica. She has to move on, and so do you."

Sampson and I were holed up at Zinny's, a favorite neighborhood dive. B.B. King's "I Done Got Wise" was wailing on the jukebox. Nothing but the blues would do tonight, not for me anyway.

What the place lacked in cheeriness, it made up for in Raphael, a bartender who knew us by name and had a heavy pour. I contemplated the Scotch in front of me. I was trying to recall if it was my third or fourth. Man, I was feeling tired. I remembered a line from one of the Indiana Jones movies: "It's not the years, honey. It's the mileage."

"Christine's not the point, though, is she, John?" I looked

sideways at Sampson. "The point is Little Alex. Ali. That's how he calls himself. He's already his own person."

He patted me on the top of my head. "The *point* is right here on your skull, Sugar. Now you listen to me."

He waited until I sat up and gave him my full attention. Then his gaze slowly drifted up to the ceiling. He shut his eyes and grimaced. "Shit. I forgot what I was going to say. Too bad, too. I was going to make you feel a whole lot better."

I laughed in spite of myself. Sampson always knew when to go light with me. It had been like that since we were ten years old and growing up in D.C. together.

"Well, next best thing then," he said. He motioned to Raphael for two more.

"You never know what's going to happen," I said, partly to myself. "When you're in love. There's no guarantee."

"Truth," Sampson said. "If you'd told me I'd have a kid, ever, I would have laughed. Now here I am with a three-month-old. It's crazy. And at the same time, it could all change again, just like *that*." He snapped his fingers hard, the sound popping in my ears. Sampson has the biggest hands of anyone I know. I'm six-three, not exactly chiseled, but not too shabby, and he makes me look slight.

"Billie and I are good together, no question about it," he went on, rambling but making sense in his way. "That doesn't mean it can't all go crazy someday. For all I know, ten years from now, she'll be throwing my clothes out on the lawn. You never know. Nah — my girl wouldn't do that to me. Not my Billie," Sampson said, and we both laughed.

We sat and drank in silence for a few minutes. Even without conversation, the mood darkened.

"When are you going to see Little Alex again?" he asked, his voice softer. "*Ali.* I like that."

"Next week, John. I'll be out in Seattle. We've got to finalize the visitation agreement."

I hated that word. *Visitation.* That's what I had with my own son? Every time I talked about it out loud, I wanted to punch something. A lamp, a window, glass.

"How the hell am I going to do this?" I asked Sampson. "Seriously. How can I face Christine — face Alex — and act like everything's okay? Every time I see him now, my heart's going to be aching. Even if I can pull it off and seem okay, that's no way to be with your kids."

"He's going to be fine," Sampson said insistently. "Alex, no *way* you're going to raise messed-up kids. Besides, look at us. You feel like you turned out okay? You feel like I turned out okay?"

I smiled at him. "You got a better example to use?"

Sampson ignored the joke. "You and I didn't exactly have every advantage, and we're just fine. Last I checked, you don't shoot up, you don't disappear, and you don't lay a finger on your kids. I dealt with all that, and I ended up the second-finest cop on the D.C. force." He stopped and smacked his head. "Oh, *wait.* You're a lame-ass federal desk-humper now. I guess that makes me D.C.'s finest."

Suddenly I felt overwhelmed by how much I missed Little Alex, but also by John's friendship. "Thanks for being here," I said.

He put an arm around my shoulders and jostled me hard. "Where else am I gonna be?"

# Chapter 42

I WOKE UP SUDDENLY to a slightly bemused flight attendant staring down at me. I remembered that it was the next morning and I was on a United jet back to L.A. Her curious expression indicated she had just asked a question.

"I'm sorry?" I said.

"Could you please put up your tray table? Put your seat forward. We'll be landing in Los Angeles in just a few minutes."

Before I had drifted off, I'd been thinking about James Truscott and how he'd suddenly appeared in my life. Coincidence? I tended not to believe in it. So I'd called a researcher and friend at Quantico, and asked her to get me some more information on Truscott. Monnie Donnelley had promised that soon I'd know more about Truscott than even I wanted to know.

I gathered up my papers. It wasn't a good idea to leave them out like that, and not like me; it was also unlike me to sleep on flights. Everything was a little upside down these days. Just a little, right?

My Mary Smith file had grown considerably thicker in just a few days. The recent false alarm was a conundrum. I wasn't even sure that Mary Smith was behind that one.

Looking at the murder reports, I had a picture of someone who was growing more confident in her work, and definitely more aggressive. She was moving in on her targets — literally. The first site, the Patrice Bennett murder, was a public space. The next time was outside of Antonia Schifman's home. Now, all indications were that Mary Smith had spent part of the night inside Marti Lowenstein-Bell's house before eventually killing her in the pool.

Anyway, here I was back in L.A. again, getting off a plane, renting a car — even though I probably could have asked Agent Page to pick me up.

Looks-wise, the L.A. Bureau field office put D.C. head-quarters to shame. Instead of the claustrophobic maze I was used to back East, this was nine stories of open floor plan, polished glass, and lots of natural light. From the cubicle they had assigned me on the fifteenth floor, I had a great view of the Getty Museum and beyond. At most field offices, I'd be lucky to get a chair and a desk.

Agent Page started hovering about ten minutes after I got there. I knew that Page was a sharp enough guy, very ambitious, and with some seasoning, he was going to make a good agent. But I just didn't need somebody looking over my shoulder right now. It was bad enough to have Director

Burns on me, not to mention the writer, JamesTruscott. My Boswell, right? Or was he something else?

Page asked if there was anything at all that I needed. I held up my file.

"This thing is *at least* twenty-four-hours cold. I want to know everything Detective Galletta has over at LAPD. I want to know *more* than Galletta has. Do you think you could —"

"On it," he said, and was gone.

It wasn't a bogus assignment I'd given him, though. I really did need to get current, and if that meant Page would be out of my hair for a while, all the better.

I pulled out a blank sheet of paper and scribbled a few questions I'd been pondering on the ride in from LAX.

*M. Lowenstein-Bell — how did someone get inside the house?*

*Does this killer have some kind of hit list? An established order? Are there other less-obvious connections between the victims? Don't there have to be?*

The most common formula in my profession is this: *How plus why equals who.* If I wanted to know Mary Smith, I had to consider the similarities and differences — the combination of the two — from site to site on every one of the murders. That meant a stop at the Lowenstein-Bell residence.

I wrote, *E-mailer? / Perp?*

I kept coming back to that point. How much intersection was there between the killer's personality and the persona in the e-mails? How *honest,* for lack of a better word, was Mary Smith's writing? And how much of it, if any, was misdirection?

Until I could figure that out, it was like chasing two suspects. If I was lucky, my next appointment would shed some light on the e-mails.

I wrote another note to myself. *Tool sets?*

Most pattern killers had two sets of tools, as did Mary Smith.

First were the tools of the actual murder. The gun was a sure thing here. We knew she used the same one each time. We weren't as sure about the knife.

And a car had to be considered. Any other way of getting in and out seemed unfeasible.

Then there were the "tools" that helped her satisfy her psychoemotional needs.

The children's stickers marked *A* or *B*, and the e-mails themselves. Usually, these were more important to the killer than the actual weapons. They were her way of saying "I was here" or "This is me."

Or, possibly, and this was the troubling part, "This is who I want you to think I am."

In any case, it was a kind of taunting — something that could be taken as "Come and get me. If you can."

I scribbled that last thought down, too.

*Come and get me? If you can?*

Then I wrote down something that kept sticking in my craw — *Truscott. Appeared six weeks ago. Who is James Truscott? What is his deal?*

Suddenly I looked at my watch. It was time to leave the office if I didn't want to be late for my first appointment. Requisitioning a Bureau vehicle would have meant one more person looking over my shoulder, and that's exactly why I'd rented a car at the airport.

I left without telling anyone where I was headed. If I was going to be acting like a homicide detective again, I was going to do it right.

# Chapter 43

THIS WAS REAL police work at least, and I threw myself into it with renewed energy and enthusiasm. Actually, I was pumped up. Professor Deborah Papadakis had my full attention as she beckoned me into her book-lined office, number twenty-two, in the Rolfe Building at UCLA. She took a neatly piled stack of manuscripts from the only available chair and set them on the floor.

"I can see you're busy, Professor. God, are you ever busy. Thank you for agreeing to meet," I said.

"Happy to help if I can." She motioned for me to sit. "I haven't seen Los Angeles so preoccupied since, I don't know, maybe since Rodney King. It's kind of sad."

Then she raised a hand and quickly added, "Although that's not the same, is it? Anyway, this is a bit unusual for me. I'm more of a short-story and personal-essay kind of person. I don't read true crime, or even mysteries for that matter. Well, I do read Walter Mosley, but he's a closet sociologist."

"Whatever you can do," I said, and handed her copies of Mary Smith's e-mails. "At the risk of repeating myself, we would appreciate your complete confidence on this." That was for my own sake as well as the investigation's. I hadn't gotten official permission to share the e-mails with her or anyone else.

Professor Papadakis poured me a cup of coffee from an old percolator, and I waited while she read, then reread, the e-mails.

Her office seemed to be a bit of prime real estate at the university. It looked out to a courtyard and sculpture garden, where students wrote and soaked up the perfect Southern California weather. Most offices in the building faced out to the street. Ms. Papadakis, with her antique pine desk and O. Henry Award on the wall, gave the impression of someone who had long since paid her dues.

Except for the occasional "hm," she was unresponsive while she read. Finally, she looked up and stared my way. A bit of the color was gone from her face.

"Well," she said with a deep breath, "first impressions are important, so I'll start there."

She picked up a red pencil, and I stood up and came around to look over her shoulder.

"See here? And here? The openings are active. Things like 'I am the one who killed you' and 'I watched you having dinner last night.' They're attention-grabbing, or at least they're meant to be."

"Do you draw any specific conclusion from that?" I had some of my own, but I was here for her perspective.

She bobbed her head side to side. "It's engaging, but also less spontaneous. More crafted. This person is choosing her words carefully. It's certainly not stream of consciousness."

"May I ask what else you see in the writing? This is very helpful, Professor Papadakis."

"Well, there's a sense of . . . detachment, let's say, from the character's own violence."

She looked up at me, as if for approval. I couldn't imagine she was usually this tentative. Her air was otherwise so earthy and grounded. "Except, maybe, when she talks about the children."

"Please, go on," I said. "I'm interested in the children. What do you see, Professor?"

"When she describes what she's done, it's very declarative. Lots of simple sentences, almost staccato sometimes. It could just be a style choice, but it might also be a kind of avoidance. I see it all the time when writers are afraid of their material. If this were a student, I would tell her to pull at those threads a bit more, let them unravel." The professor shrugged. "Of course, I'm not a psychiatrist."

"Everything but, from the sound of it," I told her. "I'm really impressed. You've added some clarity."

She dismissed the compliment with a wave of her hand.

"Anything else I can do? Anything at all? Actually, this is fascinating. Morbid curiosity, I suppose."

I watched her face as she weighed her thoughts, then opted not to continue.

"What is it?" I asked. "Please, just brainstorm. Don't worry about it. No wrong answers."

She set down her red pencil. "Well, the question here is whether you're reading a person or a character. In other words, is the detachment that I see coming from the writer's subconscious, or is it just as crafted as the sentences themselves? It's hard to know for sure. That's the big puzzle here, isn't it?"

It was exactly the question I had asked myself several times. The professor wasn't answering it for me, but she was certainly confirming that it was worth asking in the first place.

Suddenly she laughed nervously. "I certainly hope you aren't giving my assessment any critical role in your investigation. I would hate to misguide you. This is too important."

"Don't worry about that," I said. "This is just one of many factors we're taking into account. It's an incredible puzzle, though. Psychological, analytical, literary."

"You must hate having to run all over the place for these tiny crumbs of information. I know I would."

"Actually, this kind of interview is the easy part of the job," I told her honestly.

It was my next appointment that was going to be bad.

# Chapter 44

ARMED SECURITY STOPPED ME at the gate to the Lowenstein-Bell property in the Bel Air section of Beverly Hills. Two more private guards in the upper part of the driveway rechecked my ID. Finally, I was permitted to approach the house, which was on a winding road not far from the Bel Air Hotel, which I'd visited once, and found to be one of the most serene and beautiful spots I'd ever seen.

When I rang, Michael Bell himself answered. The house was more glass than anything, and I saw him coming well before he reached me. His slow shuffle spoke volumes.

It's always a balancing act with family members left behind by a murder. The time you need the most information is the time they least want to talk about what has happened. I've never found a method that feels very good to me, or probably to the person I was there to interview.

Mr. Bell didn't look particularly Beverly Hills with his bushy blond beard, jeans, sandals, and faded plaid shirt. I could almost see him as a lumberjack, or an ex-member of Nirvana or Pearl Jam, if not for the ultramodern setting. I knew from the file that he and his wife had built their house just a few years ago.

Michael Bell's manner and voice had the dulled quality of someone in the early stages of grief, but he politely welcomed me inside. "Can I offer you anything?" he asked. "I know we have iced tea. Some sun tea, Agent Cross?"

"Nothing, thanks," I said.

A middle-aged housekeeper / nanny stood nearby, waiting to help if she could. I imagined this was Lupe San Remo, who had found the body in the swimming pool.

"Nada, Lupe, gracias," Mr. Bell told her. "Quisiéramos cenar a las siete, por favor."

I followed him past an open gallery where three blond pixies were clustered onto one oversized armchair. Cassie, Anna, and Zoey, ages five, seven, and eight, according to the file. An image from *Finding Nemo* was frozen in pause on the huge plasma television.

I had interrupted, and I felt bad about that, too. I wondered if "Mary Smith" really had feelings for the victims' children. And if she did — why? What could possibly be this crazy person's motive? Why kill the mother of these small children?

"Girls, I'll be in the living room for a few minutes. You can go ahead without me." He pushed a button on a remote control and turned up the volume as the movie started again. I recognized Ellen DeGeneres's voice on the sound track, probably because I'd seen *Nemo* a dozen times with Jannie. She loved Dorry to death.

"We can talk in here," Mr. Bell said as we entered a vaulted living room. Three stories of glass wall looked out to a stunning coastal view and, closer in, the swimming pool where his wife, Marti, had been found. Michael Bell sat with his back to the pool on a cream-colored velvet couch.

"I used to love that view," he said in a quiet voice. "Marti did, too."

"Would you prefer to meet somewhere else?" I asked him straightaway.

"Thank you," he said. "It's all right. I'm trying to move around as normally as possible. For the girls. For my own sanity. It's fine. You have some questions?"

"I know you're being questioned by the LAPD. I know they've cleared you, so I'll try to keep this as short as I possibly can."

"I appreciate it. Whatever it takes," he said. "Please. Go ahead. I want to help find the person who did this. I need to feel like I'm helping, doing something."

I sat on a matching couch. A huge block of polished marble was the table between us. "I'm sorry, but I have to start with the obvious. Did your wife have any enemies that you're aware of? Anyone who's crossed your mind since this happened?"

He ran his hands over his beard, then back and forth across his eyes. "Believe me, I've thought about that. It's part of what's so ironic. Marti's one of the most popular people in town. Everyone loved her, which is so rare out here. You can check."

He stopped, and his face contorted. He was very close to losing it, and I believed that I could see his thought. *Everyone loved her. Past tense.*

His shoulders drooped. He wiped his eyes with a closed fist. "I'm sorry. I keep thinking that what's happened has sunk in, but it really hasn't."

"Take your time," I told him.

I wanted to say more; I wanted to tell him that I knew what this felt like. Not just to lose a wife, but to lose her in this way. A while back, I'd been pretty much where he was right now. If his experience was anything like mine with Maria, there was no comfort to be had anywhere, much less from a stranger, a policeman. Anything personal I could tell him at this point would only be for my own sake, though, so I didn't talk about Maria and how she was murdered.

"Dad?"

Zoey, the oldest daughter, stood in the high arch between the living room and hallway. She looked frightened, tiny, and very alone in the doorway.

"It's okay, hon," he said. "I'm okay. Come here for a sec." He opened his arms, and she went to him, taking the long way around the couch to avoid walking next to me.

She fell into his hug, and then both of them began to cry. I wondered if she had seen her father cry before. "It's okay," he said again, smoothing her hair. "It's okay, Zoey. I love you so much. You're such a good girl."

"I love you, Daddy," Zoey whispered.

"We'll do this later," I said softly. "Another time. I've got your statement on file. I don't need much more anyway."

He looked at me appreciatively, the side of his face

pressed against Zoey's head. She had softened her posture now and curled to meet the shape of his hug. I could tell that they were close, and I thought of Jannie.

"Please let me know if there's anything I can do," he said. "I do want to help."

"If I could just take a quick walk through the house, it would be useful for me," I said.

"Of course."

I turned to go, but then stopped and spoke again, only because I couldn't help myself. "You're doing exactly the right thing," I told him. "Your children will get you through this. Keep them close."

"I will. They're all I have now. Thank you. You're very considerate."

I left it at that, and if I had to guess, I'd say he knew it wasn't just a cop's advice I was offering. It was a father's, and a husband's. Suddenly I didn't want to be at this house any longer than I had to be.

# Chapter 45

AS A DETECTIVE, I would have liked to have spent hours in the Lowenstein-Bell house, to soak up all the details. Under the circumstances, I gave myself fifteen to twenty minutes.

I started by the pretty pool and stood at the deep end, staring down at the royal-blue racing lines painted on the bottom. Estimates were that Mary Smith had shot Marti Lowenstein-Bell from this position, a single bullet to the top of the head. Then she'd pulled the body over to her with a long-handled pool net.

The killer calmly stood right here and did the knife work without ever taking the body out of the water. The cuts on the victim's face had been sloppy and quick, dozens of overlapping slashes. *As though she were erasing her.*

It was evocative of what people sometimes do to photographs, the way they symbolically get rid of someone by Xing out the face. And in fact, Mary Smith had also destroyed several family photos in the office upstairs in the house.

I looked up to where I imagined the office would be, based on file diagrams.

The logical path from here to there went through the living room, then up the limestone staircase in the main entry hall.

*The killer had visited the home before the day of the murder. How exactly had that occurred? At what time? And — why? How was Mary Smith evolving?*

When I passed through the house again, Michael Bell was sitting with his three small daughters, all of them blankly watching their movie. They didn't even look up as I went by, and I didn't want to interrupt them again if I could help it. For some reason, I remembered hugging Jannie and Day right after what happened with Little Alex in Seattle.

The upstairs hallway was a suspended bridge of wood and glass that bisected the house. I followed Mary Smith's likely path up there, then down to an enclosed wing where Marti's office was easy enough to find.

It was the only room with a closed door.

Inside, the office wall had conspicuous blank spots where I imagined family photos had hung. Everything else looked to be intact.

*The killer is getting braver, taking more risks, but the obsession with families remains strong. The killer's focus is powerful.*

My attention went to a high-backed leather chair in front of a twenty-one-inch vertical monitor. This was the victim's workspace and, presumably, the place where Mary Smith sat to send the e-mail to Arnold Griner at the *L.A. Times.*

The office also had a view of the terrace and pool below. Mary Smith could have watched Marti's body floating face-down while she typed away. Did it repulse her? Put her into a rage? Or was she feeling gross satisfaction as she sat here looking down on her victim?

Something clicked for me. The destroyed photos here. The recent close call at the coffee house. Something Professor Papadakis had said about "avoidance." Something else I had been thinking about that morning. *Mary Smith didn't like what she was seeing at the murder sites, did she?*

The longer this went on, the more it reflected some powerful image from the past that disturbed her. Some part of herself she didn't want to see was becoming clearer. Her response was to devolve. I hated to think about it, but she was probably losing control.

Then I corrected myself — the killer *was* losing control.

# Chapter 46

I LAY FLAT ON MY BACK on the hotel bed that night, my head spinning in different directions, none of them worth a damn as far as I was concerned.

Mary Smith. Her pathology. Inconsistencies. Possible motivation for the murders. Nothing there so far.

Jamilla. Don't go there either. You're not even close to solving that.

My family back in D.C. Was I ever messing that up.

Christine and Alex Junior. Saddest of all.

I was aware that no part of my life was getting the attention it deserved lately. Everything was starting to feel like an effort. I had helped other people deal with this kind of depression, just never myself, and it seemed to me that nobody's very good at self-analysis.

True to her word, Monnie Donnelley had already delivered some material on James Truscott. Very simply, he checked out. He was ambitious, could be considered ruthless at times, but he was a respected member of the Fourth Estate. He didn't appear to have any connection to the Mary Smith murders.

I looked at my watch, muttered a curse, then dialed home, hoping to catch Jannie and Damon before they went off to bed.

"Hello, Cross residence. Jannie Cross speaking."

I found myself smiling. "Is this the hugs-and-kisses store? I'd like to place an order, please."

"Hi, Daddy. I knew you'd call."

"Am I that predictable? Never mind. You two getting ready for bed, I hope? Ask Damon to get on the other line."

"I'm already on. I figured it was you, Dad. You are kind of predictable. That's a *good* thing."

I caught up with the kids briefly. Damon tried to wheedle me into letting him buy a CD with a parental advisory label. No sale there, and still no word from him on the mystery girlfriend. Jannie was gearing up for her first science fair and wanted to know if I could hook her friends up to a polygraph. "Sure thing. Right after we hook up you and Damon."

Then Jannie told me something that bothered me a lot. "That writer was here again. Nana chased him off. She gave him a good tongue-lashing, called him a 'disgrace to his profession.'"

After I finished with the kids, I talked to Nana, and then I ordered room service. Finally, I called Jamilla in San Francisco. I was making the calls in reverse stress order, I knew, leaving the hard ones for last. Of course, there was also the issue of time zones to consider.

"This whole Mary Smith thing has gone national in a hurry," Jamilla said. "Word up here is the LAPD isn't even close to catching her."

"Let's talk about something besides work," I said. "That okay with you?"

"Actually, I have to leave, Alex. I'm meeting a friend . . . just a friend," she added a little too quickly. "Don't worry about it." But that sounded to me like code for *worry about it.*

"Sure, go," I said.

"Talk to you tomorrow?" she asked. "Sorry. I have to run. Tomorrow, Alex?"

I promised, and then hung up. *Just a friend,* I thought. Well, two calls down, one to go. The really hard one. I picked up the phone again and punched in numbers I knew by heart.

"Hello?"

"It's me. Alex."

Christine paused — another undecipherable response. "Hi," she finally said.

"Could I talk to Alex?"

"Of course. Hang on, I'll get him. He just finished his dinner. He's in the playroom."

I heard a rustling and then Christine's muted voice. "It's Daddy." The word gave me a strange pang — warm and regretful at the same time.

"Hi, Daddy." A whole lot of mixed feelings intensified at the excited sound of his voice, but mostly, I just missed him like crazy. I could see his small face, his smile.

"Hey, pup. What's new?"

Like any three-year-old, Little Alex wasn't quite up to

speed on the whole phone thing. It was a quick conversation, unfortunately. After a particularly long pause, I heard Christine again in the background.

"Say bye-bye."

"Bye-bye."

"See you soon," I told him. "I love you, buddy."

"Love *you,* Daddy."

Then Little Alex hung up the phone on me. With a dismissive *click,* I was back in my room, alone with the Mary Smith case, missing all the people I loved more than life itself. That was the exact thought in my head — but what did it mean?

# Part Three

# JUGGLING ACTS

# Chapter 47

MARY SMITH SAT on a park bench while her darling little Ashley monkeyed her way around the playground. Good deal. The exercise was just enough to tire her out before Mary had to pick up Brendan and Adam from their playdates; hopefully it was enough time to let Mary's brain cool down from another impossible day.

She looked at the brand-new diary on her lap, admired its nice heavy paper and the beautiful linen cover.

Journals were the one big splurge in her life. She tried to write a little every day. Maybe later, the kids would read these pages and know who she really was, besides Cook, Maid, and Chauffeur. Meanwhile, even the journal had conspired against her. Without thinking, she had written *tomatoes, baby carrots, cereal, juice, diapers* on the first page. Shoot!

That just wouldn't do. She carefully tore it out. Maybe it

was silly, but she thought this book as a sacred place, not somewhere you wanted to put a shopping list.

She suddenly realized Ashley was gone! *Oh my God, where is she?*

She was right there a second ago, and now she was gone.

Had it been just a second? She tensed. Maybe it hadn't. Maybe it was longer than a few seconds.

"Ashley? Sweetie?"

Her eyes quickly scanned the small, crowded playground. Several blonde mop tops on swings or running around, but no Ashley. The whole place was enclosed with a wrought-iron fence. *How far could she have gotten?* She headed toward the gate.

"Excuse me, have you seen a little girl? Blond hair, jeans, a red T-shirt?"

No one had, though.

*Oh, dear God, not this. No. No.*

Just then Mary spotted her. Her heart nearly burst. Ashley was tucked behind a tree near the corner of the play-ground. She coughed out a little laugh, embarrassed with herself for getting this nervous so quickly. *God, what is wrong with me?*

She walked over to her. "What are you doing over here, sweetness?"

"Playing hide and seek," she said. "Just playing, Mommy."

"With who, for gosh sake?" She fought to keep her tone in check. People were starting to stare.

"With you." She smiled so sweetly Mary could barely stand it.

She bent low and whispered against her soft cheek. "Ashley, you cannot run off like that. Do you understand? If you can't see me, then I can't see you. Okay?"

"Okay."

"Good, now why don't you go and try the jungle gym?"

Mary settled down on another bench away from the gathering storm of disapproving stares. A young mother reading the *L.A. Times* smiled over at her. "Hello."

"You must not be from around here," Mary said, giving her a quick once-over.

The woman's voice was slightly defensive. "Why do you say that?"

"First of all, no one around here is that friendly," Mary answered, then smiled. "Second of all, it takes an outsider to know one. I'm a Vermonter, myself."

The other woman looked relieved. "Baltimore," she said with a hand to her chest. "I heard everyone was friendly out here in California. They stop their cars and let you cross the street, right? You don't see that in Baltimore."

"Well, that's true."

"Of course, you don't see this, either." She held up the front page of the *Times*.

## HOLLYWOOD MURDER
## INVESTIGATION CONTINUES

"Have you heard about this?" the woman asked. "I guess you must have."

"It's hard to miss these days."

"It just makes me so sad. I know I should be afraid, too, but really, I'm just so sorry for those families."

Mary nodded solemnly. "I know. So am I, so am I. Isn't it awful? Those poor, poor children. It just makes you want to cry your eyes out."

# Chapter 48

ACCORDING TO THE STATISTICS I was reading at my desk, something like 89 percent of known female serial killers used poison, suffocation, or lethal injection on their victims. Less than 10 percent of various killers employed a gun as their weapon of choice, and none I had found on record used a knife.

*Is Mary Smith the exception that proves the rule?*

I didn't think so. But I seemed to be all alone on that.

I scanned the deskful of clippings, photos, and articles spread out in front of me like pieces from several different jigsaw puzzles.

Aileen Wuornos was a shooter. In 1989 and '90, she killed at least seven men in Florida. When she was arrested, the media dubbed her America's first female serial killer. She was probably the most famous, but nowhere near the first.

Almost half of those on record were black widows — husband-killers — or else motivated by revenge. Most had some relationship with their victims.

Bobbie Sue Terrell, a nurse, injected twelve patients with lethal doses of insulin.

Dorothea Montalvo Puente poisoned nine boarders in her home so she could get their Social Security checks.

A secretary at the field office, Maureen, poked her head in.

"You want anything from In-n-Out Burger?"

I looked up and realized it was dark already, and that, actually, I was starving.

"If they have a grilled chicken sandwich, that'd be good. And an orange juice, thanks."

She laughed merrily. "You want a hamburger or a cheeseburger?"

Since my sleep and personal life were something of a mess, I was trying to keep the junk food intake in check. I hadn't worked out in days. The last thing I needed was to get sick out here. I told Maureen never mind, I'd get something eventually.

A minute later, Agent Page was hovering at my desk. "How's it going?" he asked. "Anything yet?"

I spread my arms to indicate the breadth of information on the desk. "She doesn't fit in."

"Which was probably true for about half the female serial killers in history at the time of their activity," said Page. The young agent was impressing me more and more.

"So what about our good friends at LAPD? Anything new from them?"

"Sure is," he said. "Ballistics came back on that gun of hers. Hear this — it's a golden oldie. A Walther PPK, same one every time. There's a full briefing tomorrow if you want to be there. If not, I'll cover."

That was surprising news, and very odd — the age of the murder weapon.

"How old is the gun? Do they know?"

"At least twenty years, which deepens the mystery some, huh? Could be hard to trace."

"You think that's her reason? Traceability?" I asked, mostly just thinking out loud. Page quickly ticked off a handful of possibilities.

"She's not a professional, right? Maybe it's a weapon she's had for a long time. Or maybe she's been killing a lot longer than we think. Maybe she found it. Maybe it was her father's."

All solid guesses from a rapid-fire mind. "How old are you?" I asked, suddenly curious.

He gave me a sideways glance. "Uh, I don't think you're supposed to ask that."

"Relax," I said. "It's not a job interview. I'm just wondering. You're a lot quicker than some of the folks I see coming out of Quantico lately."

"I'm twenty-six," he said, grinning widely.

"You're pretty good, Page. Need to work on that game face, though."

He didn't alter his expression. "I've got game; I just don't need it here in the field office." Then, affecting pitch-perfect surfer-speak, he said, "Yeah, dude, I know what you're thinking about me, but now that my surfing scholarship fell through, I'm like, totally dedicated to being here."

It felt good to laugh, even if it was mostly at myself.

"Actually," I said, "I can't imagine you getting up on a surfboard, Page."

"Imagine it, dude," Page said.

# Chapter 49

AROUND 5:00 THE NEXT DAY, the briefing room at LAPD was packed to overflowing, a suitcase with way too much crap inside. I leaned up against a wall near the front, waiting for Detective Jeanne Galletta to get the madness going.

She came in walking briskly alongside Fred Van Allsburg, from my office; L.A.'s chief of police, Alan Shrewsbury; and a third man, whom I didn't recognize. Jeanne was definitely the looker in the group, and the only one under fifty.

"Who's that?" I asked the officer standing next to me. "Blue suit. *Lighter* blue suit."

"Michael Corbin."

"Who?"

"The deputy mayor. He *is* a suit. Useless as tits on a bull."

I was kind of glad to have been left out of the speechifying at the meeting — but a little wary as well. Politics were a given on this kind of high-profile homicide case. I just hoped they weren't about to start playing a larger-than-usual role here in Los Angeles.

Galletta gave me a little nod hello before she started. "All right, people, let's go." Everyone quieted down immediately. The deputy mayor shook Van Allsburg's hand and then slipped out a side door. Huh? What was that all about? It wasn't a guest appearance, more like a ghost appearance.

"Let's get the nuts and bolts out of the way first," Detective Galletta said.

She quickly ran over all the common elements of the case — the Walther PPK, the children's stickers marked with two *A*'s and a *B*, the so-called Perfect Mother victims, which was the angle the press was running with, of course. One nasty out-of-town paper had called the case "The Stepford Wife Murders." Galletta reminded us that the exact wording in the e-mails Mary had sent to the *L.A. Times* was classified information.

A few questions flew.

Does the LAPD or Bureau know of or suspect any connection between Mary Smith and other homicides in the area? *No.*

How do we know it was a single assailant? *We don't for sure, but all signs indicate as much.*

How do we know the killer is a woman? *A woman's hair, presumably the offender's, was found under a sticker at the movie theater in Westwood.*

"This might be a good time to ask Agent Cross to give us an overview of whatever profile the FBI has going. Dr. Cross has come here from Washington, where he solved cases involving serial killers like Gary Soneji and Kyle Craig."

Something like a hundred pairs of eyes shifted to look at me. I had come to the briefing as an observer, I thought, but now I was going to be put on center stage. No sense wasting the opportunity, or worse, everybody's time.

"Well, let me start by saying that I'm not yet absolutely convinced Mary Smith is a woman," I said.

*That ought to wake them up in the back rows.*

# Chapter 50

IT DID, TOO. A ripple went through the room. At least I'd gotten everybody's attention.

"I'm not saying it's definitely a male offender, but we haven't ruled that out as a possibility. I don't believe you should. Either way, though," I said, raising my voice over the low rumble, "there are a few things I can say about this case.

"I'll use *she* as a default for now. She's likely white, and in her midthirties to forties. She drives her own car, something that wouldn't get too much notice in the upscale neighborhoods where the murders happened. She's most likely educated, and most likely employed, nonprofessional. Maybe some kind of service position for which she may very well be overqualified."

I went on for a bit, then fielded some questions from the assembled team. When I was finished, Jeanne Galletta gave the floor over to ballistics for a gun report; then she wrapped up the meeting.

"Last thing," she said. "Kileen, sit down, please. Thank you, Gerry. We're not done. I'll tell you when we're done." She waited for quiet, and she got it.

"I don't need to tell you about the kind of ridiculous press coverage this is getting. I want *everyone* thinking and acting as though there's a camera on you at all times, because there probably is. Absolutely no shortcuts out there, people. I'm serious as lung cancer on that last point. S.O.P. should be a nonissue."

I noticed Galletta's eyes shift toward Van Allsburg while she spoke. Procedure had probably been the topic of their closed-door meeting with the deputy mayor. It occurred to me that this was an election year. The mayor needed a clean result on this one, and a fast one. I doubted it was going to happen that way.

"Okay, that's it for now," Galletta said, and the room came alive. She caught my eye and nodded her head toward the conference room in the back.

I had to push through the crowd to get there, wondering what she wanted to talk about.

"How's it going?" I asked as she closed the door behind us.

"What the hell was *that*?" she snapped.

I blinked. "What the hell was what?"

"Contradicting me, talking about Mary Smith as a man, confusing the issue at this time. I need these people focused, and you need to keep me informed before you start reviving dead issues out of the blue like that."

"Dead issues? Out of the blue? We talked about this. I told you my feeling."

"Yeah, and we put it away."

"No. We didn't put it away. *You* did. Jeanne, I know you're under pressure —"

"Goddam right I am. This is Los Angeles, not D.C. You have no idea."

"I *do* have some idea. In the future, if you want me to present at a briefing, and avoid any surprises, you should check in with me ahead of time. And try to remember what you said up there, about how I caught Gary Soneji and Kyle Craig."

I tried to stay calm and even supportive with my tone, but I also wasn't going to cave because of anyone's bullying.

Jeanne gritted her teeth and stared at the floor for a second. "All right. Okay. Sorry."

"And for the record, I'm not saying you need to check in with me. This is your case, but with something so big and unwieldy, there's only so much control you can have."

"I know, I know." She breathed a big sigh, not one of relief, more like a cleansing breath. Then Jeanne smiled. "You know what, how about I make it up to you? You like sushi? You have to eat, right? And I promise we won't talk about work."

"Thanks," I said. "But I'm not done for the day. Unfortunately. I need to head back to the office from here. Jeanne, I *don't* think this killer is a woman. So, who is it? Some other time for a bite, okay?"

"Some other time," Jeanne Galletta said; then she walked away hastily, the same way she'd entered the conference room earlier.

# Chapter 51

FOR THE NEXT SEVERAL HOURS I stayed focused, one of those very productive work states I wish I could put myself in every time I sat down at a desk.

I ran several theories through the VICAP system, looking for any kind of match to the rash of murders in L.A. Anything even remotely close.

Something finally came up that caught my attention. A triple murder more than six months earlier.

It had happened in New York City, though, not L.A. But the murders took place in a movie theater, the Sutton on East 57th Street, and the details were intriguing at first blush.

For one thing the murders remained unsolved. There'd been nothing even close to a solution by the NYPD. Just like the murders in Los Angeles.

There was no apparent motive for the New York killings either. That last bit was important. Maybe this series of pattern killings began a lot earlier than anyone had thought up to now. And maybe the killer was from New York originally.

I pulled up the NYPD detective notes on the case and read them through. A patron inside the movie theater, as well as two Sutton employees, had been killed that afternoon. The detective's working theory was that the theater workers had walked in on the killer just after he killed a man named Jacob Reiser, from Brooklyn. Reiser had been a film student at NYU, twenty years old.

But then something else caught my eye — the murder weapon listed in the report. Based on the bullets removed from the bodies, a Walther PPK had been used.

The gun used in the L.A. murders had also been a Walther PPK, though apparently an older model.

But there was something else that grabbed me: *The murders in New York had happened in the men's room.*

# Chapter 52

GREAT NEWS — I was accruing enough hotel points for a lifetime of free rooms. The problem was that I never wanted to see another hotel for as long as I lived. West Los Angeles didn't offer much in the way of distractions, either. I lay on the bed flipping through my notes again, a half-eaten chicken sandwich and a warm soda next to me.

When the phone rang, I gratefully picked up. It was Nana Mama.

"I was just thinking about pork chops and spoon bread," I told her. "And here you are."

"Why are you always buttering me up, Alex?" she asked. "Trying anyway. You going to tell me you're not coming home next weekend?"

"Not exactly."

"Alex —"

"I'm coming home. And believe me, there's nothing more I want than to leave this case far behind. But I'm also going to be back and forth some."

"Alex, I want you to think long and hard about how much time you really need to be out there in California. Turns out, this new job is worse than your last one."

Apparently, my post–custody trial grace period was over. Nana was back to her old self, laying it on with a trowel. Not that she was entirely wrong.

"How are the kids?" I finally asked. "Can I talk to them?" *And give my ears a rest from you, old woman.*

"They're fine and dandy, *Daddy*. Just for the record, so am I."

"Did something happen?" I asked.

"No. Just a dizzy spell. It's nothing at all. I saw Kayla Coles today. Everything's fine. Dr. Coles checked me out. I'm good for another ten thousand miles."

"If I know you, and I *do* know you, that means a big dizzy spell. Did you pass out again?"

"No, I *did not* pass out," she said, as if it was the most ridiculous idea she'd ever heard in her life. "I'm just an old woman, Alex. I've told you that before. Though, God knows, I don't look or act my age."

When I asked Nana to give me Kayla Coles's phone number, though, she outright refused. I had to wait for Damon to get on the line and Nana to get off; then I told him to go up to my desk and get me Kayla's number from my Rolodex.

"How's she seem to you?" I asked him. "You need to take care of her, Day."

"She seems pretty good, Dad. She wouldn't tell us what happened. But she went out grocery shopping and made dinner tonight. I can't tell if there's anything wrong or not. You know Nana, how she is. She's *vacuuming* now."

"She's just showing off. Go vacuum for her. Go ahead now. Help your grandmother."

"I don't know how to vacuum."

"Then this is a good time to learn."

I finished up with the kids and then called Kayla Coles, but I got her answering service. I tried Sampson next and asked if he could swing by the house and check on Nana, who had partly brought him up, too.

"No problem," he told me. "I'll show up hungry tomorrow for breakfast, how's that?"

"Sounds like a win-win to me. Also, a very believable excuse for a visit."

"She'll see right through it."

"Of course she will. Although you're a very believable hungry person."

"How're *you* doing?" he asked then. "You sound like you're at about fifty percent."

"I'm okay. More like seventy-five. There's just a hell of a lot going on out here. Big, messy case, John. Way too much publicity. I keep seeing that asshole writer Truscott, too. Though I hear he's back East again now."

"You want some backup? I could boogie out to L.A. I've got some vacation days."

"Yeah, just what I need, to piss off *your* wife. Thanks, though. I'll keep it in mind — *if* we ever get close to this Mary Smith."

A lot of my best work was with Sampson. Being with him was one of the things I missed most about the police department. I wasn't through with him yet, though. I had one more idea where he was concerned. When the time was right, I'd spring it.

# Chapter 53

I SPENT THE NEXT DAY at the FBI field office, worked from seven until seven, but maybe there was a light at the end of this particular long, dark, and creepy tunnel. Jamilla was coming to L.A., and I'd looked forward to her visit all day.

Jam insisted I not bother picking her up at the airport, and we made plans to meet at Bliss on La Cienega. When I got to the restaurant, she was standing at the bar with an overnight bag at her feet. She had on jeans, a black turtleneck, and black boots with pointy toes and steel tips. I slipped up behind her and kissed her neck. Hard to resist.

"Hey, you," I said. "You smell good. You look even better." Which Jamilla definitely did.

She twisted around to face me. "Hi, Alex. You made it."

"Was there ever a doubt?"

"Well, um, yeah," she said. "Remember the last time I was in L.A.?"

We were both hungry, so we got a table and ordered appetizers immediately — a dozen clams on the shell and an heirloom-tomato salad to share. Jamilla eats like an athlete at a training table, and I kind of like that.

"What's new on the murder case?" she asked after we'd polished off the tomatoes and clams. "Is it true she's been sending e-mails since the first murder?"

I blinked at her in surprise. The *L.A. Times* had been purposely vague about when the e-mails had begun. "Where'd you hear that? *What* did you hear?"

"Word gets around, Alex. One of those B-level security things the public doesn't necessarily know about, but everyone else does. It got up to San Francisco."

"What else have you heard? B-level stuff," I said.

"I hear this lead detective Jeanne Galletta's a hot ticket. Work-wise, I mean."

"She's no Jamilla Hughes, but yeah, she's pretty good at her job."

Jamilla shrugged off the compliment. She had my number all right. She looked pretty in the candlelight, to my eyes anyway. Now *this* was a good idea: dinner with Jam at a fine restaurant, my cell phone turned off.

We chose a bottle of Pinot Noir from Oregon, a favorite of hers, and I lifted my glass once it was poured. "Things have been complicated lately, Jam. I appreciate your being there for me. And here for me, too."

Jamilla took a sip of wine; then she put a hand on my wrist. "Alex, there's something I need to say. It's kind of important. Just listen. Okay?"

I stared across the table into her eyes and didn't know if I liked what I saw. My stomach was starting to drop. "Sure," I said.

"Let me ask you this," she said, her eyes drifting away from mine. "In your mind, how exclusive are we?"

Ouch. There it was.

"Well, I haven't been with anyone since we've been seeing each other," I said. "That's just me, though, Jamilla. You meet someone? I guess you have."

She let out a breath, then nodded. That's the way she was, straight up and truthful. I appreciated it. Mostly.

"Are you seeing him?" I asked. My body was starting to tense all over. In the beginning of our relationship, I had expected something like this, but not now. Maybe I'd just gotten complacent. Or too trusting. That was a recurring problem I had.

Jamilla winced a little, thinking about her answer. "I guess that I am, Alex."

"How'd you meet him?" I asked, then stopped myself. "Wait, Jam. You don't have to answer that."

She seemed to want to though. "Johnny's a lawyer. *Prosecution,* of course. I met him on one of my cases. Alex, I've only seen him twice. Socially, that is."

I stopped myself from asking more questions, even though I wanted to. I didn't have a right, did I? If anything, I'd brought this on myself. Why had I done it, though? Why wasn't I able to commit? Because of what happened to Maria? Or Christine? Or maybe to my own parents, who had broken up in their twenties and never even seen each other again?

Jamilla leaned across the table and spoke softly, keeping this confidential, just between us. "I'm sorry. I can tell I've hurt you, and I didn't want that. We can finish dinner and talk about this if you want. Or you can go. Or I can go. Whatever you want, Alex."

When I didn't answer right away, she asked, "Are you mad at me?"

"No," I answered a little too fast. "I'm surprised, I guess. Maybe disappointed, too. I'm not quite sure what I am. Just to get it straight — are you telling me you want to see other people, or was it your intention to break things off tonight?"

Jamilla took another sip of her wine. "I wanted to ask you how you felt about it."

"Right now? Honestly, Jam? I don't think I can continue like we've been. I'm not even sure of my reasons. I've always been pretty much — one person at a time. You know me."

"We never made any promises to each other," she said. "I'm just trying to be honest."

"I know you are. I appreciate it, I really do. Listen, Jamilla, I think I need to go." I kissed her on the cheek, and then I left. I wanted to be honest, too. With Jamilla and with myself.

# Chapter 54

I LEFT IT ALL BEHIND, everything, and flew up to Seattle for the weekend.

As I drove from the airport toward the Wallingford neighborhood where Christine and Alex lived, I grappled with the idea of seeing her now. What other choice did I have?

I brought no presents, no bribes, just as she had done when Alex lived with me in Washington. Christine was letting me see Alex, and there was no way I could resist. I wanted to be with him for a while — I needed it.

The house was on Sunnyside Avenue North, and I knew the way by now. Christine and Ali were sitting on the porch steps when I got there. He ran down the walk to meet me like a little tornado, and I scooped him up. There was always a fear of finding a different boy than the one I last saw. All that dissolved the second I had him in my arms.

"Man, you're getting heavy; you're getting so big. *Ali.*"

"I gotta new book," he told me, grinning. "A hungry caterpillar that eats anything. It pops up. Then it *eats* you!"

"You can bring your book with you today. We'll read." I gave him another squeeze and saw Christine watching from a distance, arms folded. Finally, she smiled and raised one hand in a wave.

"Want some coffee?" she called. "Need some before you two take off?"

I squinted at her, a silent question in the still, fragrant air.

"It's okay with me," she said. "C'mon. I won't bite." Her tone was bright, probably for my sake as well as Ali's.

"Come on, Daddy." He climbed out of my arms, took my hand. "I'll show you the way."

So I followed them inside. Was this a good idea? I'd never actually been inside before. The house was tastefully cluttered. Several Arts and Crafts–style built-ins overflowed with books and some of Christine's art collection. It was more informal and comfortable-looking than her home outside D.C. had been.

I was struck by how naturally both of them moved through this space that was so foreign to me. *I don't belong here.*

The kitchen was open, very bright, and smelled of rosemary. A small herb garden thrived on the windowsill.

Christine set Alex up with a sippy cup of chocolate milk and then put two mugs of steaming coffee on the table between us.

"Seattle's drug of choice," she said. "I drink way too much of it. I should switch to decaf in the afternoons or something. Maybe in the mornings," she added with a laugh.

"It's good. The coffee. Your house looks great, too."

The chitchattiness was striking in its banality, and almost as uncomfortable as a real conversation might have been right now. I vowed not to ask Christine about the weather, but this was weird for both of us.

Little Alex slipped off his chair and came back with his new book. He climbed onto my lap.

"Read. Okay? Careful, it pops up and eats you!"

It made for a good distraction and also put the focus on him, where it was supposed to be. I opened the cover and began.

" 'In the light of the moon a little egg lay on a leaf.' "

Alex put his head against my chest, and as I felt my voice reverberate into him, my heart melted a little. Christine watched while I read. She smiled, clutching her mug with both hands. *What might have been.*

A couple of minutes later, Alex had to go to the bathroom, and he asked me to go with him. "Please, Daddy."

Christine came over and whispered near my ear. "He's having trouble hitting the toilet bowl with his pee. He's a little embarrassed about it."

"Oh," I said. "Fruit Loops. You have any?"

Fortunately, Christine had a box, and I took it into the bathroom with Alex.

I threw a couple into the bowl. "Here's a cool game," I said. "You have to put your pee right in the middle of a Fruit Loop."

He tried, and he did pretty good — hit the bowl anyway.

I told Christine the trick when we came out, and she smiled and shook her head. "Fruit Loops. It's a guy thing, right?"

185

# Chapter 55

THE REST OF MY DAY in Seattle was less stressful and a lot more fun. I took Little Alex to the aquarium, and it was easy, and gratifying, to throw myself into the time I had with him. He stared wide-eyed at the tropical fish and made a mess of his chicken fingers and ketchup at lunch afterward. For all I cared, we could have spent the day in a bus terminal waiting room.

I loved watching him be himself, and also grow up. Every year it got better. *Ali. Like the great one.*

My mind didn't get too weighed down again until we were back at the house that night. Christine and I talked for a while on the front porch. I didn't want to go inside, but I didn't want to leave yet. And if I wasn't imagining it, her eyes were a little red. Ever since I'd known her, she'd had mood swings, but they seemed to be getting worse.

"I guess it's my turn to ask if you're all right," I said. "Are you okay?"

"I'm fine, Alex. Just the usual. Trust me, you don't want to hear about my stuff."

"Well, if you mean romance, then you're right. But otherwise, go ahead."

She laughed. "Romance? No, I'm just a little overextended these days. I do it to myself, always have. I'm working way too hard."

I knew she was the new head at a private school nearby. Other than that, I really didn't have a clue what Christine's life looked like anymore — much less why she had been crying before I got back to the house with Alex.

"Besides," she said, "we agreed last time I would ask about *you*. How are you doing? I know it's hard, and I'm sorry for that, for everything that's happened."

I told her in the briefest possible terms about the Mary Smith case, Nana's recent dizzy spell, and that Jannie and Damon were doing fine. I left Jamilla out of the conversation, and she didn't ask.

"I've been reading about that terrible murder case in the paper," Christine said. "I hope you're being careful. It surprises me that a woman could be a killer."

"I'm always careful," I told her. There was all kinds of irony going on here. Obviously, my job stood for a lot between Christine and me, and none of it was good.

"This is all so strange, isn't it?" she said suddenly. "Was it harder than you expected, being here today?"

I told her that seeing Alex was worth whatever it took, but that honestly, seeing her was hard, too.

"We've certainly had easier times than this, haven't we?" she asked.

"Yes, just not as parents."

She looked at me, and her dark eyes were so intelligent, as they always had been. "That's so sad, Alex, when you put it that way."

I shrugged, with nothing to say.

She put a tentative hand on my forearm. "I'm sorry, Alex. Really. I hope I'm not being insensitive. I don't know what you're feeling, but I do think I understand the position you're in. I just —" She mustered up her next thought. "I just wonder sometimes what kind of parents we would have made. Together, I mean."

That was it. "Christine, you either *are* being insensitive or you're trying to tell me something."

She sighed deeply. "I'm doing this all wrong. As usual. I wasn't going to say anything today, but now I have. So, okay, here it is. I want Alex to have a two-parent life. I want him to know you, and believe it or not, I want you to know him. For everyone's sake. Even mine."

I took a step back, and her hand fell limply away. "I don't know what to say to that, Christine. I think it's obvious that I wanted the same thing. You're the one who decided to move out here to Seattle."

"I know," she said. "That's what I really wanted to speak with you about. I'm thinking of moving back to Virginia. I'm almost sure that's what I'm going to do."

My mind, finally, was completely blown.

# Chapter 56

VANCOUVER WAS ONE of the Storyteller's favorite cities — along with London, Berlin, and Copenhagen. He flew up there on Alaska Air and arrived just in time to wait on a long line with about five hundred "visitors" from Korea and China. Vancouver was crawling with Chinese and Koreans, but that was about the only thing he didn't like about the beautiful Canadian seaport, and it seemed a minor complaint.

He had some movie business in town that took up most of the day and also put him in a dark mood. By five or so that night he was in a wretched state of mind, and he needed to get the bottled-up anger out somehow.

*Know what I need? To tell somebody what's going on, to share.*

Maybe not tell everything, but some of it — at least an idea of how incredible this whole thing was, this totally strange period of his life, this wilding, as he'd come to call it, this story.

There was this foxy red-haired producer he knew who was in Vancouver to shoot a TV movie. Maybe he should connect with her. Tracey Willett had her own wilding period in Hollywood, starting when she was eighteen and continuing into her late twenties. She'd had a kid since and had apparently cooled her jets some.

But she kept in touch with him, and that had to mean something. He'd always been able to talk to Tracey, and about almost anything.

So he called her, and sure enough, she said she'd love to have dinner and drinks with him. About an hour later, Tracey called back from the movie set. The movie shoot was running late. Not her fault, he knew. Probably some hack director's fault. Some disorganized, arrogant, glorified art director two or three years out of film school.

So he didn't get to see Tracey until past eleven, when she came over to his room at the Marriott. She gave him a big hug and a sloppy kiss, and she looked pretty good for having worked all day. "I missed you, sweetcakes. I missed you so much. Where have you *been?* You look great by the way. So thin, *good* thin, though. The lean-and-hungry look, right? It suits you."

He didn't know whether Tracey was still into blow, or booze, or whatever, so he had a little of everything on hand, and that's what they did — just about everything. He knew right away she wanted to fool around, because she told him she was horny for one of the stunt men on the movie and because of the way she sat on the couch, legs set apart, looking him up and down with those bedroom eyes of hers, hungry eyes, just as he remembered. Finally, Tracey pulled up her top and said, "Well?"

So he took her to bed, where she complimented his new lean body again. Tracey did a little more coke; then she took off her blouse to let him admire her tits some more. He remembered the drill with Tracey — you had to talk about how sexy she was and touch her everywhere for about twenty minutes, then at least thirty minutes of very energetic humping because Tracey couldn't have an orgasm to save her life, and was always getting *so close,* but never quite there, so keep going, *harder, faster, harder, faster, oh baby, baby, baby.* And when he came inside her, she seemed to like it, and she held him close as if they were a couple again, even though they had never really been a couple.

Once the sexual preliminaries were out of the way, it was his turn to really get off. They were out on his terrace overlooking the city, and Tracey had her head on his shoulder. Very romantic and cute, in a pathetic sort of way, like going on a date with Meg Ryan, or Daryl Hannah maybe.

"I want to tell you a little about what I've been up to," he finally said. Until then, everything had been about her.

"I want to hear all about it, sweetie. Only I can't leave the kid too late back at my hotel. The nanny threatens to quit."

Now that he remembered, Tracey was kind of a selfish bitch most of the time.

"Does anybody know about the two of us tonight?" he asked.

"No. Duh. So what are you up to? Something big, of course. You're due."

"Yeah, it's kind of a mystery thing. It's big, all right. Really different though. Nothing anything like it before. I'm writing the story myself. The story of stories."

"Wow, that's great. You're writing it yourself, huh?"

"Yeah. You know those murders in L.A.? Mary Smith?"

She knew a little but not everything, since she'd been up in Vancouver for four weeks, so he quickly filled her in.

"You bought the rights? Wow! That's great. And what, you want *me* to produce?"

He shook his head in disbelief.

"From *who*, Tracey? Who would I buy the rights from?"

"Oh, right. Well, so what's the deal then?"

"So I can talk to you? Really talk?"

"Of course you can talk to me. Tell me your big idea, your story. I love thrillers."

*This is it. Go or no-go? What is it going to be?*

"I planned those murders, Tracey. I'm Mary." Wow. It was out. Just like that. I'm Mary. Holy shit!

She looked at him real funny, funny peculiar, and suddenly he knew this had been a very bad idea, and old Tracey wasn't the crazy one — *he was*. He'd just blown his whole deal. And for what? To let off a little steam with an old girlfriend? To vent? Confess?

She was staring at him as if he had two heads, at least that many. "Come again? What are you saying?"

He laughed, faked it the best he could, anyway.

"It's a *joke*, Trace. We're high; I made a joke. Hey, let me give you a ride home. You've got the kid at your hotel, the nanny and whatever. I hear you. And you're a good mommy, right?"

# Chapter 57

THEY DIDN'T TALK MUCH in the car, so he knew how big a mistake he'd made, and now he wondered if he'd made other mistakes along the way. Maybe important ones that would get him caught. Like way back in New York City. The movie-theater shootings.

He finally spoke. "I've been under a lot of stress lately, you know."

She muttered, "Sure. I hear you."

Man, she was making him paranoid, and a little nuts, actually. They'd been friends for a long time, though. "So how old is the kid now?"

"Uhmmm, four and a half. He's great. Stefan."

She was really scaring him. Now what? What the hell should he do? This wasn't a "Mary Smith" scene. Tracey wasn't even in his story. This was bad news.

Suddenly he pulled his rented Volvo over to the side of the road. Now what?

"What's the matter?" she asked. "What?"

"You'd better get out right here, Trace. I'm not kidding you. Get out! Walk the rest of the way!"

"Walk? Are you crazy. What are you talking about?"

"Get out of the car! Right now. *Get out before I throw you out!*"

That got her moving. She threw open the passenger's door and stumbled outside, cursing him like a truck driver. It was cold out there, and she had both arms wrapped around her. Then she started to cry. "You're crazy. You know that? I thought we were friends."

She started to run away on the dark residential side street somewhere between the Marriott and her hotel.

The Storyteller got out of the car and found himself following close behind. "Tracey, wait! Hey. Tracey."

He caught up to her easily. "Hey, hey. I'm sorry for scaring you, baby. I'm really sorry. Hey, you okay?" And then he shot her in the throat, and once she was down on the sidewalk, he shot her again in the head.

And this time it wasn't good, didn't feel good at all.

This time it felt kind of bad, scared the hell out of him.

Because the story was taking over, the story was writing itself, and the story didn't seem to care who got hurt.

# Chapter 58

AS I FLEW FROM SEATTLE back to Los Angeles the next day, it struck me again how darkly appropriate the Mary Smith case was as a backdrop to my entire life. I was also starting to feel like some kind of record-setter for complicated or failed relationships. The only closure I had reached with Christine was that we would speak more soon. It excited me to think about having Little Alex — Ali — closer by, but I wasn't about to get attached to the idea. Christine had proved herself too changeable in the past for me to trust that anything she said might happen for sure.

As it turned out, I got sucked back into the murder case even before I made it through the terminal at LAX.

A television news report caught my ear, and I stopped to watch the next development unfold.

I couldn't look away as a talking head reported, "At a press conference this morning, lead detective on the

Hollywood Stalker case, Jeanne Galletta, denied the existence of any so-called kill list."

Hollywood Stalker was a media moniker that had emerged lately for Mary Smith. As for a "kill list," I had no idea what the TV reporter was talking about.

"LAPD is urging area residents to remain calm and go about their business. Many people, however, aren't buying it.

"One citizens' group appeared at the local precinct, demanding to see the 'kill list,' which police claim doesn't even exist. Either way, and whoever you choose to believe, one thing is clear: The Stalker has this community" — she inserted a reporterly pause — "very much on edge. Lorraine Solie, reporting live from Beverly Hills."

*Kill list?* What the hell was this? Had the LAPD found out something and then not shared it with us? It wouldn't be the only time.

The first person I was able to reach at the FBI field office was David Fujishiro, another special agent assigned to the murder case.

"It's way, way out in left field," he told me. "There's this supposed list with twenty-one names, starting with Patrice Bennett, Antonia Schifman, and Marti Lowenstein-Bell. The idea is that it's Mary Smith's agenda."

"And everyone in L.A. wants to know if they're on it?" I asked. "One of the twenty-one?"

"Right. And it gets even better than that. The rumor is that anyone on the list can *buy their way off* by sending a hundred thousand dollars to a post office box in Orange County that doesn't seem to exist. We've checked it all out, not that anyone believes us. People are actually threatening legal action against the LAPD."

"But there's no truth to the rumor, David? You're sure?"

"Not that we know of. But hey, what the hell do we know? We're only the FBI."

"This case is getting its own social life," I said. "Has anybody spoken to Detective Galletta about the list?"

"I don't know, but — *what?*" There was a pause on the line. "Hang on, Alex."

"David? What's happening?"

I could hear voices in the background, but nothing distinct. Agent Fujishiro came back on and told me to wait another second. "Something's up," he added.

"Wait!" I yelled, but it was no good. He was gone again.

More voices came, then a general rumbling, rising in pitch. What the hell was happening?

Then I heard Fujishiro saying "Yeah, I've got him right here on the phone."

"Alex? Fred Van Allsburg needs to talk to you right now. Hold the line."

I was never glad to hear from Van Allsburg, but his voice had a no-bullshit tension to it.

"What's going on?" I said.

"That's what we're trying to figure out right now. All we know at the moment is that Arnold Griner at the *Times* just got another e-mail. Can you get over to the *L.A. Times* office right away?"

"Not if there's a new murder scene, I can't. I need to see it now."

"I'm not going to negotiate this, Alex. We'll get word to you as soon as we know what's what. Meanwhile —"

I couldn't help myself — I cut him off. "Sir? Hello? Can you hear me?"

I hung up in the middle of Van Allsburg shouting that he could hear me fine.

Then I called Agent Page and told him to put me on hold until we knew if Mary Smith had a new victim.

# Chapter 59

SUZIE CARTOULIS WASN'T PAYING much attention to the real world as she backed out of the driveway that morning. Her thoughts were on an unfinished pool cabana in the back-yard of the house in Pacific Palisades, and the blankety-blank contractor who wasn't returning any of her phone calls, who never returned her calls, only her husband's. Two more days like this and she was going to fire the guy's ass. Right after she set it on fire.

Another car, idling just past a neighbor's cedar hedge, came into sight at the last second. Suzie braked hard to avoid hitting the jerk who was parked there. Her heart thudded. That certainly would have been an auspicious way to start her day, a fender bender ten feet from her driveway.

She gave a quick wave into the rearview mirror.

"Sorry!" My bad.

Then she put her silver Mercedes wagon in drive and started down the cul-de-sac toward Sunset. The other car pulled out as well and began to follow, but Suzie Cartoulis didn't notice.

Her focus had shifted to the nine-year-old boy in the backseat. "Are you all right, Zach? I didn't mean to stop so suddenly like that."

"I'm fine, I'm fine, I'm fine."

"All right. Just checking, sweetie. How about a little music? What do you want to hear?"

She tried not to be overbearing, but it was hard sometimes. Zachary was such a sensitive boy, and he didn't react well to being ignored, either. Maybe if he had a little brother or sister, but that wasn't going to happen any time soon. Not now that Suzie had become the ten-o'clock anchor. She had finally gotten into the inner sanctum of recognizable faces in L.A. — no small feat for a former weathergirl from Tucson, thank you very much — and she wasn't going to let another pregnancy slow her down right now. Especially since New York was apparently very interested in her as well.

As if on cue, the phone rang.

Caller ID showed her husband's cell number, and she juggled the headset up to her ear.

"Hi. Where are you, honey?" She spoke through a frown she was glad Gio wasn't there to see.

"Miami. I think we're wrapping up. I have to shoot up to Palm Beach in a minute. Of course, there's another hurricane on the horizon, so I want to vamoose out of here. We just need a few signatures, but it looks like the contract's a go."

"Great," she said with hollow enthusiasm. She was supposed to know what project he was talking about, but they all blended together. Something about a shopping mall in southern Florida. Was that right? Was Vero Beach in south Florida? The Treasure Coast? This was their game; he spoke about his work as if she cared, and she pretended to.

"So I should be home tonight instead of Monday, which would be nice. Maybe play a little golf this week? Wiatt finally invited me to Riviera."

"Mm-hm."

"How's the little dude?"

"He's right here. Hang on."

Suzie surrendered the phone to the backseat. "It's Daddy. Be nice."

She was already rearranging today's schedule in her head. Get someone else to cover the mayor's press conference on the ongoing murders. Have the housekeeper pick up Zach after tennis practice. Call Brian, see if he can get away; then call the Ramada and ask for an early check-in. Get laid properly once more before her all-business-all-of-the-time husband got back to town.

Make it an afternoon to remember.

# Chapter 60

To: agriner@latimes.com

From: Mary Smith

To: Suzie Cartoulis:

People in Los Angeles watch you on television every day, reporting the news, acting like you really know what's going on. That's what you do so well. Acting, pretending, faking it with flair. But today will be a little different, Suze. Today you will be the news.

They'll say that Suzie Cartoulis and her handsome, former-beach-volleyball-champ lover were found slain in a hotel room. That's how you people talk, isn't it? Slain? But no matter what they say on the news, no one will ever know just how you looked at me when I killed you. The incredible fear, the confusion, and what I took to be *respect*.

It was different this morning outside your fancy house in Pacific Palisades. You almost bumped into me with your highly polished silver Merc wagon, and you looked right through me. You *did*, Suze. Trust me on that. I remember these kinds of things.

Then, just like the others, you went on with your day like I wasn't even there. I had a feeling today might be the last one for you. Then I was sure of it.

First I watched you say good-bye to your darling little boy for the last time. He probably can't appreciate everything you do for him — all the sacrifices — but he'll think about it later, when someone else has to take him to school or to practice the next time he goes. You're right about one thing though, *you should have made more time in your life for Zachary. Coulda, shoulda.*

Then I followed you to the hotel in West Hollywood. At first I didn't know why you went there, but I figured out pretty quickly that you weren't going to die alone. That delicious-looking blond man you met — you two were perfect for each other. Central casting all the way.

I could tell just by looking that he's the kind of somebody you are. Am I right? He went to

the Olympics, after all. He's an exec at your
network. Another fast-tracker. And now you have
another thing in common. You're both *dead* somebodies. Killed by a nobody you couldn't even see
when you looked right at her.

I gave you two some quality time before I
came up there for you. Enough time to feel safe
in your little cocoon of deceit. Maybe even
enough to do what you had in mind for your
sneaky little rendezvous. Then, when I came in,
I saw him first. That was a bit of good luck.
Know why? I wanted you to see him die. It put
the fear of God on your face before I shot you —
and then I got to cut that fear away, one piece
at a time, until you weren't afraid anymore.

You weren't anything anymore.

You were nothing, Suzie Cartoulis.

Just like me.

# Chapter 61

I WAS STILL ON THE ROAD when word came about Mary Smith's latest — a *triple* homicide this time, the killer's deadliest strike to date, at least as far as we knew for certain. I was still chasing down leads on the triple homicide in New York, but progress was slow, and suddenly I was off to another crime scene.

Susan Cartoulis, a prizewinning newscaster, had been found dead, along with her lover, in a room at the Ramada Plaza Suites in West Hollywood.

The dead man was Brian Conver, a sports producer at the same network where Ms. Cartoulis worked. A second woman, Mariah Alexander, a college student who attended Southern Cal, had also been killed. What was that all about?

I asked Agent Page to read Mary Smith's latest e-mail message over the phone while I drove. The text made clear that the newswoman had been the primary target. Mr. Conver was never mentioned by name, and there was no reference whatsoever to any Mariah Alexander.

"What do we know about Susan Cartoulis?" I asked Page. "Does she fit the MO?"

"Basically, yeah. She fits right into the puzzle. Married with one son, good-looking woman, high profile in the city. She was a ten-o'clock anchor for a local affiliate. Also the honorary chair of the Cedars-Sinai pediatric burn unit capital campaign. Nine-year-old son. Another perfect mom."

"With a boyfriend on the side."

"Well, I guess nobody's perfect. Is that what Mary's trying to tell us?"

"Maybe," I said.

The press was going to eat up this one, as if they weren't already overfed. It made me feel even sorrier for Susan Cartoulis's husband and her young son. Her murder and infidelity would be trotted out for the public in great detail.

"Do you think that has anything to do with it?" Page asked. "Perfect mothers who aren't so perfect after all? Hypocrisy on the home front? Something as simple as that?"

"If that's Mary Smith's point, she's being pretty murky about it. Especially for someone who's so deliberate in getting her message out there in her e-mails. Plus, as far as we know, most of the murdered women actually live up to their reputations."

"As far as we know," said Page. "Stay tuned on that one, yeah?"

"All right, why don't you do a little digging around about the others. See if you can find any dirty little secrets we missed. Try Arnold Griner. I'll bet he has an inside line or two. That's his job, right?"

"The forensics of gossip, huh?" Page said, and laughed. "I'll see what I can do. See if I can get Griner to talk about anything besides himself."

"Who was the other victim? Mariah Alexander."

"Yeah, that really sucks. She was a maid at the hotel. College kid. We think Mary got in the room with her passkey."

"One other thing," I said. "If anyone asks, you haven't heard from me and you don't know where I am."

Page paused on the line. "I'm not going to lie if someone asks me, but I won't volunteer anything. Anyway, I'm on my way out of the office."

"Good enough. By the way, you're doing a terrific job."

"For a surfer boy, huh?"

"Exactly, dude."

# Chapter 62

I FOLLOWED KARL PAGE'S DIRECTIONS toward the Ramada in West Hollywood and deliberately left my phone in the car when I got there. I didn't want to be reached by anybody at the Bureau right now, not even Director Burns's office.

The stark Art Deco lobby was quiet and depressing. Dreary, dried-up palms loomed over rows of boxy chocolate-brown couches, all of them empty. Two elderly women at the front desk were the only customers in sight.

Whoever was in charge here — Jeanne Galletta, I hoped — had gotten a good cap on the scene. The only indication that a major investigation was under way one story up was the two officers stationed at the elevator. I took the stairs to the murder scene, two at a time.

The second-floor hallway was thick with LAPD personnel. Several of them wore gloves, white booties, and "Crime

Scene Unit" polo shirts. The faces were all stressed and drawn.

A uniformed officer gave me the once-over. "Who are you?" he asked. His tag said Sandhausen. I flashed him my creds without comment and kept moving past him. "Hey!" he called out.

"Hey yourself," I called back, and kept going.

When I got to room 223, the door was wide open.

A row of cartoonish stickers, Mary Smith's calling card, was affixed to the outside — two glittery-winged fairies and another unicorn, which was stuck right over the peephole.

Two stickers were marked with an *A*, the other with a *B*.

A maid's cart stood parked off to the side.

"Is Jeanne Galletta around?" I asked another young officer as she pushed past me into the hall. The sheer number of people coming and going here was disconcerting.

The female officer gave me a petulant look. "I think she's downstairs in the office. I don't know."

"Find out," I said, suddenly losing my patience. "Let her know Alex Cross is looking for her. I'll be in here."

I steeled myself before I stepped inside the hotel room. There's a necessary detachment at any murder scene, and I can feel it like a second skin that I put on. But there's a necessary balance, too. I never wanted to forget that this was about human beings, not just bodies, not just vics. If I ever got immune to that, I'd know it was time to look for another career. Maybe it was time anyway.

What I found was a scene just as predictably brutal as I had come to expect from Mary Smith.

Plus a couple of nasty surprises that I wasn't prepared for.

209

# Chapter 63

THE BATHROOM WAS A HORROR.

Mariah Alexander, the nineteen-year-old hotel maid, lay collapsed backward in the tub, her head at a nearly impossible angle to her torso. Her throat was torn open where a bullet had erased any possibility of a scream. Her long, curly black hair was streaked with her blood. It looked as though the girl's carotid artery had been nicked, which would explain the blood spurts that extended all the way up the wall.

A heavy set of keys lay on the tile floor near the dead girl's dangling feet. My first guess was that Mary Smith had pulled a gun on the young woman, forced her to unlock the hotel-room door, then backed her up into the bathroom and shot her — all in quick succession.

Susan Cartoulis and Mr. Conver would likely have been in the bedroom at that point, just a short hallway away.

Someone — probably Conver — had come to see what was going on.

If the bloodstains on the carpet were any indication, Mary Smith had intercepted Conver halfway between the bedroom and bathroom.

His body, however, was now arranged on the bed next to Susan Cartoulis. The lovers lay faceup, side by side, on top of the covers.

Both of them were nude — another first for Mary Smith — although it was likely they were undressed when she got there.

Pillowcases were draped across the two victims' hips and over Ms. Cartoulis's chest, in an odd suggestion of modesty.

Man, this was a wacky and confusing killer. The inconsistencies boggled the mind, mine anyway.

It got even stranger. *The king-size bed was perfectly made.* It was possible that Cartoulis and Conver hadn't used the bed while having sex, but soft drinks and a condom wrapper on the nightstand indicated otherwise.

Did Mary Smith actually make the bed after she murdered three people? If so, she was good at it. Nana had long ago made sure I knew the difference between a real hospital corner and a lazy one. Mary Smith knew the difference as well.

The tidily arranged covers were soaked with blood, particularly around Ms. Cartoulis. Both victims had sustained gunshot wounds to the head, but Cartoulis's face had also been brutalized with a blade — in Mary Smith's usual manner, and as promised in the e-mail. I could just about make out Conver's last, strained expression of terror, but

Cartoulis's face had so many cuts it looked like a single open wound.

It reminded me of the murders at Antonia Schifman's house — neat *and* sloppy at the same time.

One killer, two completely different impulses.

What the hell had she been thinking? What did she want out of this?

The most disturbing new wrinkle came a few minutes later. A yellow leather Coach wallet with Susan Cartoulis's driver's license and credit cards lay open on a chair near the bed.

As I looked through the wallet, I saw that it was neatly filled with one thing and another, but that there were several empty plastic sleeves. The empty spaces sent tension up and down my spine. "Goddammit," I said out loud. "Photographs."

One of the Crime Scene Unit staff turned to me. "What's up? You find something?"

"Do we know where Susan Cartoulis's husband is?" I asked.

"He's supposed to be on a plane, coming home from Florida. Why?"

"I need to know if this woman carried family photos in her wallet."

My question was a formality; I was almost certain I knew the answer. This would be the second time in as many incidents that Mary Smith had been interested in family photos. She'd gone from leaving the children entirely alone to either destroying or stealing their photographs. Meanwhile, her methodology was increasingly erratic, and her e-mails seemed more confident than ever.

How slippery a slope was this going to be from here on? And where was it taking me?

I didn't think I could live with myself if Mary Smith started turning on kids before we caught up to her. But that's what I was afraid might happen next.

# Chapter 64

"CAN I SEE YOU for a minute, Dr. Cross? We need to talk."

I looked up to see Detective Jeanne Galletta standing in the door. Her expression was strained; I thought that she looked older than the last time we met, and thinner, as if she'd lost ten pounds she hadn't needed to shed.

We went out into the hall. "What's going on? Don't tell me something else has happened."

"I don't want to go wide with this yet," she said in a low, tired voice, "but there's a woman who saw a blue Suburban leaving the hotel parking lot in a big hurry. Happened around two o'clock. She didn't notice much else. I wonder if you could interview her, and then we could compare notes. Before I do anything with this."

It was a good move on her part. I'm pretty sure she was thinking the same thing I was: The D.C. sniper case in 2002 had included a massive public search for what turned out to be the wrong vehicle, a white van with black lettering. It was an investigative and public-relations nightmare, exactly the kind of mistake LAPD wouldn't want to make now.

"And could you do it right now? That would be helpful. I'd appreciate it," she added. "If I'm going to run with this, I don't want to wait."

I hated to leave the crime scene. There was a lot of work to be done. If Jeanne weren't wearing her stress so plainly, maybe I would have said no.

"Give me five minutes to finish up here," I told her. "I'll be right down."

Meanwhile, I asked Jeanne to do me a favor and follow up with Giovanni Cartoulis about the missing photos in his wife's wallet. There was frustratingly little we could do with the information from him, but it was important to know if Mary Smith had stolen family pictures. Also, Giovanni Cartoulis needed to be eliminated as a suspect, as all the previous husbands had been. Jeanne and her people had been handling this, but I was satisfied with the reports. The LAPD was doing a good job.

"What?" Jeanne asked, standing very still in the hallway and staring at me. "What are you thinking? Tell me. I can handle it. I *think*."

"Take a deep breath. Don't give in to this crap. You're running the case as well as anyone possibly could, but you look like hell right now."

She knitted her eyebrows. "Um . . . thanks?"

"You look good, just not as good as usual. You're pale, Jeanne. It's the stress. Nobody understands that until they get hit with it."

Jeanne finally smiled. "I look like a fucking raccoon. Big dark smears around my eyes."

"Sorry."

"It's okay. I've got to run."

I thought about her earlier dinner invitation and my clumsy decline. If we had stood there a few seconds longer, maybe I would have reciprocated the invitation for later, but Jeanne — and the moment — was already gone.

And I had an interview to do.

A blue Suburban, right?

# Chapter 65

IT WASN'T THE FOOT-LONG SERPENTINE tattoos up and down both of Bettina Rodgers's arms, or the half-dozen piercings on her face that made me doubt what she had just told me. Actually, Bettina was as good a witness as you get. It was more the fact that eyewitness accounts are notoriously sketchy and unreliable. FBI research has shown them to hover around 50-percent accuracy, even just a few minutes after an incident — and this was at least two hours later.

That said, Bettina's confidence in what she had seen was unwavering.

"I was in the parking lot, starting my car," she told me for the third time. "And the Suburban tore out behind me, over that way, toward Santa Monica Boulevard. I turned around to look 'cause it was going so fast.

"I know for sure it was dark blue, and I know it was a Suburban 'cause my mom used to have one. I've ridden in it a

217

million times. I remember thinking it was kind of funny, 'cause it was like my mom was driving crazy like that."

She paused. "The Suburban took a sharp left out of the parking lot. That's all I know. Can I fucking go now?"

That was about as much as Jeanne Galletta had gotten out of her, but I pressed on with a few more questions of my own.

"Any markings on the car?" I asked. "Bumper stickers, dents, anything at all?"

She shrugged. "I mostly just saw it from the side, and like I said — it flew by super fast. For a Suburban. I didn't see the license plate or anything."

"How about the driver? Anything you noticed? Was there anyone else in the car? More than one person?"

She fiddled absently with one of the thick silver rings in her eyebrow while she thought about that. Her makeup was heavy and mostly black, except for the pale white cast of her face powder. I didn't know too much about Bettina, but she put me in mind of the urban vampire culture I'd investigated a few years back on a case. One thing I'd learned then was how sharp some of these people were despite the goth-slacker stereotype.

Finally, Bettina shook her head. "I want to say it was a woman, 'cause that would make sense, right? I mean, *Jesus shit,* we're talking about that fucked-up Hollywood Stalker wench, aren't we? Don't bother to lie, I *know* it's her. One of the other cops told me already."

I didn't respond, letting her think some more until she shrugged again. "Blue Suburban goin' like a bat out of hell, left turn, that's all I really know for sure. That's my final answer."

The fact that she wasn't inclined to fill in details actually boosted my confidence in her. It's incredible how many people do the opposite, sometimes just to please the interviewer. A few minutes later, I thanked Bettina for her time and help, and let her go.

Then I found Jeanne Galletta to tell her my thoughts. We met in an unused guest room on the second floor. Jeanne told me that another hotel patron had corroborated the story.

"Around two o'clock, he saw a large, dark-blue SUV tearing out of the parking lot from his room on the third floor. He couldn't see too much, but he said it might have been a woman driver."

"That doesn't mean it was Mary Smith," I said. "But if it was, this would be huge for us. At least two people saw the same vehicle leaving in a hurry."

Jeanne nodded silently, weighing the idea. "So then the sixty-four-thousand-dollar question remains: How big do we go with this?"

There were risks either way, and I puzzled it out loud, partly for her and partly for myself.

"Time's not on our side. Mary Smith hasn't shown any signs of slowing down. Just the opposite, in fact. She seems to be evolving. This is a chance to use the press to our advantage and speed up the search — if that's what you want.

"On the other hand, people are already scared, and they're going to react to every blue Suburban they see, probably to every blue SUV. If this blows up in your face, then it's one more reason for the public not to trust the Department. But if it gets you Mary Smith, then everything's okay and you're a hero."

"Russian roulette," she said dryly.

"Name of the game," I said.

"By the way, I don't want to be a hero."

"Goes with the territory."

She finally smiled. "America's Sherlock Holmes. Didn't I read that somewhere about you?"

"Don't believe everything you read."

I could almost hear the clock ticking inside Jeanne's head, but maybe it was her heartbeat.

"All right," she said, looking at her watch. "Let's do it up. I'm going to have to clear this with the Department, but if I go now, we can get in a press conference before the early news."

She paused at the door. "Jesus, I hope this isn't a mistake I'm making."

"Just go," I said.

"Come with me, Alex. Okay?"

"Okay," I said. "In spite of the Sherlock Holmes remark."

# Chapter 66

THIS WAS BIG, no doubt about that, anyway. Even James Truscott was on hand. The news conference on the blue Suburban got covered by everybody and their big brother, and was sure to be the lead item on every report until something else even more dramatic turned up on the L.A. murder case. Hopefully, it would be the capture of the Suburban, and then Mary Smith, male or female.

I didn't appear in the small group on camera with Detective Jeanne Galletta, but I met up with her minutes afterward. She was getting attagirls all around, but she broke away to come over and see me.

"Thanks for the help. The wise counsel," she said. "So did I look like a fricking raccoon on national TV?"

"No, you didn't. Well, yeah, you did." Then I smiled. "I remember you saying one time, *you have to eat, right?* You still interested?"

Jeanne's worried look returned suddenly. "Oh, Alex, not tonight." Then she winked and grinned. "Gotcha. Yeah, we could eat, I guess. What are you in the mood for? Actually, I'm starving now. Italian sound good?"

"Italian always sounds good to me."

Jeanne's apartment was on the way to the restaurant, and she insisted we stop. "I need to check out my face in my own mirror, with lighting I trust and know," she explained. "This will only take five minutes, maybe seven minutes tops. Come up. I won't jump your bones, I promise."

I laughed and followed her into a redbrick building somewhere off of Santa Monica.

"Maybe I *will* jump your bones," she said as we walked up the stairs to her apartment.

Which is exactly what happened as soon as she shut the door behind us. She spun around fast, grabbed me, kissed me, and then let me go again.

"Hmmm. That was kind of nice. But I'm just messing with you, *Doctor*. Ten minutes, just like I promised."

"Seven."

And then Jeanne scooted down the hall to her bedroom and the lighting she could trust. I'd never seen her so loose and lively; it was almost as if she was a different person away from the job.

It took her a little more than seven minutes, but the wait was worth it, the transformation kind of startling, actually. She'd always struck me as attractive, but she looked kind of tough at work, and definitely all-business. Now she wore a silk T-shirt with jeans and sandals, her hair was still wet from a quick shower, and Detective Jeanne Galletta seemed softer, another side of her revealed.

"I know, I know, I look like hell," she said, only we both knew different.

She hit her forehead with the palm of her hand. "I forgot to offer you a drink. Oh, God, what is it with me?"

"We only had five minutes," I said.

"Right. Good point. You always, *usually,* say just the right thing. Okay then, let's go. The night awaits us."

The thing of it was, I could still feel the impression of Jeanne's body against mine, and her lips. Also, I was unattached now, wasn't I? *Was I?* To be honest, I was starting to get a little confused myself. But she was herding me out the door into the hallway — and then Jeanne whirled around on me again. This time I was ready for her and took her in my arms. We kissed, and it was longer and more satisfying than the first time. She smelled terrific, felt even better, and her brown eyes were beautiful up close like this.

Jeanne took my hand, and she started to pull me back into her apartment.

I stopped her. "You just got dressed to go out."

She shook her head. "No, I got dressed for you."

But then I gathered it together, got hold of my senses, and said, "Let's go eat, Jeanne."

She smiled and said, "Okay, let's eat, *Alex.*"

# Chapter 67

AT 4:00 IN THE MORNING, a twenty-two-year-old actress named Alicia Pitt left Las Vegas and headed for L.A. The open casting call started at 9:00, and she didn't want to be blond chick number three hundred and five in line — the part would already be gone before she even got to read.

Her parents' Suburban, which the highly imaginative Pitts called Big Blue, was a gas-guzzler without a conscience. Other than that it was a free ride, so all in all, the price was close to being right. Once Alicia got some kind of real work, maybe she could afford to actually live in L.A. Meanwhile, it was this endless back-and-forth for auditions and callbacks.

Alicia ran her lines as she drove west on I-10, trying not to glance too much at the dog-eared script on the seat next to her. The familiar ritual continued almost all the way to L.A.

"'Don't talk to me about pride. I've heard everything I need to from you. You can just —'"

Wait, that wasn't it. She looked down at the script, and then up again at the road and passing traffic.

" 'Don't talk to me about pride. I've heard it all before from you. There's nothing you can tell me now that I'll believe. You can just —' *Oh, shit!* What are you *doing,* Alicia? You numbskull!"

Somehow, she had shuttled off the highway and then onto an exit ramp. It brought her down to a traffic light at an unfamiliar intersection.

She was in L.A., but this definitely wasn't Wilshire Boulevard.

It wasn't anywhere she'd ever been, from the look of it. Abandoned buildings mostly, and one burned-out car sitting on a far curb. A taxi, actually.

Then she saw the men, boys, whatever they were. Three of them, standing on the corner and staring her way.

*All right, all right,* she thought. *Don't freak out, Alicia. Just get yourself turned around and back on the highway. You're right as rain; everything is cool.*

She willed the red light in front of her to change as she craned her neck, looking for the ramp back onto the highway.

One of the young guys had wandered out into the intersection now, his head tilted for a better view through her windshield. He wore baggy cargo pants and a sky-blue sweat jacket; he couldn't have been more than sixteen, seventeen.

Then the two others came along slowly behind. By the time Alicia thought to run the red light, the boys were standing in front of the hood of her car, blocking the way. Oh, great. Now what?

# Chapter 68

SHE SQUEEZED HER EYES SHUT for just a half second. What were you supposed to do in this situation? And why had she never gotten around to buying a cell phone? Um, maybe because she was almost dead broke.

When she opened her eyes again, the one in the blue jacket was at her side window, a menacing look on his face, a tattoo of a red dragon on his neck.

She screamed in spite of herself — just a small yelp, but enough for him to see how scared she was.

Then her panic level crept even higher. It took her a moment to realize the kid in blue was saying something. His hands were held up flat, in a "calm down" sort of gesture.

She cracked the window. "W-what?" she said, unable to keep her voice from quivering.

"I said, 'you lost?'" he asked. "That's all, lady — *you lost? You look — lost.*"

Alicia choked back a sob. "Yes. I'm so sorry." It was a bad habit; she apologized for everything. "I'm just looking for —"

"'Cause I *know* you don't live around here," he said. His expression shifted, and hardened again. The others laughed at the joke. "This your car?"

Fear and confusion locked Alicia into subservience, which she hated. All she could think to do was answer his question. "It's my parents'."

The guy in blue rubbed his chin whiskers as if considering her answer. "Lotta people looking for a car just like this one," he said. "Don't you read the papers? Watch TV?"

"I'm just trying to get to Westwood. For an audition. A TV movie. I got off the highway before I was supposed to —"

He howled with laughter, turning away from the car to his group, and then back again. His movements were casual and slow. "She's trying to get to Westwood to be in a movie. A *film*. Damn, that's about exactly what I expected. 'Cause I know you ain't got no interest in anything or anybody 'round here."

"Nah, man," said one of the other boys. "She do her killing in the rich neighborhoods."

"I got no problem with that," said another. "Kill the rich, eat the rich, whatever."

"What are you saying?" She looked at each of them now, desperate for any kind of clarity, a clue about what she should say or do to get out of there. Her wild-eyed gaze fell on the rearview mirror. *Could I back out of here? Fast? Really, really fast? Pedal-to-the-metal kind of thing?*

The kid at her window lifted his jacket to show a pistol

tucked into the waistband of his jeans. "You *don't* want to do that," he said.

The idea that she could be murdered before she had her morning coffee came over Alicia with an ugly reckoning. "Please, I just . . . please. D-don't h-hurt me," she stammered.

She could hear the helplessness in her own voice. It was like listening to someone else, someone pathetic. God, she was supposed to be an actress.

The man in blue nodded slowly, in a way she couldn't decipher. Then he stepped back from the car and put out his hand to let her pass.

"Highway's that way," he said. The other two moved off to the side, too.

Alicia felt as if she might faint from relief. She gave the men a watery smile. "Thank you. I'm so sorry," she said again.

Her hands were shaking on the steering wheel, but at least she was safe.

The Suburban had barely inched forward when, with a sickening crack, the front windshield shattered into a spiderweb of about a million glass pieces.

An instant later, a heavy metal pipe smashed through the driver's-side window.

Paralysis overtook Alicia. Her arms and legs wouldn't function. She couldn't even scream.

The impulse to floor the accelerator got to her brain a moment too late — about a second after her car door flew open and large, powerful hands dragged her out onto the street.

Alicia landed on her back, the air rushing out of her lungs in a gasp.

"What kind of stupid are you?" she heard someone say — and then she felt a shock of pain on the side of her head. Then she saw a pipe rise up high and come down really fast, a blur aimed right at the center of her forehead.

# Chapter 69

EVERYTHING HAD CHANGED suddenly and dramatically on Mary Smith. Jeanne Galletta was out; she was completely off the case. She'd been reassigned.

I tried going to bat for her, but within hours of Alicia Pitt's murder, she was history on Mary Smith. That evening, Police Chief Shrewsbury announced that he would be personally overseeing the Hollywood Stalker murders, and that Detective Galletta was on temporary leave pending an investigation into the unfortunate murder of a young Las Vegas woman driving a blue Suburban.

Jeanne was inconsolable, but she was getting the full spectrum of experiences on the case, including a turn as sacrificial lamb. "The mayor of Las Vegas telling the mayor of L.A. to tell the chief of police how to run an investigation?" she ranted to me. "When did this stop being about professionals doing good work?"

"Somewhere around the dawn of time," I said.

The two of us met for a drink around 8:00 that night. She picked the spot, and said she wanted to make sure I had everything I needed from her on the murder investigation. Of course, she also wanted to vent.

"I know Alicia Pitt's my fault, but —"

"Jeanne, stop right there. You aren't responsible for what happened to that woman. It might have come as a result of a decision you made, but that's not the same thing. You made the best call you could. The rest is politics. You shouldn't have been taken off the case, either."

She didn't speak for several seconds. "I don't know," she finally said. "That poor girl is dead."

"Do you have any vacation time?" I asked her. "Maybe you should use it."

"Yeah, like I'm going to leave town now," she said. "I may be off the case, but —"

She didn't finish her sentence, but she didn't need to. I had been in her position before. It's best not to say out loud that you're going to break the rules. Just go ahead and break them.

"Alex, I'm going to need my space," she said. "That's why I wanted to meet you here."

"I understand completely. You know where to reach me," I told her.

Jeanne finally cracked a half smile. "You're a really good guy," she said. "For FBI."

"You're okay for a cop. For LAPD."

Then she reached across the table and put her hand on mine. But she quickly took her hand away.

"Awkward," she said, and smiled again. "Sorry, if I'm being goofy."

"You're being human, Jeanne. That's different, right? I wouldn't apologize for it."

"All right, I won't apologize anymore. I have to go, though, before I cry or something incredibly embarrassing like that. You know where to reach me, if you need to."

Then Jeanne got up from the table. She turned back before she got to the door. "I'm not off this case, though. I'll be around."

# Chapter 70

WEIRD.

When I got back to my room that night, an envelope was waiting for me at the front desk.

It was from James Truscott.

I opened it on my way to my room, and I couldn't stop reading the contents all the way there.

SUBJECT: WOMEN ON DEATH ROW IN CALIF.

There were fifteen at the moment, and Truscott included a brief write-up on each of them.

The first woman was Cynthia Coffman. In 1986, she and her boyfriend robbed and strangled four women. She'd been sentenced in 1989 and was still waiting. Cynthia Coffman was forty-two years old now.

At the end of the long note, Truscott said that he planned

to visit some of the women in prison. I was welcome to tag along if I thought it might be useful.

After I finished reading the pages, I leafed through them a second time.

What was with James Truscott? And why did he want to be my Boswell? I wished he would just leave me alone, but that wasn't going to happen, was it?

# Chapter 71

THE PHONE IN MY HOTEL ROOM woke me at just past
2:30 in the morning. I was having a dream about Little Alex
and Christine, but I forgot most of it as soon as I heard the
first ring.

My first coherent thought: *James Truscott*.

But it wasn't him.

Around 3:00 A.M. I was driving through an unfamiliar
Hollywood neighborhood looking for the Hillside condo
complex. I might have found it sooner in daylight, and if my
mind hadn't been racing the whole way there.

Mary Smith's game had changed again, and I was struggling
to understand it. Why this murder? Why now? Why these
two victims?

The condo complex, when I finally found it, looked to
have been built in the seventies. The units were flat-roofed
three-story structures in dark cedar, with fat columns for legs

and open parking underneath. There was also parking on the street, I noticed, and that would offer an intruder privacy.

"Agent Cross! Alex!" I heard from across the lot.

I recognized Karl Page's voice from somewhere in the dark. My watch read 3:05.

He caught up with me under a streetlight. "Over this way," he said.

"How'd you hear about it?" I asked him. Page was the one who had called me in my hotel room.

"I was still in the office."

"When the hell do you sleep?"

"I'll sleep when it's over."

I followed the young agent through a series of right and left turns, to where a square of buildings faced a common garden and pool area. Several residents, many of them in nightclothes, were gathered around one of the front doors. They were craning their necks and whispering among themselves.

Page pointed to a third-floor unit where the lights were on behind drawn curtains. "Up there," he said. "That's where the bodies are."

We made our way past the officers on duty and up the front stairs — one of two ways into the building.

"*Check.*" Page shorthanded his response to the stickers on the apartment door as we passed inside. Marked with two *A*s and a *B*. This was Mary Smith all right. The stickers always made me think of that clown doll in *Poltergeist* — benign on the outside but completely ominous in context. Child's play turned inside out.

The door opened onto a good-size living room. It was

crowded with cardboard moving boxes and haphazardly arranged furniture.

In the middle of the room, a man lay dead, facedown over a stack of fallen boxes. Several dozen books had spilled onto the sand-colored carpet, several of them streaked with blood. Copies of *The Hours* and *Running with Scissors* lay near the body.

"Philip Washington," Page told me. "Thirty-five; an investment banker at Merrill Lynch. Well-read, obviously."

"You too, I guess."

There was no arranging the body this time, no artful tableau. The killer might have been in a hurry given all the neighbors so close by, the lack of sufficient cover.

And Philip Washington wasn't the only target. Nearby, another body lay faceup on the floor.

This was the one I couldn't reconcile, the murder that would dog me.

The victim's left temple showed an ugly wound where the bullet had entered, and the face had been repeatedly slashed in Mary Smith's signature style. The flesh around the forehead and eyes was crisscrossed with knife marks, and the cheeks, constricted in a scream, had both been punctured.

I stared at the body, just beginning to piece together what had happened, and the events that had led up to it. Two questions burned in my mind. *Did I have some hand in causing this murder? Should I have seen it coming?*

Maybe the victim I was staring at had the answer — but *L.A. Times* writer Arnold Griner wouldn't be able to help us again on the Mary Smith case. Now Griner was one of the victims.

Part Four

# THE BLUE SUBURBAN

# Chapter 72

I HAD BARELY BEGUN walking the crime scene when I met up with Maddux Fielding, LAPD's deputy chief in charge of the Detective Bureau and also Jeanne Galletta's replacement on the case. With his shock of silver-gray hair and the same deep-brown eyes as Jeanne's, Fielding looked as though he could have been Jeanne's father.

He struck me as professional and focused from the start. He also seemed to be something of an asshole.

"Agent Cross," he said, shaking my hand. "I've heard a lot about your work in D.C." Something in the way he said it didn't exactly sound like a compliment.

"This is Special Agent Page," I said. "He's been assisting me while I'm in L.A."

Fielding made no response at all, so I pushed on.

"What do you make of all this?" I asked him. "I know

you're just getting started with the case, but I'm assuming you're up to speed on the priors."

The last part wasn't intended as a dig, but it hung in the air as if it were one. Fielding turned down the corners of his mouth and looked at me over the tops of heavy-rimmed bifocals. "This isn't my first serial case. I'm good to go."

He took a self-important deep breath. "Now, as to your question, I'm prepared to believe this is Mary Smith's work and not some copycat. I have to wonder if she didn't want Arnold Griner dead from day one. I believe she did. The questions, of course, would be why and how this motive is related to the previous incidents."

Everything he said made some sense, especially that Griner might have been a target from the start. I turned to Page. "How about you?"

I was beginning to wonder what he thought, which he may or may not have recognized as a mark of my growing confidence in him.

"Griner and Washington just moved in," Page said, flipping through a small notebook. "Three days ago, in fact. I know Griner changed all his info and kept everything unlisted, so Mary would have had to go to at least a little trouble to keep up with him. That's consistent with the stalking aspect, right? And even though Griner doesn't fit the victim profile, he's been part of Mary Smith's landscape all along. She started with him, and now, I don't know, maybe she's ending with him. Maybe this represents some kind of closure for her. Maybe her story is over."

"Doubtful," Fielding said, without even looking at Page. "Too much anger expressed here. Too much rage in Griner's murder. Have you seen *The Grudge*? Not important. Forget I said it."

"What about the blue Suburban?" I asked. "Any progress there?" As of that afternoon, LAPD hadn't turned up anything promising, which was a little surprising given the urgency.

Fielding pulled out a handkerchief, took off his glasses, and began to polish them before he spoke. "Nothing yet," he finally said. "But as long as you brought it up, let me make one thing clear. I'm not Detective Galletta. I'm her boss, and I'm not going to be checking in with you at every turn. *If* the Bureau wants to take full jurisdiction on this case, they could argue for it. After the way things have gone around here, I'd almost welcome it. But until then, you just do your job and try not to screw up my investigation any more than you did Detective Galletta's. I hope we're clear."

It was bald cop-to-cop loyalty. Without asking a single question, he decided I had wasted the case for Jeanne. I'd seen this kind of thing before, even understood it a little. But I couldn't keep quiet now.

"Little piece of advice," I told him. "You should know what you're talking about before you start throwing accusations around. You're just going to make your own job harder."

"I don't see how that's possible at this point," he said curtly. "Now I think we've covered everything. You know how to reach me if you have questions, or hell, even if you have something that will help us out."

"Absolutely."

I could have punched him in the back of the head as he

walked away. It was maybe the only thing that could have taken our first meeting to a lower level.

"Great guy," Page said. "Lots of personality, social skills, the whole package."

"Yeah, I'm all warm and fuzzy inside."

Instead of dwelling on it, I turned back to the work. If the lines of communication with LAPD were going to be strained further, we needed our own analysis more than ever. Page didn't ask me to, but I walked him through my process. We worked in a spiral out from the bodies, as anyone else would, but much more slowly.

First we covered the condo, inch by inch; then we worked out to the hallway, front and back stairs, and then the grounds around the building.

I was curious to see how Page's patience held, or if everyone his age was too hurry-up to do this work right. Page did just fine. He was really into the case.

We were outside when we got word from the Bureau's electronic surveillance unit. At 5:30 that morning, another e-mail had shown up at Arnold Griner's *L.A. Times* address.

A letter from Mary Smith had arrived — written to the man she had just killed.

# Chapter 73

To: agriner@latimes.com

From: Mary Smith

To: Arnold Griner:

Guess what? I followed you home to your new apartment, after you had dinner with friends at that Asia de Cuba place on Sunset.

You parked under the building and took the stairs up the back. Huffing up a single flight? I could see that you're out of shape, Arnold. And out of time, I'm afraid.

I waited outside until your apartment lights came on, and then I followed. I wasn't as afraid anymore, not like I used to be. The gun used to feel strange and unwieldy in my hand. Now it's like I barely know it's there.

You haven't installed a dead bolt on your

back door. Maybe you've been meaning to but you've been too busy with the move; or maybe you just felt a little safer in the new place so it didn't seem to matter. You'd be right about that last part. It doesn't matter — not anymore.

It was dark in the kitchen when I came in, but you had the lights and TV on in the living room. There was also a carving knife on the counter next to the sink, but I left it where it was.

I had my own, which is something you probably already knew about me — *if* you read my other e-mails.

I waited for as long as I could bear to in the kitchen, listening to you and your companion. I couldn't hear exactly what you were saying to each other, but I liked the sound of your voices. I even liked knowing that I'd be the last person to ever hear them.

Then the nervousness started to come back. It was just a little at first, but I knew it would get worse if I waited much longer.

I could have left the condo right then if I wanted to, and you'd never even have known I was there.

That's one way you're like the others. No one seems to know I'm around until their time comes. The Invisible Woman, that's me. That's a lot of us, actually.

When I waltzed into the living room, you both

jumped up at the same time. I made sure you saw the gun, and you stayed still after that. I wanted to ask if you knew why I came for you, why you *deserved* to die, but I was afraid I wouldn't finish if I didn't do it right away.

I pulled the trigger, and you fell flat on your back. Your roommate screeched; then he tried to run. I couldn't imagine where he thought he was going to escape to.

I shot him, and I think he may have died immediately. You both seemed to just die. Not much fight in you, especially considering what a snippy, nasty little man you are.

Good-bye, Arnold. You're gone, and know what else? You're already forgotten.

# Chapter 74

THE STORYTELLER HAD TO STOP the stream of murders now. He knew that; it was part of the plan, and the plan was a good one. What a pity, though, what a shame. He was just getting good at this, and he hadn't been good at anything for a long time.

Anyway, congratulations were in order. Praise for him was all over the TV, and in the newspapers, of course. Especially the *L.A. Times*, which had made that piece-of-shit Arnold Griner into such a saint and martyr. Everyone recognized the Storyteller's masterpiece — only it was so much better than they knew.

And he did want to celebrate, only there was still no one he could tell. He'd tried that in Vancouver and look what had happened. He'd had to kill a friend, well, an acquaintance, an old humpty-dump of his.

So how would he celebrate? Arnold Griner was dead, and that made him laugh out loud sometimes. The ironies were building up now, including some subtle ones, like Griner getting his e-mails, then being his messenger to the police, then getting it himself. In real life — as opposed to what had been written in the latest e-mail — the little prick had begged for his life when he saw who it was, when he finally understood, which made his murder even more satisfying. Hell, he hadn't killed Griner and his companion right away. It had taken close to an hour, and he'd loved every minute of the melodrama.

So what would he do now?

He wanted to party, but there really was no one he could talk to about this. Boohoo, he had no one.

Then he knew exactly what he wanted to do, and it was so simple. He was in Westwood anyway, so he parked in a lot and walked over to the wonderfully tacky Bruin Theater, where *Collateral* was playing. *Tom Cruise, oh, good.*

He wanted to go to the movies.

He wanted to sit with *his* people and watch Tom Cruise pretend he was a big, bad killer without any conscience or regrets.

*Oohh, I'm scared, Tom.*

# Chapter 75

"MR. TRUSCOTT CALLED for you. He said he'd like an interview. Said it was important. That he'll come to the house if you like. He wondered if you received his notes about the women on death row."

I frowned and shook my head. "Ignore Truscott. Anything else happen while I was away?"

"Did Damon tell you he and his friend broke up?" Nana asked me quietly. "Did you even know he had a girlfriend?"

We were sitting in the kitchen that Saturday afternoon on my first day back. I looked over toward the living room to make sure we were still alone.

"Is that the girl he's been talking to so much on the phone?" I asked.

"Well, not anymore," she said. "Just as well, I'm sure. He's too young for any of that." She got up humming "Joshua Fit the Battle of Jericho" and turned her attention to a pot of chili she had going on the stove.

I was distracted by the chili itself, and the fact that she had used ground turkey instead of her usual beef or pork. Maybe Kayla Coles had worked some magic and finally gotten Nana to do something new to take care of herself. Good for Kayla.

"When did Damon tell you he had a girlfriend?" I asked, unable to completely drop the subject. I was more curious about it than I was reluctant to show how out of the loop I had become with my older son.

"He didn't tell me; it just sort of presented itself," Nana said. "It's not something teenagers talk about directly. Cornelia's been to the house a couple of times. To do homework. She's very nice. Her mother and father are lawyers, but I didn't hold that against her." She laughed at her little joke. "Well, maybe I held it against her just a little."

*Cornelia?* Nana the expert, and Alex the outsider. All my good intentions and the promise I'd made myself to do things differently had been swallowed up by whatever it was that always — *always* — seemed to drag me back to the Job.

*Missed out on Damon's first breakup. Can't get that one back. Cornelia, we hardly knew ya.*

It was good to be home anyway. The kitchen was soon overflowing with the smells of Nana's cooking, exponentially so, as I was being received back with a party for friends and family. Besides the chili, there was Nana's famous corn bread, two kinds of garlicky greens, seasoned steaks, and a batch of caramel bread pudding that was a rare show-off treat. Apparently, Dr. Coles hadn't completely gotten through to her about the taking-it-easy part.

I tried to help without getting in the way, while Nana checked her watch and just about flew around the kitchen. I would have been more excited if I felt I deserved a party. Not only was I out of the running for father of the year, but my return trip to L.A. was already booked.

# Chapter 76

"LOOK WHO'S HERE with the family! Will you look at this. Where's my camera?"

Sampson and Billie arrived early with three-month-old Djakata, whom I hadn't seen since she was a newborn. John, beaming, lifted her out of the Snugli on Billie's chest and put her in my arms. What a sight this was — Sampson with his baby girl. *Papa Bear,* I thought. *And Mama and Baby Bear.*

"What a rare beauty," I said, and she was — with cocoa skin and soft little swirls of dark hair all over her head. "She has the best of both of you. What a doll."

Jannie came around and slipped between us to get a good look at Djakata. She was at the age where it sets in that she may have babies of her own someday, and she was starting to take a perspective.

"She's so teensy-tiny," she said, her voice tinged with awe.

"Not too tiny," Sampson said. "Hundredth percentile

height and weight. Takes after her father. She'll be as big as Billie when she's *five*."

"Let's just hope she doesn't get your hands and feet, poor thing," Nana leaned in and said. Then she winked at Billie, who was already considered part of our family.

An intense feeling of homecoming overtook me right then and there. It was one of those transcendent moments that grabs you a little by surprise and reminds you all at once about the good things. Whatever else happened, there was this, where I needed to be, where I belonged.

*Snapshot — remember the feeling for the next time I need it.*

The feeling of intimacy didn't last long, though, as the house soon began filling up with other guests. A few of my old guard from DCPD were the next to show up; Jerome and Claudette Thurman came with Rakeem Powell and his new girlfriend, whose name I didn't catch. "Give it a week," Sampson told me on the side. "If she's still around, then you can worry about it."

Aunt Tia and my cousin Carter were the first actual family to come, followed by a string of warm and familiar faces, several of them bearing some vague resemblance to my own.

The last to arrive was Dr. Kayla Coles, and I greeted her at the door myself.

"Annie Sullivan, I presume?"

"Excuse me? Oh, I get it. The Miracle Worker."

"The Miracle Worker — the one who got my grandmother to put turkey in her chili. I'm guessing that was your work. Well done."

"At your service." She curtsied playfully in her turquoise dress, which looked very comfortable even while it clung to her. Kayla didn't usually show off much of herself, and I couldn't help noticing. She definitely looked different than she did in her usual preppy-practical work clothes.

Instead of a medical bag, she carried a large covered crock.

"Now *this* might be your biggest trick yet," I said. "Bringing someone else's food into Nana's kitchen? I want to see this."

"Not just the food; I brought the recipe, too."

She turned the crock around to show a white index card taped to the side.

"Heart-healthy baked beans for a woman who knows all too well how to cook with bacon fat."

"Well, come on in," I said with a sweeping gesture. "At your own risk."

The sounds of Branford Marsalis Quartet's *Romare Bearden Revealed* ushered us through the house, where the party was gathering up steam and everyone looked glad to see Dr. Kayla, who happened to be a saint in the neighborhood. I couldn't help feeling a little giddy. At the end of the week I'd be on another plane. But for now, this was as good as it gets.

# Chapter 77

I FOUND SAMPSON AND BILLIE just as he was opening a beer in the kitchen, and I took it out of his hands. There was something I wanted to get out of the way with the big man before the festivities really got rolling.

"Follow me. I need to talk to you — before either of us has a drink," I told him.

"Ooh, mysterious," Billie said, and laughed at the two of us, the way she usually does. Billie is an ER nurse, and she's seen it all.

"Come on upstairs," I said to John.

"I already had a drink," John said. "This is number two."

"Come anyway. We'll just be a minute, Billie."

From my office in the attic, I could still hear the music muted through the floor. I recognized Dr. Kayla's laugh amid the indistinct thrum of party voices.

Sampson leaned against the wall. "You wanted to see me, sir? In your office?"

He had on a funny T-shirt from his basketball team in the older men's league at St. Anthony's. It said, "*Nobody moves, nobody gets hurt.*"

"I didn't want to mix work with the party," I said.

"But you can't help yourself." Sampson grinned. "Can you?"

"I'm not home for too long. I have to go back to L.A., and I don't want to wait on this anymore."

"Well, that's a good hook," he said. "What's the pitch? Let's hear it."

"Basically? Director Burns and I want you to think seriously about coming to work at the Bureau. We want you to make the move, John. Were you expecting it?" I asked.

He laughed. "More or less, of course. You've been hinting around enough. Burns looking to blackify the Bureau, sugar?"

"No. Not that I'd mind."

What Burns wanted at the Bureau was more agents who knew the value of fieldwork, and people he could trust, his team. If I could recruit only one person, I'd told him, John Sampson would be my first choice. That was good enough for Burns.

"I've already got the go-ahead from the director's office," I said. "Ron Burns wants the same things I do. Or maybe it's the other way around."

"You mean he wants me?" Sampson asked.

"Well, we couldn't get Jerome or Rakeem, or the crossing

257

guard at the Sojourner Truth school. So yeah, he'll settle for you."

Sampson laughed loudly, one of my favorite sounds. "I miss you, too," he said. "And believe it or not, I have an answer. I want you to come back to the Washington PD. How's that for turnaround? You're right about one thing — we do have to get back together. One way or the other. I guess I vote for the other."

I couldn't help laughing out loud, too; then John and I banged closed fists, agreeing that we needed to work together again, one way or the other.

I told Sampson that I'd think about his surprising proposal, and he said he'd think about mine, too. Then Sampson swung open the office door and let in the music from downstairs.

# Chapter 78

"ARE WE ALLOWED to have a drink now?" said Sampson. "It's a party, sugar. You do remember parties?"

"Vaguely," I said.

Two minutes later, I had a beer in one hand and a rib dripping homemade barbecue sauce in the other. I found Jannie and Damon in the dining room playing Thirteen with a cousin of theirs, Michelle, and Kayla Coles. To be honest, though, it was Kayla who drew me over.

"Are you ignoring our guests?" I asked the kids.

"Not these two," Jannie deadpanned, with a nod to Kayla and Michelle.

"No, they're whipping my butt too much to be ignoring me," Kayla said, sending Jannie and Damon into conspiratorial laughs. There it was again. A woman and my kids, getting along. What was it about that? What was I missing?

I gave Dr. Kayla a long look as she shuffled and dealt the

cards. She was incredibly grounded, and good-looking without trying to be. The thing of it was, I liked her. I'd liked Kayla for a long, long time, ever since we were kids growing up in Southeast. And so?

"You looking at my cards?" she asked, breaking through my reverie, or whatever it was supposed to be.

"Not at your cards," Jannie broke in. "At you, Dr. Kayla. He's sneaky like that."

"All right, that's enough kidding around. I'm out of here. I have to go help Nana," I said. I rolled my eyes for Kayla's benefit, and then I walked away. Quickly.

"Don't go," Kayla said. But I was already through the doorway.

As I headed to the kitchen, there was only one thing on my mind, though. How could I get Kayla alone at the party? And where was I going to take her on our first date?

# Chapter 79

I TOOK KAYLA to Kinkead's on purpose. It had been my and Christine's favorite spot, but before that, it had been *my* favorite spot, and I was reclaiming it. Kayla arrived less than five minutes after I did, and I liked that. She was on time, no game-playing. She had on a black wrap cashmere sweater, black slacks, and kitten-heel sling-backs, and she was kind of dazzling again. In her own way.

"I'm sorry, Alex," she said as she walked up to me at the bar. "I'm punctual. I know it's a big bore and takes all the mystery out of things, but I just can't help myself. Next time, and there will be a next time, I'll force myself to be fashionably late. At least ten minutes, maybe fifteen."

"You're forgiven," I said, and suddenly I felt incredibly relaxed. "You just broke the ice, huh?"

Kayla winked. "I did, didn't I? Just like that. God, I'm good, aren't I? Sneaky, just like you are."

"You know the axiom that men don't like women who threaten them because they're too smart?" I said. "You're scary smart."

"But you're the exception that proves the rule, right? You like smart women just fine. Anyway, I'm not that smart. Tell you why — my theory anyway."

"Tell away. I'll have a beer, Pilsner on tap," I said to the bartender.

Kayla continued, "I see all these supposedly supersmart people at the hospital, doctors and researchers who are complete disasters in their personal lives. So how smart can they really be? What, they're smart because they can memorize facts and other people's ideas? Because they know every rock-and-roll song ever recorded? Or the storyline for every episode of *Bewitched*?"

I rolled my eyes. "You know the storylines of *Bewitched*? You know people who know the storylines of *Bewitched*?"

"My God, no. Maybe *ER*. And *Scrubs*."

"I know a lot of R & B songs," I told her. "Haven't figured out life too good, though."

Kayla laughed. "I disagree. I've met your kids, Alex."

"Have you met Christine Johnson?"

"Stop it. Anyway, I *have* met her. She's an impressive woman. Completely. A little messed-up right now."

"All right, I'm not going to argue. I could make a good case against myself, though."

We talked like that, laughed a lot, drank some, ate good food. Interestingly, we stayed away from talk about Nana and the kids, maybe because that would have been too easy. As always, I enjoyed Kayla's sense of humor, but most of all, her confidence. She was comfortable in her own skin, not defensive. I liked being out on a date with her.

We were finishing an after-dinner drink when she declared, "This has been nice, Alex. Very nice and easy."

"Surprised?" I asked her.

"No, not really. Well, maybe a little bit," she admitted. "Maybe a lot."

"Want to tell me why?"

"Hmm. I guess because I knew you had no idea who I was, even though you probably thought that you did."

"When I see you, you're usually working," I said. "You're being Dr. Kayla of Neighborhood Health Services."

"Take two aspirin, don't you *dare* call me at home," she said, and laughed. "I guess what's hard is that lots of people confide in me, but most of the time, I don't get to confide back."

I smiled. "You have anything you'd like to tell me?"

Kayla shook her head. "I think that I said it already. This has been good. I enjoyed tonight even more than I thought I would."

"Right. And there *will* be a next time. That's what you said."

She gave me the most delightful wink. "Wasn't I right about that?"

"You were right. If you'll see me again."

"Oh, I'll see you, Alex. Of course I will. I want to see how this turns out."

# Chapter 80

THE NEXT AFTERNOON, when I got back to the West Coast, the L.A. Bureau field office was buzzing about the latest in the Mary Smith case, but also about me, which wasn't good news, to put it mildly.

Apparently, word had gotten around that Maddux Fielding and I hadn't exactly hit it off after he replaced Jeanne Galletta. The Bureau-LAPD relationship had always been tenuous, more functional on some cases than others, and this was a definite downturn.

The general gossip/debate, from what I gathered, was about whether or not Agent Cross from D.C. had waltzed in with nothing to lose, and then cavalierly screwed things up for the LAPD.

I let it bother me for about five minutes; then I moved on.

Mary Smith, aka the Hollywood Stalker, aka Dirty Mary, was turning out to be one of the busiest, fastest-moving —

and fastest-changing — murder cases anyone could remember. Even the old hands were talking about it. Especially now that there was a little controversy mixed in with the moments of dizzying mayhem.

Another e-mail had arrived the morning I got to town. I hadn't seen it yet, but the word was that this one was different, and LAPD was already scrambling to respond. Mary Smith had sent a warning this time, and her message had been taken very seriously.

We gathered in the fourteenth-floor conference room, designated weeks ago as the Bureau's Mary Smith nerve center. Photos, newspaper clippings, and lab reports lined the walls. A temporary phone bank sat along one side of a huge cherry table that dominated the room with both its length and width.

The meeting was to be run by Fred Van Allsburg, and he breezed in ten minutes after the rest of us got there. For some reason his late arrival made me think of Kayla Coles and how she liked to be punctual at all times. Kayla believes that people who are habitually late don't have respect for others — or at least, for clocks.

Fred Van Allsburg had a dusty old nickname — the Stop Sign. It dated back to a United States–Central American heroin corridor he'd shut down in the late eighties. From what I knew, he had done little of note since then except climb the bureaucratic ladder. Having worked with him now, I had no more respect for him than the job required, per his rank and seniority.

I think he knew that, so it caught me off guard when he started the meeting the way he did.

"I just want to say a few things before we get going," he

began. "As you all know by now, we're quasi on our own where LAPD is concerned. Maddux Fielding seems intent on going it alone if he can, and he's outdoing himself at being a huge pain in the ass. Isn't that right, Alex?"

A knowing chuckle went around the room. Heads turned my way. "Uh, no comment," I said, to more laughter.

Van Allsburg raised his voice to quiet everyone. "As far as I'm concerned, we keep our lines of communication open, and that means full and timely disclosure to LAPD on anything we know. If I hear about anyone doing any petty withholding, they'll find themselves back in fingerprints on their next case. Fielding can run his end of things how he likes. I'm not going to let that compromise our own professionalism. Is that clear to everybody?"

I was pleasantly surprised by Van Allsburg's response to the situation. Apparently, he had allegiances of his own, even if it meant sticking by me.

We then moved on to Mary Smith's new e-mail. He used the conference room's projection system to put the message up on the big screen where we could all see it.

As I read it through, I was struck not by what she had written, but by what she seemed to be saying to us. It was the same thing I'd noticed before, in her earlier messages, but much plainer now, like a steady drumbeat that had gotten louder over time.

*Come and get me,* she was telling us.

*Here I am. Just come and get me. What's taking you so long?*

And she'd sent the e-mail to the late Arnold Griner, the dead letter office, so to speak.

# Chapter 81

To: agriner@latimes.com

From: Mary Smith

To: The one who will be next:

We've already met, you and I, so how about
that?

Do you remember? I do.

You gave me an autograph the other day, and
you were so full of your perky, charming manner-
isms. You seemed so approachable, so down-to-
earth. I don't want to say where we met, but you
wouldn't remember anyway. I told you how much I
liked your movies, and you smiled as though I
hadn't said anything at all. It reminded me of
how invisible I can be to you people.

It wasn't the first time you looked right
through me, either. You didn't see me at the day

care yesterday, or at the gym today. Not that I'd really expect you to.

It's like I'm the opposite of you in every way. Is that a *clue* I smell burning?

Everyone knows who you are, and no one knows who I am. I'm not famous or movie-star beautiful or any of the things you are. I don't have flawless skin or a trademark grin. By all reports, you are a better mother than Patsy Bennett was, a better actress than Antonia Schifman, a better wife than Marti Lowenstein-Bell, and surely more famous than that up-and-comer Suzie Cartoulis.

You are exactly who they mean when they say "she has everything." You do — and I'll bet that you know it, even if you forget from time to time.

There's only one thing I have that you don't. *I know something.* I know that by noon two days from now, you'll be dead. You'll have a bullet in your brain and a face that no one could recognize, not even your own beautiful children, not even the adoring public that flocks to your films.

But I didn't tell you any of that when we met.

I just smiled, almost curtsied, and thanked you for being you. I walked away knowing that the next time you look at me, it will be in a different way.

Next time, *I won't be invisible,* I promise you that much.

And I keep my promises — just ask Arnold Griner.

# Chapter 82

"WHAT DO WE THINK about this?" Van Allsburg asked the room, and then he stared directly at me. "You have more cases like this one than anyone else here. What's going on? What is she up to now?"

I just went ahead and said it. "She wants to be caught."

I felt I needed to stand to address the group. "Most likely, this is a person who feels completely isolated. The reaction to eliminate the people she fixates on is paradoxical. She, he, or it destroys what she can't have. Over time, it's making her feel worse. Some part of Mary may know that, and doesn't want to do this anymore, but she lacks the self-control to stop on her own."

"And the latest e-mail?" Fred asked.

"Another sign that the killer is conflicted. Maybe the conscious mind believes it's taunting the authorities while the subconscious is drawing a map for us to follow. That's the only thing I can come up with that makes sense of what's happened, and I'm not even sure if it makes sense."

"What about the counterpossibility?" asked David Fujishiro. "That she's trying to deliberately mislead us, throw us off with fiction."

"You're right. That is a real possibility," I said. "And what it leaves us with is every conceivable outcome *except* what's in the e-mail. I think we have an obligation to take the message at face value first, and consider the alternatives second. But David has just stated the other logical possibility. Of course, we don't know if she's logical."

Several agents, including my buddy Page, scribbled notes while I spoke. I was aware of my stature here, if not exactly comfortable with it.

"Do we know what LAPD's doing with this? I'm talking about the latest threat," asked an agent in the back, one of several faces I had never seen before. I looked over to Van Allsburg for a response.

"They've got a very large internal task force up and running. That much we know for sure. They're working on a database of potential targets. But you take every name-above-the-title actress in this town, even just sticking to the ones with families, and you've got a long list on your hands.

"Plus, LAPD's going to be a little trigger shy about the panic factor. Outside of increased patrols and some awareness-raising, there's not a hell of a lot they can do for all of these women and their families — except keep after Mary Smith. Someone has to catch her. And you know what? I want it to be us, not LAPD."

# Chapter 83

DISNEYLAND WAS CHOCK-FULL of ironies for any good mother. "The Happiest Place on Earth," the brochures called it, and maybe it could be, but with the large, electric crowds, it also had to be one of the easiest places to lose a child.

Mary tried not to give in to her worry. *Worrying just makes bad things happen. Worrywarts are the saddest people in the world. I should know.*

Besides, this day was supposed to be about fun and family. Brendan and Ashley had been looking forward to it — for like forever and a day. Even little Adam was bucking up and down in his stroller, squealing with a wordless excitement.

Mary kept close watch on her older two as they led the way along Main Street USA, with its candy-colored shops and other attractions. Each of them held one side of a park map. This was adorable, since neither of them knew what they were looking at. Ever since Adam was born, they liked to play at being older.

"What do you want to do first, my three little pumpkins?" she asked them. "We're *here*. We're finally at Disney, just like I promised."

*"Everything,"* Ashley said breathlessly. She watched slack-jawed as Goofy, the real *Goofy,* went ambling past on Main Street.

Brendan pointed to a little boy about his own age wearing Mickey Mouse ears with *Matthew* embroidered across the brim.

"Can we get those?" he asked hopefully. "Can we please, please, please?"

"No, I'm sorry, sweetie. Mommy doesn't have enough money for that. Not this trip. Next time for sure."

She wondered suddenly why she hadn't thought to pack sandwiches. The trip to Disney was going to cost far more than she could afford. If something went wrong at home between now and her next paycheck, she'd be in deep doo-doo.

But that was just more to worry about. *Stop. Stop. Not today. Don't ruin everything, Marsey-doats.*

"I know just what we should do," she said gently, taking the map from their hands.

Shortly, they were floating through the It's a Small World boat ride, something Mary hadn't done since she was Brendan's age.

But it was still the same, and that was comforting. The cool and the dark were as soothing as she remembered, and she still loved all the smiling animatronic faces that never changed. There was something reassuring about the ride, about Disneyland. She loved being here with the kids, and she'd kept her promise.

"Look at *that!*" Brendan squealed, pointing to a jolly-looking Eskimo family, waving from their snow-covered home.

Brendan and Ashley probably didn't even remember snow, she realized, and Adam had never seen it at all. The gray and the endless cold from back home were like another world now, like the black-and-white part of *The Wizard of Oz.* Except Dorothy went back, and Mary never would. Never again. No more snow-covered mountains. It was all a million miles away, right where it belonged. From now on it was going to be nothing but California sunshine — and smiling Eskimos, and Goofy.

"Excuse me, ma'am, please step out," said an attendant, breaking her reverie.

"Mommy!"

Mary winced in frustration. She had missed out on half the ride, thinking about other things. What was the last part she remembered? *The Eskimo family. Snow. Oh, yes, snow.*

"Ma'am? Please. Others are waiting."

Mary looked up at the uniformed worker, who gave her a look of utter politeness.

"Can we go around again?" she asked.

He smiled obligingly. "Sorry, but we're not allowed to let people do that. You'll have to get back in line."

"Let's go!" Brendan cried. "C'mon, Mommy. No scenes. *Please?*"

"All right, all right," Mary said. Her voice was tense, and she was a little embarrassed.

She winked to the attendant. "Kids," she said conspiratorially, then jogged across the platform to catch up with her crew, her lovies.

# Chapter 84

LUNCHTIME CAME QUICKLY, and Mary was terribly disappointed to find she had only twelve dollars and change in her purse. A small pizza and a drink to share were going to have to be it for herself and the kids.

"There's green stuff on it," Ashley said as Mary set the food on the table.

"It doesn't taste like anything," she said. She wiped away the flecks of oregano with her napkin. "There. All the green's gone, all gone now."

"It's *under* the cheese, too. I don't want it, Mommy. I'm hungry, I'm really hungry!"

"Sweetie, this is lunch. There won't be anything else until we get home."

"I don't care."

"Ashley."

"No!"

Mary took a deep breath and counted to five. She tried to get control of herself, tried so hard. "Look at your brother. He likes it. It's so yummy."

Brendan smiled and took another bite, the picture of obedience. Ashley only ducked her chin and completely avoided Mary's eye contact.

Mary felt the tension building in her shoulders and neck. "Ash, honey, you have to have at least one bite. Ashley! You have to try it. Look at me when I'm speaking to you."

Mary knew with all her heart she should just let it go. Not eating was a self-correcting problem. Ashley's problem, not hers. "Do you know how much this cost?" she said in spite of herself. "Do you know what *everything* costs here at *Fantasyland?*"

Brendan tried to intervene. "Mommy, don't. Mommy, Mommy."

"Do you?" she pressed. "Have any idea?"

"I don't care," Ashley fired back. The little bitch, the awful girl.

The tension took hold, shooting from her shoulders down into her arms and legs. Mary felt a sharp prickling in her muscles, and then all at once, a release.

*Ashley didn't want the food? Fine. Just fine.*

Her hand swept across the table.

"Mommy!" Brendan cried out.

Paper plates and slices of pizza slid to the concrete patio floor. The one soda tipped over, its sudsy contents sloshing onto the open stroller where Adam was sitting. His shriek was almost instantaneous. It resonated with Mary's own.

"Do you see what you've done? Do you?"

She barely heard any of it. Her voice was like something on the other side of a door, and the door was closed, and locked.

Oh, this wasn't how it was supposed to be. She and the kids were at Disneyland for God's sake. This was so wrong, so wrong. Everything she'd worked so hard for was going down the toilet. This was a nightmare. What else could possibly happen to spoil everything?

# Chapter 85

IF MARY SMITH'S LATEST E-MAIL was to be believed, we were down to forty-eight hours or less to stop the next homicide.

To make the impossible situation even worse, we couldn't be everywhere at once, not even with hundreds of agents and detectives on the case.

One lead in particular had emerged, and we were going to run with it. That's all Fred Van Allsburg had told us. I wasn't sure we needed another meeting to discuss it, but I showed up, and now I was glad I did.

We'd managed an end run around Maddux Fielding's unofficial closed-door policy at LAPD. A member of their blue-Suburban detail was on the phone when I got there.

The LAPD detail consisted of two lead detectives, two-dozen field agents, and a clue coordinator, Merrill Snyder, who was on the line with us.

Snyder started with his overview of the search. His voice had a subtle touch of New England. "As you know, DMVs don't track by color, which is the only specification we have on Mary Smith's alleged Suburban," he told the group.

"That's left us with just over two thousand possible matches in Los Angeles County. As a matter of triage, we've been focusing on civilian call-ins. We're still getting dozens every day — people who own a blue Suburban and don't know what to do about it; or people who've seen one, or thought they might have seen one, or maybe just know someone who's seen one. The hard part is recognizing the worthwhile point zero zero one percent of calls from the other ninety-nine point ninety-nine."

"So why did this one spike?" I asked.

It was a combination of things, Snyder told us. Plenty of leads had some individual compelling detail to them, but this one had a convergence of suspicious factors.

"This guy called in about his neighbor, who's also his tenant. She drives a blue Suburban, of course — and goes by the name Mary Wagner."

Eyebrows bobbed around the room. This was the stuff coincidence was made of, but it wouldn't have shocked me to know that our killer — with her penchant for public attention — was actually using her own first name.

"She's a virtual Jane Doe," Snyder went on. "No driver's license here, or in any state for that matter. The plates on the car are California, but guess what?"

"They're stolen," someone muttered from the rear.

"They're *stolen*," said Snyder. "And they don't track. She probably got them off an abandoned car somewhere.

279

"And then, lastly, there's her address. Mammoth Avenue in Van Nuys. It's only about ten blocks from that cybercafe where the one aborted e-mail was found."

"What else do we know about the woman herself?" Van Allsburg asked Snyder. "Any surveillance on her?"

An agent in front tapped some keys on a laptop, and a slide came up on the conference room screen.

It showed a tall, middle-aged white woman, from a vantage point across a parking lot. She wore what looked like a pink maid's uniform. Her body was neither thin nor fat; the uniform fit but still looked too small for her mannish frame. I put her age at about forty-five.

"This is from earlier this morning," Fred said. "She works in housekeeping at the Beverly Hills Hotel."

"Hang on. *Housekeeping?* Did you say housekeeping?"

Several heads turned to where Agent Page was sitting perched on the window ledge.

"What about it?" Van Allsburg asked.

"I don't know. Maybe this sounds crazy —"

"Go ahead."

"Actually, it was something in Dr. Cross's report," Page said. "At the hotel where Suzie Cartoulis and Brian Conver were found. *Someone made the bed.* Perfectly." He shrugged. "It's almost too neat, but . . . I don't know. Hotel maid . . ."

The silence in the room seemed to intimidate him, and the young agent shut up. I imagined that with more experience, Page would come to recognize this kind of response as interest, not skepticism. Everyone took the theory in, and Van Allsburg moved on to the next slide.

A tight shot of Mary Wagner.

In close up, I could see the beginnings of gray in her dark, wiry hair, which was tamed at the nape of her neck in an un-fashionable kind of bun. Her face was round and matronly, but her expression neutral and distant. She seemed to be somewhere else.

The mutterer from the rear spoke up again. "She sure doesn't look like much."

And she didn't. She was no one you'd notice on the street. Practically invisible.

# Chapter 86

AT 6:20 THAT NIGHT, I was parked up the block from Mary Wagner's house. This could definitely be something, our big break, and we all knew it. So far, we'd been able to keep the press away.

A second team was in the alley behind the house, and a third one had trailed Wagner from work at the Beverly Hills Hotel. They had just sent word that she'd stopped for groceries and was nearly home.

Sure enough, a blue Suburban, puffing smoke from the exhaust pipe, pulled into the driveway a couple of minutes later.

Ms. Wagner hoisted two plastic bags from the truck and went inside. She appeared to be a strong woman. It also looked as though she was talking to herself, but I couldn't tell for sure.

Once she'd gone inside, we pulled down the street for a better view.

My partner for the evening was Manny Baker, an agent about my age. Manny had a good reputation, but his monosyllabic responses to polite conversation had long since dropped off to silence. So we settled in and watched the Wagner house in the gathering dusk.

Ms. Wagner's rented bungalow was in poor shape, even for a marginal neighborhood. The gate on the chain-link fence was completely missing. The lawn overgrew what remained of the brick edging along the front walk.

The property was barely wider than the house itself, with just enough room for a driveway on the south side. The Suburban had nearly scraped the neighbor's wall when she pulled in.

Jeremy Kilbourn, the man who had called in to us about the Suburban, lived next door and owned both houses. We'd learned from him that Ms. Wagner's bungalow had belonged to his mother until she died fourteen months prior. Mary Wagner moved in shortly after that and had been paying cash rent, on time, ever since. Kilbourn thought she was "a weird chick" but friendly enough, and said she kept mostly to herself.

Tonight, his house was dark. He had taken his family to stay with relatives until Mary Wagner was checked out.

As dusk changed to night, it grew quiet and still on the street. Mary Wagner finally turned on a few lights and seemed to settle in. I couldn't help thinking, *life of quiet desperation.*

At one point, I got out my Maglite and my wallet, and I stole a glance at the pictures I had of Damon, Jannie, and Little Alex, wondering what they were doing right now. In the dark, I didn't have to worry about the goofy grin it put on my face.

For the next several hours, I divided my attention between Mary Wagner's unchanging house and a file of case notes in my lap. The notes were more of a prop than anything else. Everything there was to know about Mary Smith was already lodged in my head.

Then I saw something — *someone,* actually — and I almost couldn't believe my eyes.

"Oh, no," I said out loud. "Oh, Jesus!"

Poor Manny Baker almost jumped out of his seat.

# Chapter 87

"HEY! *TRUSCOTT!* Stop right there! I said *stop*." I got out of the car as I saw the writer and his photographer approaching Mary Wagner's house. What in hell were they doing here?

We were about the same distance from the bungalow, and suddenly Truscott started to run for it.

So did I, and I was a lot faster than the reporter, and maybe faster than he thought I might be. He gave me no other choice — so I tackled him before he got to the front door. I hit him at the waist, and Truscott went down hard, grunting in pain.

That was the good part, hitting him. What a mess, though, a complete disaster! Mary Wagner was sure to hear us and come out to look, and then we'd be blown. Everything was going to unravel in a hurry now. There wasn't much I could do about it.

I dragged the reporter by his feet until we were out of sight from the Wagner house, and hopefully out of sound.

"I have every right to be here. I'll sue you for everything you have, Cross."

"Fine, sue me."

Because Truscott had started to scream at me, and his photographer was still snapping pictures, I put him in a hammerlock, and I ran him even farther up the street.

"You can't do this! You have no right!"

"Get her! Take that camera away!" I called to the other agents coming up from the rear.

"I'm gonna sue your ass! I'll sue you and the Bureau back to the Dark Ages, Cross!" Truscott was still shouting as three of us finally carried him around the first corner we reached. Then I cuffed James Truscott and shoved the writer into one of our sedans.

"Get him out of here!" I told an agent. "The camerawoman, too."

I took one last look into the backseat before Truscott was hauled away. "Sue me, sue the FBI. You're still under arrest for obstruction. Take this lunatic the hell out of here!"

A few minutes later, the narrow side street was quiet again, thank God.

Frankly, I was amazed — stunned — Mary Wagner, this supposedly careful and clever murderess, seemed not to have noticed.

# Chapter 88

MARY WAGNER GOT A LOT MORE SLEEP that night than any of the rest of us. James Truscott spent the night in jail, but I was sure he'd be out in the morning. His magazine had already put in a complaint. He hadn't missed much of anything, though. There was nothing new to report when the relief team finally came at 4:00 A.M.

That gave me enough time to get to my hotel for a two-hour nap and a shower before I was back on the road again.

I got to the Beverly Hills Hotel just past 7:00. Mary Wagner's work shift started at 7:30.

This was definitely getting interesting now, and also weirder by the minute.

The luxury hotel, a pink stucco landmark in Hollywood, sat nearly obscured behind a wall of palms and banana trees on Sunset Boulevard. The inside echoed the outside, with its

pink-everything lobby and ubiquitous banana-leaf wall-
paper.

I found the security chief, Andre Perkins, in his office on
the lower level. I had deliberately arranged for only one contact at the hotel.

Perkins was a former Bureau agent himself. He had two
copies of Mary Wagner's file on his desk when I got there.

"She pretty much reads like a model employee," he told
me. "Shows up on time, keeps up with the work. As far as I
can gather, she just seems to come in, do her thing, and
leave. I can ask around some more. Should I?"

"Don't do it yet, thanks. What about her background?
Anything for me there?"

He pulled out Wagner's original application and a couple
of pages of notes.

"She's been here almost eight months. It looks like she
was legitimately laid off from a Marriott downtown before
that. But I made some calls on the earlier stuff, and it's all
wrong numbers or disconnected. Her social security number's a fake, too. Not all that unusual for a maid or porter."

"Is there anyone who can say for sure that she was actually on the premises during all of her shifts?" I asked.

Perkins shook his head. "Just the cleaning records."

He looked over his papers again.

"She definitely keeps up with her quotas, which she
wouldn't be able to do if she was ducking out a lot. And her
comment cards are fine. She's doing a good job. Mary Wagner
is an above-average employee here."

# Chapter 89

PERKINS LET ME USE HIS FAX machine to send copies of Mary Wagner's time sheets over to the Bureau for cross-referencing. Then he set me up with a maintenance uniform and a name tag that said "Bill."

Bill stationed himself in the basement, within sight of the stocking area where housekeeping loaded up on paper products and cleaning materials. Just after 7:30, the new shift filtered in.

All of them were women, all in the same pink uniform. Mary was the tallest in the group. *Big-boned,* that's what some people would call her. And she was white, one of the few on the housekeeping staff.

She certainly looked strong enough for the physical work Mary Smith had done — manipulating Marti Lowenstein-Bell's body in the swimming pool, moving Brian Conver from the hotel room floor to the bed.

Bill stood maybe twenty yards away from her, facing a fuse panel, his face partially hidden behind its door.

Wagner went about her work quietly and efficiently while the others chatted around her, most of them talking in Spanish. She stuck mostly to herself, just as Perkins had described. Hers was the first cart onto the freight elevator.

I didn't follow her upstairs. The hotel corridors would offer no cover, and my priority was to interview her at home later, as myself. That meant a limited surveillance for Bill at the hotel.

My best opportunity came during the lunch hour, when the staff cafeteria was filled to capacity. Mary sat by herself at a table near the door, eating a tuna salad sandwich, writing in a clothbound book, presumably a journal of some kind. I wanted to see that journal. Her conversations with the people around her seemed to be little more than polite hellos and good-byes. The perfect employee.

I decided to pull myself out at that point, and went back to Perkins's office in the basement. I gave him a courtesy debriefing. As we were talking, my beeper went off.

"Excuse me." I got Karl Page in the crisis center.

"I thought you'd want to know right away — yeah, just a second, I'll be there — her time sheets check out perfectly. Mary Wagner *wasn't* at work for at least two hours before and two hours after every estimated time of death. No exceptions. Cha-ching!"

"Okay, thanks. I'm out of here. She's working today."

"When did you last see her?"

"About ten minutes ago. I have to go, Page." Perkins was looking at me expectantly, and I didn't want him asking too many questions. The receiver was halfway back to the cradle when I heard Page shout, "Wait!"

I gave Perkins a *sorry* with my eyebrows. Sometimes Agent Page could be a little exasperating, almost as if he was trying too hard.

"What, Karl?"

"Mary Smith's last e-mail, Alex. The murder that's supposed to happen by twelve tomorrow."

"Yeah, I got it," I said, and hung up the phone. I already knew what Page was trying to tell me.

Tomorrow was Mary Wagner's day off.

# Chapter 90

I WAS ALREADY CONVINCED it was crucial that I try to speak with Mary Wagner before the trauma of an arrest. That was my strong gut response on this strange case. I knew LAPD was going to be under a lot of pressure to move quickly, though. It meant I had to move even faster if I could.

I hurried back to the Bureau and found Van Allsburg in his office. "Don't ask me. Not my call," he said, after I'd made my case for the interview. "If Maddux Fielding wants to move in on her —"

"Then do me one favor," I said.

Minutes later, we were on the phone in Fred's office. I knew Maddux Fielding probably wouldn't take my call, but Van Allsburg got patched through right away.

"Maddux, I've got Alex Cross here. He's making a pretty good argument for holding off on Mary Wagner, just long enough to interview her."

"How much more do you think we're going to get on her?" Fielding asked. "It's done. We've got plenty to take her in."

"It's all circumstantial," I said into the speakerphone. "You'll have to let her go."

"Yeah, well I'm working on that."

"What do you mean?" I asked, already starting to fume. "What aren't you telling us, Maddux? What's the point of shutting us out?"

He ignored my legitimate question with one of his trademark stony silences.

"Listen, between LAPD and the Bureau, she's under constant surveillance; she hasn't shown any sign of making a move. We know her timetable. Let me just talk to her at home. This could be a last chance to get her in a nondefensive state." I hated the conciliatory tone of my voice, but I knew the interview with Mary could be important.

"Detective, I know you and I have our disagreements," I said, "but we're both going for a quick resolve here. This is what I do best. If you'll just let me —"

"Be at her house by six," he said suddenly. "I'm not making any promises to you though, Cross. If she doesn't go home after work, or if anything else changes, that's the end of it. We grab her."

By the time I had arched my eyebrows, there was a click on the line and the call was over.

# Chapter 91

SHE DIDN'T BOTHER to use the chain lock. I heard it rattle on the back of the front door as she opened it.

"Mary Wagner?"

"Yes?"

Her large feet were bare, but she still wore the pink maid's uniform from the Beverly Hills Hotel. She smiled engagingly before she knew who I was.

"I'm Agent Cross with the FBI." I held up my ID, which included my shield. "May I come in and ask you a few questions? It's important."

Her tired face sagged. "It's about the car, isn't it? Lord, I wish I could just paint that thing or trade it in or something. I've been getting all kinds of embarrassing looks — you wouldn't believe."

Her manner was more outgoing than anything I'd seen at the hotel, but she had the beleaguered, animated quality of a public-school kindergarten teacher with way too many students.

"Yes, ma'am," I said. "It is about the car. Just a formality; we're following up on as many blue Suburbans as we can. May I come in? It won't take long."

"Of course. I don't mean to be rude. Please, come on inside. Come."

I waved to Baker on the curb.

"Five minutes," I called out, mostly just to let Ms. Wagner know I wasn't alone at her house. Hopefully, the unmarked LAPD units up and down the street were more invisible to her eyes than mine.

I stepped inside, and she closed the door behind me. Adrenaline shot through my body in an instant. Was this woman a killer, possibly an insane one? For some strange reason, I didn't feel threatened by her.

The neatness of the house made a strong first impression on me. The floors were recently swept, and I saw no signs of clutter anywhere.

A wooden cutout hung in the front hallway. It was in the shape of a curtsying farm girl with the word *Welcome* stenciled across her skirt. The relative disrepair outside, I suddenly realized, was the landlord's domain. This was hers.

"Please sit down," she said.

Mary Wagner gestured me toward the living room through an archway to my right. A mismatched sofa and love seat took up most of the room.

Her television was on mute, and a can of Diet Pepsi and a half-eaten bowl of soup sat on the worn redwood coffee table.

"Am I interrupting your dinner?" I asked. "I'm real sorry about that." Not that I was going to leave.

"Oh, no, no, not at all. I'm not much of an eater." She quickly turned off the TV and cleared the food away.

I stayed in the hall and glanced around while she put the dishes on the kitchen counter in the back. Nothing looked out of place. Just a regular house that was almost too neat, uncluttered, spick-and-span clean.

"Would you like something to drink?" she called out from the other room.

"Nothing, thanks."

"Water? Soda? Orange juice? It's no bother, Agent Cross."

"I'm fine."

Her journal was probably here in the house, but nowhere that I could see. She'd been watching *Jeopardy!* on TV.

"Actually, I'm out of orange juice, anyway," she said genially, coming back toward me. She was either completely comfortable or very good at faking it. Very odd. I followed her into the living room, and we both sat down.

"So, what can I do for you?" she asked in a kindly tone that was oddly unsettling. "I'd like to help, of course."

I kept my own tone casual and nonthreatening. "First of all, are you the only driver for your car?"

"Just me." She smiled as though the question was vaguely funny. I wondered why.

"Has it been outside of your supervision at any time in the past six weeks or so?"

"Well, when I sleep, of course. And when I'm at work. I do housekeeping at the Beverly Hills Hotel."

"I see. So you need the car for transportation to work."

She fingered the collar of her uniform and eyeballed the pad in my hand as though she wanted me to write that part down. On an impulse, I went ahead and did it.

"So I guess the answer is yes," she went on. "Technically, it has been outside of my . . . whatever you said. *Supervision*." Her laugh was a tiny bit coy. "My purview."

I scribbled a few more notes of my own. *Eager to please? Busy hands. Wants me to know she's intelligent.*

As we continued, I watched her as much as I listened. Nothing she said was really out of the ordinary, though. What struck hardest was the way she concentrated on me. Her hands kept landing in different places, but her brown eyes didn't travel very far from my own. I got the impression she was glad I was there.

When I stood up at the end of the interview, as if to leave, her face dropped.

"Could I bother you for that glass of water?" I asked, and she brightened visibly.

"Coming right up."

I followed her as far as the doorway. Everything in the kitchen was neatly arranged, too. The counters were mostly empty, except for a four-slice toaster and a set of country kitsch–style canisters.

The dish rack next to the sink was full, and there were two steak knives among the clean silverware.

She filled a glass at the tap and handed it to me. It tasted slightly soapy.

"Are you originally from California?" I asked conversationally. "From around here?"

"Oh, no," she said. "Nowhere near as nice as this."

"Where'd you move from?"

"The North Pole." Another coy laugh and a shake of the head. "At least, it might as well be."

"Let me guess. Maine? You strike me as a New Englander."

"Can I get you a refill?"

"No, thank you. Really, I'm fine."

She took the water glass out of my hand, not yet half empty, and turned toward the sink.

That was when all hell broke loose.

First, I heard heavy footsteps and a loud shout coming from just outside.

Almost immediately, the back door burst open with a crash of splintering wood and glass. I heard the front door crashing in as well.

Then police officers streamed into the kitchen from both sides, flak jackets on, their weapons drawn and pointed at Mary Wagner.

# Chapter 92

MARY DROPPED THE WATER GLASS, but I didn't even hear it break. Suddenly the kitchen was filled with loud shouting, as well as Mary's frightened screaming.

"Get out of my house! I didn't do anything! Get away from me, please! Why are you here?"

I held up my badge in front of me, unsure if the LAPD assault team even knew who I was.

"Get down on the floor!" The lead officer's pistol was pointed at Mary's chest. "Get down. *Now!* On the floor!"

In a matter of seconds, Mary Wagner was a total wreck. Her eyes were unfocused, and she didn't even seem to hear the officer shouting at her.

"Get down!" he shouted again.

She backed up, still screaming, with her arms and shoulders in a hunched, defensive position.

I could only watch as her bare foot came down on a piece

of the broken water glass. She yelped pitifully, then jerked to one side as if she'd been slapped.

Her free foot slipped in the water, and twisted under her. With a fast pinwheeling of arms, she went down hard.

The police assault team was on her in a second. Two officers rolled Mary over and handcuffed her from behind. Another one read her rights, the words probably coming too fast for her to understand.

Someone took my elbow and spoke in my ear. "Sir, could you come with me, please?"

I ignored whoever it was.

"*Sir?*" The officer grabbed at me again, and I angrily shook him off.

"She needs first aid." But no one seemed to hear me, or if they did, pay any attention.

"Ma'am, do you understand everything I've told you?" the arresting officer asked. She nodded shakily, still facedown on the floor. I was fairly certain she didn't understand any of this.

"Ma'am, I need you to say yes or no. Do you understand everything I've told you?"

"Yes." It came out as a gasp. Her breathing was ragged. "I understand. You think I did something bad."

That was enough. I pushed my way through the cops and knelt down next to her.

"Mary, it's me. Agent Cross. Are you all right? Mary? Do you really understand what's happening now?"

She was still panicked but not dissociated. I made sure the shard was out of her foot, then wrapped it in a dish towel and helped her sit up.

She looked around, wide-eyed, as if scanning the room for anything familiar.

"Mary, they're placing you under arrest. You need to go with them now. Do you understand what I'm saying?"

"All right, we got it." A cop maybe half my age stepped in.

"Just give me a second here," I said.

"No, sir," he answered. "We are to take the suspect into immediate custody."

I turned away from Mary and kept my voice low. "What do you think I'm trying to help you do here?"

"Sir, my instructions are clear, and unequivocal. Please step away. This is our arrest."

My only alternative to giving in was a truly ugly scene. I thought seriously about it, but knew my argument wasn't with the arresting officers — it was with their boss. Anyway, the damage was already done.

Within seconds, they had Mary Wagner on her feet and were pushing her out the door. The stained dish towel lay crumpled on the floor, where a long red smudge marked the linoleum.

"First aid!" I yelled after them, not that they could hear me anymore, not that they gave a damn about what I had to say.

I swear, I wanted to hit someone. My frustration and anger boiled over, and I knew where to take it; I wheeled on the nearest sergeant.

"Where the hell is Maddux Fielding?" I shouted at the top of my voice. "Where is he?"

# Chapter 93

"BACK OFF, CROSS!"

Fielding said it before I even reached him. He was out on the sidewalk in front of Mary Wagner's house, conferring with one of his arresting officers.

The block had been transformed from suburban normalcy into the kind of police scene most people never see, or want to.

A dozen or more black-and-whites clogged the street, most of them with their flashers still rolling.

Bright-yellow crime scene tape was being strung across the chain-link fence, and a barrier of sawhorses bracketed the property, holding back a fast-growing crowd of lookyloos who wanted to see a little true-crime history in the making.

*Mary Smith lived right in that house. Can you imagine? In our neighborhood?*

I saw that a couple of news vans were already on site as

well. I wondered if Maddux Fielding had prearranged a little coverage for his Big Get, and it made me even angrier.

"What was the purpose of that?" I yelled at him.

All I could see was his smug expression as he grudgingly turned to look at me.

"You compromised a key interview, not to mention her personal safety and mine. Both unnecessarily. I could have been shot. She could have been shot. You made a carnival out of this arrest. You're a disgrace to the LAPD."

I didn't know or care who was listening in; I just hoped it was embarrassing to Fielding. Maybe this was a language that he spoke. His face remained inscrutable.

"Agent Cross —"

"Do you know what you may have just done to your chances for a confession?"

"*I don't need one!*" he finally shouted over me. "I don't need one because I have something better."

"What are you talking about?"

He nodded condescendingly. Information was the valuable currency here, and he had it. What the hell was he holding back?

"You can probably see I'm busy," he told me. "I'll make my report available to the Federal Bureau — as soon as it's ready."

I couldn't walk away. "You gave me time for this interview. I had your word!"

He had already turned away but now pivoted back on me. "I said if anything changed, it was over. That's precisely what I said to you."

"So what changed, goddammit?"

He took a beat. "Fuck you, Agent Cross. I don't have to give you answers."

I lunged at him, and it was probably exactly what he wanted. Two of his monkeys stepped between us and pulled me back. Just as well, but it would have felt good to erase that cynical sneer off his face, even better to briefly rearrange some of his features. I shook off the two officers and walked away.

Before I'd even begun to calm down, though, I was dialing my cell phone.

"Jeanne Galletta."

"It's Alex Cross. Do you know anything about the Mary Wagner arrest?"

"Fine, thanks. How are you?"

"Sorry. But do you, Jeanne? I'm at her house right now. It's an incredible mess. You wouldn't believe how it went down."

Jeanne paused. "I'm not on that case anymore."

"Would I get a different answer in person?"

"You might."

"Then give me a break. Please, Jeanne. I need your help. I don't have time to run around."

Her voice finally softened. "What happened out there? You sound really upset."

"I am upset. Everything blew up. I was right in the middle of interviewing her when LAPD burst in like a damn clown car at the circus. It was ridiculous, Jeanne, and unnecessary. Fielding knows something, and he won't say what."

"I'll save you a step," Jeanne said. "She's the one. She did those murders, Alex."

"How do you know? How does LAPD know? What is going on?"

"You remember the hair that was found at the movie theater when Patrice Bennett was killed? Well, they pulled one off Mary Wagner's sweater from her locker at the hotel. The results just came through. It's the same hair. Fielding ran with it."

My mind raced, placing this new bit of information alongside everything else. "I see you're doing a good job staying off the case," I finally said.

"Can't help what I overhear."

"So did you overhear where they took her?"

Jeanne hesitated, but only for a couple of seconds. "Try the Van Nuys station on Sylmar Avenue. You better hurry. She won't be there long."

"I'm on my way."

# Chapter 94

I GOT RIGHT OVER to the Van Nuys station, but I was stonewalled: I was told to my face that Mary Wagner wasn't being held there.

There was nothing I could do to budge LAPD: They had this woman, their suspect, and they weren't sharing her. Even Ron Burns couldn't, or wouldn't, help me out.

I wasn't able to see Mary until the next morning. By that time, LAPD had transferred her to a temporary holding facility downtown, where they kept her completely tied up in interrogation — without any real progress, as I had predicted.

One sympathetic detective described her to me as somewhere between despondent and catatonic, but I still needed to see Mary Wagner for myself.

When I arrived at the downtown facility, the assembled press corps mob was twice the size of anything we'd seen so far. Easily. For weeks, the Hollywood Stalker case had made national headlines, not just local ones. Mary Wagner's mug shot was everywhere now, a blank-eyed, disheveled woman looking very much the part of a killer.

The last thing I heard before I switched off my car radio was ridiculous morning-talk-show banter and psychobabble about why she had committed murders against rich and famous women in Hollywood.

"How about Kathy Bates? She could play Mary. She's a great actress," one "concerned" caller asked the talk show host, who was all too glad to play along.

"Too old. Besides, she already did *Misery*. I say you get Nicky Kidman, get her to slap on another fake nose, wig, thirty pounds, and you're good to go," replied the DJ. "Or maybe Meryl Streep. Emma Thompson? Kate Winslet would be strong."

My check-in at the station house took almost forty-five minutes. I had to speak with four different personnel and show my ID half a dozen times just to reach the small interrogation room where they were going to bring Mary Wagner to me. Eventually — in their own sweet time.

When I finally saw her, my first reaction, surprisingly, was pity.

Mary looked as though she hadn't slept, with bruise-colored half-moons under her eyes and a drooping, shuffling walk. The pink hotel uniform was gone. She now wore shapeless gray sweatpants and an old UCLA sweatshirt flecked with pale yellow paint the same color as her kitchen.

Vague recognition flickered in her eyes when she saw me.

I was reminded of some of the Alzheimer's patients I regularly visited at St. Anthony's in D.C.

I told the guard to remove her cuffs and wait outside.

"I'll be okay with her. We're friends."

"Friends," Mary repeated as she stared deeply into my eyes.

# Chapter 95

"MARY, DO YOU REMEMBER ME from yesterday?" I asked as soon as the guard was back out in the hallway. I had pulled up a chair and sat across from her. The plain four-by-eight table between us was bolted to the floor. It was  chilly in the small room, with a draft from somewhere.

"You're Mister Cross," she said dully. "FBI Agent Cross. Excuse me, I'm sorry."

"Good memory. Do you know why you're here?"

She tensed, though it was barely discernible from her otherwise flat affect. "They think I'm that woman. They're accusing me of murder." Her gaze fell to the floor. "*Murders*. More than one. All those Hollywood people. They think I did it."

I was actually glad she said "they." It meant I could still be a potential ally in her mind. Maybe she'd tell me some of her secrets after all, and maybe not.

"We don't have to talk about that if you don't want to," I said.

She blinked once, and seemed to focus a little. She squinted her eyes at me, then looked down at the floor.

"Would you like anything? Are you thirsty?" I asked. I wanted her to feel as comfortable as possible with me, but I was also feeling an urge to help this woman. She looked and sounded so terrible, possibly impaired.

Now she looked up, her eyes searching mine. "Could I have a cup of coffee? Would it be too much trouble?"

The coffee arrived, and Mary held the paper cup with her fingertips and sipped at it with an unexpected kind of delicacy. The coffee seemed to revive her a little, too.

She kept sneaking glances at me, and she absently smoothed her hair against her head. "Thanks." Her eyes were a little brighter, and I saw a shade of the friendly woman from the day before.

"Mary, do you have any questions about what's going on? I'm sure you must."

Immediately, a pall came over her. Her emotions were palpably fragile. Suddenly, tears welled up in her eyes, and she nodded without speaking.

"What is it, Mary?"

She looked up to the corner of the ceiling, where a camera was watching us. I knew that at least a half-dozen law enforcement personnel and psychiatric specialists were tucked away less than ten feet from where we sat.

Mary seemed to guess as much. When she did speak, it was in a whisper.

"They won't tell me anything about my *children*." Her face contorted as she fought back more tears.

# Chapter 96

"YOUR CHILDREN?" I asked, somewhat confused, but going along with what she'd said.

"Do you know where they are?" Her voice was wavery, but her energy had increased quite a bit already.

"No, I don't," I answered truthfully. "I can look into it. I'll need some more information from you."

"Go ahead. I'll tell you what you need to know. They're too young to be on their own."

"How many children do you have?" I asked her.

She seemed dumbfounded by the question. "Three. Don't you already know?"

I took out my pad. "How old are they, Mary?"

"Brendan's eight, Ashley's five, and Adam's eleven months." She spoke haltingly while I wrote it all down.

*Eleven months?*

It was certainly possible she had given birth a year ago, but somehow, I doubted it very much.

I checked the ages to be sure about what she'd said. "Eight, five, eleven months?"

Mary nodded. "That's right."

"And how old are you, Mary?"

For the first time, I saw anger show on her face. She balled her hands into hard fists, closed her eyes, and struggled to compose herself. What was this all about?

"I'm twenty-six, for God's sake. What difference does that make? Can we get back to my kids now?"

*Twenty-six? Not even close. Wow. There it was. The first opening.*

I looked at my notes; then I decided to take a little leap with her. "So Brendan, Ashley, and Adam live at home with you. Is that right?"

She nodded again. When I got something right, it seemed to calm her down tremendously. Relief spread over her face, then seemed to continue down into her body.

"And were they home yesterday when I was there?"

She looked confused now, and the anger that had ebbed away edged back. "You know they were, Agent Cross. You were right there. Why are you doing this?"

Her voice rose as she spoke. Her breath had gone shallow. "What have you people done with my children? Where are they right now? I need to see them. *Right now*."

The door opened, and I held my hand up to the guard without taking my eyes off of Mary. It was obvious her pulse had quickened as the agitation seemed to take hold.

I took a calculated risk with her.

"Mary," I said gently, "there were no children in the house yesterday."

Her response was immediate, and extreme.

She sat bolt upright and screamed at me, her neck muscles straining. *"Tell me what you've done with my children! Answer me this instant! Where are my kids? Where are my kids?"*

Steps sounded on the floor behind me, and I stood up so I could be the first one to reach her.

She was raving now, screaming over and over.

"Tell me! Why won't you tell me?" Now she had started to sob, and I felt sorry for her.

I slowly walked around the table. *"Mary!"* I shouted her name, but she was completely unresponsive to the sound of my voice, even to my movement toward her.

"Tell me where my kids are! Tell me! Tell me! Tell me! This instant!"

"Mary —"

I leaned over and took her by the shoulders, as gently as I could under the circumstances.

"Tell me!"

"Mary, look at me! Please."

That's when she went for my gun.

# Chapter 97

SHE MUST HAVE SEEN THE HOLSTER tucked inside my jacket. In a split second, she reached up and her hand was on the butt of my Glock.

"No!" I yelled. "Mary!"

I instinctively knocked her back into her chair, but the gun wrenched free from the holster and she had it. I caught a flash of her eyes, which were glazed and crazy.

I dove at her, grabbing her wrist with one hand and the gun with the other. I continued to yell her name.

Next, the two of us fell over the chair as it went down with a loud crack.

I was vaguely aware of people scrambling all around us. My focus stayed on her.

She strained, red-faced, slamming my side with her free fist. I now had a knee on her chest and one hand still on her wrist, pinning the gun to the ground, but she was as strong as she looked.

And her finger was already wrapped around the Glock's trigger. She squirmed hard, turning the barrel of the gun toward herself — and tilting her head to meet it. She knew exactly what she was doing.

"No! Mary!"

With a rush of adrenaline, fighting an equal surge of resistance from her, I managed to lift her gun hand toward the ceiling. Then I smashed it back down, very hard, against the floor.

The Glock fired once into the wall of the interrogation room, even as it fell out of her grasp. I snatched it up, the shot still ringing in my ears, the side of my face numb.

There was a brief, suspended moment of near silence.

Mary stopped struggling immediately, and then, in an unbelievable echo of the previous day's events, the police descended on her like a small army. They picked her up as she flailed once again, arms and legs whipping crazily.

I could hear her unchecked sobs as they carried her away.

"My babies, my babies, my poor babies . . . Where are my children? Oh, where? Oh, where? What have you done with my children?"

Her voice receded down the hall until a heavy door slammed with great finality, and she was gone. Not surprisingly, I didn't get the chance for another interview.

To make matters worse, if that was possible, I saw James Truscott as I left the building about an hour later. He was among the throng of reporters gathered outside waiting for any tidbit of news.

He yelled at me, "How did she get your gun, Dr. Cross? How'd that happen?" Somehow, Truscott had already gotten the story.

# Chapter 98

I COULD ONLY WONDER about the causes and the full extent of Mary Wagner's mental illness and the obvious torment and stress it was putting on her. There certainly hadn't been any time for a meaningful psych evaluation, and my part in the investigation was coming to an end now, whether I liked it or not. And, to be honest, I had mixed feelings.

By early that afternoon, Mary's state of mind was a moot point. LAPD's search of her house had turned up a holy trinity of evidence.

A Walther PPK, discovered under a blanket in her attic crawl space, had already shown a preliminary ballistic match to the weapon used in the murders.

CSI had also found half-a-dozen sheets of children's stickers and, most significant, stolen family photographs from Marti Lowenstein-Bell's office and Suzie Cartoulis's purse. Both Michael Bell and Giovanni Cartoulis had positively identified the photos as having belonged to their murdered wives.

"And best of all, most important anyway," Fred Van Allsburg told the small group of agents assembled in his office, "twelve o'clock came and went today without incident. No new victim, no new e-mail. It's *over*. I think I can safely say that."

The mood was grimly congratulatory. Just about everyone was glad to leave this one behind, but the details of the case would haunt most of the team for some time, just as the D.C. sniper case still lingered in the J. Edgar Hoover Building back East. It's an unsatisfying and unpleasant feeling, but also part of what drives us to do better.

"Alex, we owe you one on this." Van Allsburg finally came over to me. "Your work on the case was invaluable. I have to say that. I see why Ron Burns likes you close to home."

A few uneasy laughs went through the room. Agent Page reached from behind and patted my shoulder. He would go far in the Bureau, if he could keep his passion for solving crimes.

"I'd still like to take a peek at that final evidence LAPD found. And maybe get a real interview with Mary Wagner," I said, diverting back to what *I* thought was most important.

Van Allsburg shook his head. "Not necessary."

"There's no reason for me not to stick around another day —" I started to say.

"Don't worry about it. Page and Fujishiro are good for the details; I can back them up. And if we really need you again, there's always frequent-flier miles, right?" His tone was artificially bright.

"Fred, Mary Wagner wouldn't talk to anyone before I came. She trusts me."

"At least, she did," he said. "Probably not anymore." It was a blunt statement, but not aggressive.

"I'm still the only person she's opened up to. I hear LAPD is getting nowhere with her."

"Like I said, you're just a plane ride away if we need you back. I spoke about it with Director Burns and he agrees. Go home to your family. You have kids, right?"

"Yes, I have kids."

Hours later, packing my bag at the hotel, I was struck hard with another kind of realization: Actually, I couldn't wait to get home. It was a huge relief that I'd be back in D.C. again, with no immediate travel plans.

But — and the *but* was important — why had that fact been so far from my mind in Van Allsburg's office? What were these blinders I wore, and how did I keep forgetting I had them on? What kind of dramatic wake-up call did I need before I got the message?

On the way to the airport I figured out another piece. It just hit me. The *A*'s and *B*'s on the children's stickers at the crime scenes. I knew what the letters meant. Mary's imaginary children's names — Ashley, Adam, Brendan. Two *A*'s and a *B*.

I phoned it in on my way out of L.A.

# Part Five

# END OF STORY

# Chapter 99

THE STORYTELLER WAS DONE KILLING. *Fini.* It was over, and no one would ever know the whole truth about what had happened. *End of story.*

So he threw himself a party with some of his best buddies from Beverly Hills.

He told them he'd just gotten a gig writing a screenplay for an A-list director, a big, dopey thriller based on a dopey bestseller. He'd been given license to change anything he didn't like, but that was all he could say about it right now. The director was paranoid — so what's new? But a big party was definitely in order.

His friends thought they understood what was going down, which gave him some idea how little they knew him. His best friends in the world — and hell, none of them knew him at all. None of them suspected he could be a killer. How fricking unbelievably crazy was that? No one knew him.

The party was at the Snake Pit Ale House, a bar on Melrose where they'd held a fantasy football league during his early days in L.A., soon after he'd arrived from Brown University to act, and maybe dabble at writing scripts — serious, worthy stuff, not box-office crap.

"The order of the night is free beer," he said as each of his buds arrived at the bar, "and wine for the wussies among you. So I guess it's vino all around?"

Nobody drank wine, not one of the fourteen pals who came to the bash. They were all glad to see him out and about, and also about his new gig — though some of the more honest ones admitted they were jealous. Everybody started calling him "A-list."

He and David and Johnboy and Frankie were still at the bar when it closed at a little past two. They were overanalyzing a movie called *We Don't Live Here Anymore.* They finally more or less stumbled outside and exchanged Hollywood hugs on the street next to Johnny's fucking Bentley — talk about A-list — the spoils of the last movie he'd produced, a 400-million-dollar grosser worldwide, which made all the rest of them sick because all he'd done was buy a dipshit graphic novel for fifty thousand then sign up the Rock for ten mil. Genius, right? Yep — 'cause it worked.

"Love ya, man. You're the best, you sick, obnoxious, ostentatious bastard. You too, Davey!" he yelled as the silver Bentley pulled away from the curb and sped west.

"I know — I'm just a *bastard* right now," David yelled back. "But I have dreams of being sick, obnoxious, and ostentatious, too. And *talented* — which is what's holding me back in this town."

"Hey, man — I hear you, I feel ya," he yelled.

"Seeya, A-list! Ya hack!"

"I'm just a storyteller!" he yelled back.

Then he was kind of floating down a side street to his own car, a seven-year-old Beamer. Not a Suburban. He was definitely three sheets to the wind. Happy as a pig out of a blanket — humming Jimi Hendrix's "The Wind Cries Mary." An in-joke that only he would get.

Until suddenly he began to sob, and he couldn't make himself stop, not even when he was sitting on the lawn of some grungy apartment building with his head down between his legs, bawling like a baby.

And he was thinking, *Just one more, just one.*

*One more kill and I'll be good.*

# Chapter 100

THE NEXT MORNING, he couldn't sleep, and he drove up and down Melrose — past L'Angelo, which used to be Emilio's; the Groundling Theater where Phil Hartman got his start; Tommy Tang's; the original Johnny Rockets; the Blue Whale. His city, man. His and Proud Mary's.

It was around 5:30 or so when he bounced into the Starbucks on Melrose, which used to be The Burger that Ate LA back in the day. Man, he did not like Starbucks, but they were open, the greedy little Yuppie bastards. The numbers dictated that they be open, right? The numbers ran everything these days.

And here he was — proving the number crunchers right. Five-thirty in the A.M. and he was already making their day.

God, he despised these dipshit coffee places, the new McDonald's, overpriced rip-offs. He remembered when a cup of coffee was fifty cents, which seemed about right. But

"Sumatra blend" — now that was worth two-fifty if it was worth a nickel. For a *tall,* which really meant a *small.*

And the goateed schmo minding the store was too busy setting up shop to give any attention to his paying customer, his early bird, the day's first sucker.

He let it go for a minute or so, but the jerk was starting to piss him off royally.

"Be right back," he finally told the superbusy "barista" behind the counter, and the guy still hardly noticed him. What an ass and a half. No doubt, an actor out of work. Too good for the job, right? With an attitude — which was supposed to be a good thing these days.

A minute later, he reentered the Starbucks with a piece in his jacket pocket. He was starting to rev-up now. This was probably stupid, definitely not too smart, but God, it felt pretty good.

*Hey, pal, my gun is getting thirsty.*

Right then and there, the decision was made. This arrogant fuck wannabe actor was going down for the count. He was tomorrow's headlines today.

"Hey, buddy, I'm waiting here for some coffee. You got any coffee at Starbucks?"

The barista didn't look up from his busy work even then, just waved a free hand. "Be with ya."

The Storyteller, *the* Storyteller, heard the door open behind him. Another sucker arrives.

"Hey, morning, Christopher." A woman's chirpy voice came from behind. He didn't even turn to look at her. Screw her, too.

"Hiya, Sarah," called the counter guy. And he was suddenly all chirpy, too.

*Now* the jackass came to the front, now he wakes up. *For Sarah.*

And that's when he shot the dude in the chest, right in the Starbucks apron.

"Forget the coffee, Christopher. Don't need it now. I'm already wired."

Then he turned to see about the woman. First time he ever looked at her.

Chirpy-looking blonde, maybe midthirties, wearing a black leather jacket over black pedal pushers, black thongs, too.

"Hey, morning, Sarah," he said, casual-like and friendly as a cocker spaniel off its leash in the park. "Wearing black for the funeral?"

"Excuse me —"

And he shot her, too. Twice. Then one more for the barista.

*Just one more kill, right?* he was thinking. *Well, maybe two more.*

He robbed the cash register, took Sarah's ratty buckskin pocketbook, and off he went into the early morning L.A. smog, heading west, across Stanley, Spaulding, Genessee.

*Mary Smith rides again, right?*

# Chapter 101

I LOOKED AT JANNIE in the rearview mirror. "The Spy Museum, huh?" I asked.

She nodded. "Absotootly!"

Jannie had drawn Saturday afternoon in our little lottery. Tonight was mine, Sunday day was Nana's, and Sunday night was Damon's time to howl. The Cross Family Weekend was all mapped out, and it was already under way.

We spent the afternoon learning about ninja, cloak-and-dagger, and shadow spies, a construct I must have missed in my classes at Quantico. The kids tested their powers of observation in the School for Spies, and even I was impressed with some of the future-world props and models they had in the 21st Century section.

Since dinner was my choice, I decided to introduce everyone to Ethiopian food. Jannie and Damon did fairly well with some of the more exotic tastes — except for the *kitfo*, essentially steak tartare. Still, they liked eating with their fingers, which Nana called "real down-home cooking."

When Jannie and Nana went off to the ladies' room, Damon turned to me. "You know, you could have invited Doctor Coles. If you wanted," he said, then shrugged.

I was touched by the man-to-manness of Damon's remark. I'd even say it was adorable, except that he'd hate it if I saw it that way. "Thanks, Day," I said, playing it straight. "Kayla and I are having dinner on Tuesday. I appreciate the thought."

"She's a good lady. Everybody thinks so. You need somebody, you know."

"Yeah, I know."

"And she's the only person I've ever seen who can make Nana do stuff she doesn't want to."

I laughed, liking that he had noticed so much about Kayla, and his observations were mostly sharp and true.

"What's so funny?" Nana asked, suddenly at the table again. "What did I miss?"

"What is it?" Jannie asked, demanded actually. "I want to know what's going on. Was it about the Spy Museum? You two mocking me? I will not be mocked."

"Guys' privilege," Damon said.

"I bet it was about Doctor Coles." Jannie's voice turned to a squeak as her instincts landed her in exactly the right place. "We like her, Daddy," she said, when I had neither confirmed nor denied her guess.

"Yeah, but you like everyone."

"Guess where I got that from?"

"We need to have her over for dinner," Nana piped up.

"Just not Tuesday," Damon told her.

Jannie grinned, and her eyes got wide. "Yeah. Tuesday night is date night. Right, Daddy? Am I right?"

# Chapter 102

TUESDAY NIGHT *WAS* A DATE NIGHT with Kayla Coles.

And then so was Thursday.

At a little past 1:00 in the morning, I was sitting with Kayla on her front porch. We'd been out there talking for at least a couple of hours. Kayla had just recruited me to do some work for the Children's Defense Fund in D.C. She used statistics to make her points — just like Nana did: forty million uninsured in America, a new baby born uninsured every minute of every day. Sure I would help — whatever I could do. Even if the circumstances hadn't been what they were.

"What are you doing Saturday?" she asked. Just the question, in her sweet voice, made me smile. "This *isn't* about the Children's Defense Fund by the way."

"I was hoping you'd come over for one of Nana's home-cooked meals," I said.

"Don't you need to ask Nana?"

I laughed. "It was her idea. Or one of the kids. But Nana's definitely part of the conspiracy. She might even be the ring-leader of the gang."

If the universe wanted me to stop dating, its message was getting garbled. All day Saturday, I was a little nervous about Kayla coming over, though. This meant something, didn't it? Bringing her home — under these circumstances.

"You look *good*, Daddy," Jannie said from the door to my room.

I had just rejected a shirt onto the bed and pulled on a black V-neck sweater, which I had to admit looked pretty good. It was a little embarrassing to be caught in the act of preening, though. Jannie invited herself in, flopped down, and watched while I finished up.

"What's going on?" Damon wandered in next and sat beside Jannie on the bed.

"Anybody ever hear of privacy around here?"

"He's getting all handsome for Doctor Kayla. All duded-up and such. I like him in black."

My back was to them now, and they spoke as if I weren't there, their voices just a little stagy.

"Think he's nervous?"

"Mm-hm. Probably."

"You think he'll spill something on himself during dinner?"

"Definitely."

I turned on them with a roar and grabbed them both before they could separate and squirm away. They exploded into screams of laughter, forgetting, for an instant, that they had outgrown this kind of horseplay. I rolled them both around on the bed, going for all the ticklish spots I knew from past tickle fests.

"You're going to get all wrinkly!" Jannie yelled at me. "Dadd-eee! Stop!"

"That's okay," I said. "I'll have to change anyway . . . when I spill something on myself!"

I chased them all the way down to the kitchen; then we pitched in to help Nana with the parts that she would let us. Adding a leaf to the dining table. Putting out the good china and new candlesticks.

Nana was showing off a little, maybe a lot. Fine by me; I've got no problem eating her finest. Never have.

After dinner, which was pretty amazing — two herb-roasted chickens with oven fries, asparagus, mesclun salad, and coconut cake — Kayla and I got out of there. We took the Porsche, and I drove out to the Tidal Basin and then up to the Lincoln Memorial. We parked, then strolled the length of the Reflecting Pool. It's a beautiful, tranquil spot at night. For some reason, not too many tourists make it there after sunset.

"Everything was perfect," she said as we approached the Washington Monument. "Back at your house."

I laughed. "A little too perfect for my taste. Didn't you think they were trying too hard?"

It was Kayla's turn to laugh. "What can I say? They like me."

"Three dates in a week. Had to give them ideas."

Kayla smiled. "Gave me some ideas. Want to hear?"

"Like what? Give me an example, a for-instance."

"My house isn't far."

"You're a doctor. Must know a lot about human anatomy."

"And you're a psychologist, so you know the human psyche, right?"

"Sounds like a lot of fun."

And it was.

But then the Job got in the way again.

# Chapter 103

"I'LL BE OUT THERE TOMORROW. That's the best I can do. I'll book a flight to L.A. right now."

I couldn't believe the words were coming out of my mouth, even as they did.

I had been on the phone with Fred Van Allsburg for less than a couple of minutes, and my response was pretty much automatic, almost as if I'd been programmed to answer in a certain way. What was this, *The Manchurian Candidate*? What part was I playing? Good guy? Bad guy? Somewhere in between?

I was definitely eager to meet with Mary Wagner again, drawn by curiosity, almost as much as by obligation. The LAPD hadn't been able to get her to talk to them, apparently not for days. So they wanted me to come back to California to consult. And I needed to do it — something still bothered me about the murder case, even if Mary was as guilty as she appeared to be.

Of course, I wanted the trip to be as short as possible. In fact, I left everything packed except my toothbrush when I got to the hotel in L.A. It probably helped me feel as though the trip was more temporary.

Anyway, my interview with Mary Wagner was scheduled for ten o'clock the following morning. I thought about calling Jamilla, but decided against it, and right then I knew that it was completely over between us. A sad thought, but a true one, and I was sure that we both knew it. Whose fault was it? I didn't know. Was it useful or important to try to place blame? *Probably not,* thought Dr. Cross.

I spent the night going over the past week's reports and transcripts, which Van Allsburg had messengered over to me. According to everything I read, the three children — Brendan, Ashley, and Adam — seemed to be the only thing on Mary's mind.

It made my direction pretty clear. If the children were all that Mary could think about, that's where we'd begin tomorrow morning.

# Chapter 104

AT 8:45 IN THE MORNING, I found myself in a different but identical-looking room to the one where I had last interviewed Mary Wagner.

The guard escorted her in exactly on time — almost to the second. I could see right away that several days of interrogation had taken a toll.

She wouldn't look at me, and sat stoically while the officer cuffed her to the table.

He then took a position inside the room, next to the door. Not my first choice, but I didn't argue it. Maybe if there was a second interview, I'd try to loosen things up.

"Good morning, Mary."

"Hello."

Her voice was neutral, a minimal show of following the rules. Still no eye contact though. I wondered if she had served time before. And if she had, for what?

"Let me tell you why I'm here," I said. "Mary, are you listening to me?"

No response from her. She clenched and unclenched her teeth, staring at a single point on the wall. I sensed that she *was* listening but trying not to show it.

"You already know that there's a significant amount of evidence against you. And I think you also know that there are still some doubts about your children."

She finally looked up, and her eyes burned into my skull. "Then there's nothing to talk about."

"Actually, there is."

I pulled out my pen and laid a blank piece of paper on the table. "I thought you might like to write a letter to Brendan, Ashley, and Adam."

## Chapter 105

MARY CHANGED IN A BEAT, just the way I'd seen her do before. She looked up at me again, her eyes and mouth noticeably softer. A familiar vulnerability showed across her features. When she was like this, it was hard not to feel something for Mary Wagner, no matter what she had done.

"I'm not allowed to remove your handcuffs," I said, "but you can tell me what you'd like to say. I'll write it for you, word for word."

"Is this a trick?" she asked, and she was practically pleading for it not to be. "This is some kind of trick, isn't it?"

I had to choose my words carefully.

"No trick. It's just a chance for you to say whatever you want to say to your kids."

"Are the police going to read it? Will you tell me? I want to know if they are."

Her responses fascinated me, a mix of high emotion and control.

"All of your conversations in here are recorded," I reminded her. "You don't have to do this if you don't want to. It's up to you. Your choice, Mary."

"You came to my house."

"Yes, I did."

"I liked you."

"Mary, I like you, too."

"Are you on my side?"

"Yes. I am on your side."

"The side of justice, right?"

"I hope so, Mary."

She looked around the room, either weighing her options or searching for the right words, I didn't know which. Then she turned back. Her eyes locked onto the piece of paper between us.

"Dear Brendan," she said in a whisper.

"Just Brendan?"

"Yes. Please read this to your brother and sister, because you're the big boy in the family."

I took it down verbatim, writing fast to keep up with her.

"Mommy has to be away from you for a while, but it won't be long, I promise. *Promise.*

"Wherever you are now, I know they are taking good care of you. And if you get lonely, or want to cry, that's okay, too. Crying can help let the sadness out. Everyone does it sometimes, even Mommy, but only because I miss you so much."

Mary paused, and a pleased look came over her, as if she

341

had just seen something sweet. Her eyes were fixed on the far wall, and she had an almost heartbreaking smile on her face.

She continued, "When we're all together again, we'll go for a picnic, your favorite. We'll get whatever we want to eat and drive out somewhere pretty and spend the whole day. Maybe we'll go swimming, too. Whatever you want, sweetie pie. I'm already looking forward to it.

"And guess what? You have a guardian angel watching over you all the time. That's me. I give you good-night kisses in your dreams when you go to sleep at night. You don't have to be afraid because I'm right there with you. And you're right here with me."

Mary stopped, shut her eyes, and sighed loudly.

"I love you very, very much. Love, Mommy."

By now, she was leaning much closer to the table than when we'd begun. She held on to the letter with her eyes — still speaking to me in a soft voice. A whisper.

"Put three *X*'s and three *O*'s at the bottom. A kiss and a hug for each of my babies."

# Chapter 106

THE MORE I HEARD, the more I doubted that Mary Wagner could have invented these three children entirely. And I had a bad feeling about what might have happened to them.

I spent the afternoon trying to track the children down. The Uniform Crime Report came back with a long list of child victims matched to female killers in recent decades. I've heard and read somewhere that shoplifting and the killing of one's own children are the only two crimes that American women commit in equal numbers to men.

If that was true, then this thick, voluminous report only represented *half* of the child murders on record.

I gritted my teeth, literally and figuratively, and did another run through the disturbing database.

This time, I searched for multiple homicides only. With that list compiled, I started wading through.

A few of the more famous names jumped out right away: Susan Smith, who had drowned both her sons in 1994; Andrea Yates, who killed all five of her children after several years of struggling with psychosis and profound postpartum depression.

The list went on and on. None of these female perpetrators could be considered the victims in their cases, but the dominance of severe mental-health issues was clear.

Smith and Yates were both diagnosed with personality and clinical disorders. It was easy to imagine the same could be true of Mary Wagner, but a reliable diagnosis would take more time than we were likely to have together.

That particular question was sidelined a few hours into my research.

I clicked onto a new page and, sadly, found exactly what I was looking for.

A triple homicide in Derby Line, Vermont, on August 2, 1983. All three victims were siblings:

*Beaulac, Brendan, 8*

*Beaulac, Ashley, 5*

*Constantine, Adam, 11 months.*

The killer, their mother, was a twenty-six-year-old woman, with the last name Constantine.

First name, *Mary.*

I cross-referenced the homicide report for local media coverage.

It brought me to an article from a 1983 *Caledonian-Record* in St. Johnsbury, Vermont.

There was also a grainy black-and-white trial photo of Mary Constantine, seated at a defendant's table.

Her face was thinner and younger, but the detached, stony expression was unmistakable, that look she had when she didn't want to feel something, or had felt too much. Jesus.

The woman I knew as Mary Wagner had killed her own children more than twenty years ago, and as far as she was concerned, it had never happened.

I pushed back my chair and took a deep breath.

Here I was, finally, at the center of the labyrinth. Now it was time to start finding my way back out.

# Chapter 107

"NINETEEN EIGHTY-THREE, HUH? Jeez, that's not even *this century*. All right, hang on a second. I'll try to help you out. If I can."

I sat through several minutes of tapping keys and riffling paper on the other end of the phone line.

The tapper and riffler was an agent named Barry Medlar, of the Bureau's Albany field office. He was the coordinator of Albany's Crimes Against Children Unit. Every FBI office has a CAC unit, and Albany has oversight for Vermont. I wanted to get as close to the source as I possibly could.

"Here we go," Medlar said. "Hold on, here she is. . . ."

"Constantine, Mary. Triple homicide on August second, arrested on the tenth. Let me scroll the rest of this. Okay, here we go. Sentenced NGRI on February first of the following year, with a state-appointed attorney."

"Not guilty by reason of insanity," I muttered.

So she hadn't been able to afford her own defense; no legal bells and whistles on her behalf. Not guilty by reason of insanity can be a tough plea to prove. It must have been a fairly clear-cut case for it to go that way.

"Where did she end up?" I asked.

"Vermont State Hospital in Waterbury, probably. I wouldn't have any transfer records here, but that ward isn't exactly overflowing. I can get you a name and number if you want to find out."

It was tempting to pull a little no-I-want-YOU-to-find-out attitude, but I preferred to make the calls myself anyway. I took down the number for Vermont State Hospital.

"What about Mary Constantine's MO?" I asked Medlar. "What have you got on the actual murders?"

I heard more turning pages and then, "Unbelievable."

"What is it?"

"Didn't your Mary Smith use a Walther PPK out there in L.A.?"

"Yeah, why?"

"Ditto here. Walther PPK, never recovered, either. She must have dog-boned it."

I was scribbling notes furiously the whole time he talked. To say the least, he had me riveted.

"All right, Agent Medlar, here's what I need. Get me a contact for whatever Mary Constantine's local police department would have been. I also want everything you've got on file there. Send whatever's electronically available right now and fax the rest.

"And I mean everything. I'm going to give you my cell number in case you find anything else worth mentioning. I'll be on the move."

I stuffed some papers into my briefcase while I was still talking to Medlar.

"One other thing. What airlines fly to Vermont, anyway?"

# Chapter 108

EIGHTEEN HOURS AND THREE THOUSAND MILES later, I was sitting in the small, cozy living room of Madeline and former sheriff Claude Lapierre, just outside Derby Line, Vermont. It was a tiny village, as sweet as a calendar photo, and literally pressed up against the Canadian border. In fact, the local Haskell Free Library and Opera House had been accidentally built *on* the border, and guards were sometimes stationed inside to prevent illegal crossings.

Not the kind of place you'd imagine would keep law enforcement very busy, though. Mary Constantine had lived there all her life — right up until she killed her three young children, a horrifying crime that had made national headlines twenty years ago.

"What would you say you remember most about the case?" I asked Mr. Lapierre.

"The knife. For sure the knife. The way she cut up that

poor little girl's face, after she killed all three of them. I was Orleans County sheriff for twenty-seven years. It was the worst thing I ever saw. By far, Agent Cross. By far."

"I actually felt kind of sorry for her." Mrs. Lapierre sat next to her husband on the couch, which was covered in a denim-blue fabric. "For Mary, I mean. Nothing good ever happened to that poor woman. Not that it excuses what she did, but . . ." She waved her hand in front of her face instead of finishing the thought.

"You knew her, Mrs. Lapierre?"

"The way everybody knows everybody around here," she said. "This is a community of neighbors. We all depend on one another."

"What can you tell me about Mary before all this happened?" I asked both of them.

Claude Lapierre started. "Nice girl. Quiet, polite, loved boating. On Lake Memphremagog. Not a whole lot to tell, really. She worked at the diner when she was in high school. Served me breakfast all the time. But so very quiet, like I said. Everyone was pretty surprised when she got pregnant."

"And even more surprised when the father stuck around," Mrs. Lapierre said.

"For a while, anyway," her husband quickly added.

"I assume that was Mr. Beaulac?"

They both nodded.

"He was ten years older than her, and she was all of seventeen. But they did make a go of it. Tried their best. Even had a second kid together."

"Ashley," Mrs. Lapierre said.

"Nobody was really bowled over when he finally took off. If anything, I would have expected it sooner."

"George Beaulac was a real bum," said Mrs. Lapierre. "Took a lot of drugs."

"Do you know what happened to him? Did he see Mary or the kids again?"

"Don't know," said Claude, "but I'm inclined to doubt it. He *was* a bum."

"Well, I need to find him," I muttered, more to myself than to either of them. "I really need to know where George Beaulac is now."

"Up to no good for sure," said Mrs. Lapierre.

# Chapter 109

I DIDN'T BOTHER TAKING NOTES after that. Whatever wasn't already written down, I wouldn't need. A whirring sound had been coming from the kitchen, and I finally asked Mrs. Lapierre about it. I never would have guessed what the sound was. Turned out she was making venison jerky in a dehydrator.

"Where were Mary's parents during all of this?" I asked, moving back to more pertinent questions.

Again, Mrs. Lapierre shook her head. She topped off my coffee cup while her husband continued.

"Rita died when Mary was about five, I guess. Ted raised her, pretty much on his own, though he didn't seem to put a lot of effort into it. Nothing illegal, just real sad. And then he died, too, the year Brendan was born, I think."

"He smoked like a chimney," Madeline said. "Lung cancer took him. That poor girl never got a break."

After George Beaulac left, Mary fell in with another local man, a part-time mechanic by the name of John Constantine.

"He started running around on her almost as soon as she got pregnant," Madeline said. "It was no great secret. By the time Adam was six months old, John was gone for good, too."

Claude spoke now. "If I had to guess, I'd say that's when she really went downhill, but who knows. You don't see someone for a while, you just assume they're busy or something. And then one day, boom. That was it. She must have snapped. It felt sudden, but it probably wasn't. I'm sure it was building up over a long period."

I sipped my coffee and took a polite bite of scone. "I'd like to go back to the day of the murders now. What did Mary have to say when she was caught, Sheriff?"

"This is more piecework than anything, just my memories. We never got a peep out of Mary about the murders after her arrest."

"Anything you can tell me would be helpful. Try to think, Sheriff."

Madeline took a deep breath and put a hand flat on top of her husband's on the couch cushion. They both had the solid quality of old farm stock, not unlike what I'd seen in Mary at times.

"It looks like she took them for a picnic that day. Drove way out in the woods. We found the spot later, just by luck. That's where she shot them. One, two, three, in the back of the head.

"The ME thinks she laid them down, like maybe for a nap, and I'm guessing she did the older two first, since the baby couldn't run away."

I waited patiently for him to go on. I knew that the

passage of time didn't make this kind of thing any easier to remember and talk about.

"She carefully wrapped them each in a blanket. I still remember those old army blankets she used. Terrible. Then it looks like she took them home and did the knife work on Ashley there. All over her face and just on her for some reason. I'll never forget it. I'd like to, but I can't."

"And were you the first one to find them?" I asked.

He nodded. "Mary's boss called and said he hadn't seen Mary for days. Mary didn't have a phone at the time, so I said I'd go over. I thought it was just a courtesy call. Mary came to the door like there was nothing going on, but I could smell it right away. Literally. She'd put them all in a trunk in the basement — in August — and just left them there. I guess she blocked that smell out like everything else. I still can't explain any of it. Not even now, after all these years."

"Sometimes there is no explanation," I said.

"Anyway, she didn't put up any resistance whatsoever. We took her in quietly."

"It was a huge story, though," Madeline said.

"That's true. Put Derby Line on the map for about a week. Hope it doesn't happen again now."

"Did either of you see Mary after she was committed?"

Both Lapierres shook their head. Decades of marriage had clearly linked them.

"I don't know anyone who ever visited her," Madeline told me. "It's not the kind of thing you want to be reminded about, is it? People like to feel safe around here. It wasn't that anyone turned their back on her. It was more like . . . I don't know. Like we never knew Mary in the first place."

# Chapter 110

VERMONT STATE HOSPITAL was a sprawling, mostly red-brick building, unassuming from the outside except for its size. I had been told that almost half of it was unused space. The women's locked ward on the fourth floor held forensic patients, like Mary Constantine, but also civilly committed patients. "Not a perfect system," the director told me, but one borne of small population size and shrinking budgets for mental health care.

It was also part of the reason Mary had been able to escape.

Dr. Rodney Blaisdale, the director, gave me a quick tour of the ward. It was well kept, with curtains in the dayroom and a fresh coat of paint on the concrete-block walls. Newspapers and magazines were spread on most end tables and couches: *Burlington Free Press, The Chronicle, American Woodworker.*

It was quiet — so quiet.

I'd been on locked wards many times before, and usually the general noise level was like a constant buzz. I had no idea until now how oddly comforting that buzz could be.

It occurred to me that Vermont State had the still, slow-moving quality of an aquarium. Patients seemed to come and go in response to the quiet itself, barely speaking, even to themselves.

The television was on a low volume, with a few women watching the soaps through what looked like Haldol-glazed eyes.

As Dr. Blaisdale took me around, I kept thinking about how vivid a scream would be in here.

"This is it," he said as we came to one of many closed doors in the main hallway. I realized I had stopped listening to him, and tuned back in. "This was Mary's room."

Looking through the small observation window in that steel door, I found no clue that she had ever been there, of course. The platform bed held a bare mattress, and the only other features were a built-in desk and bench, and a stainless-steel blunt-edged shelf mounted to the wall.

"Of course, it didn't look like this then. Mary was with us for nineteen years, and she could do a lot with very little. Our own Martha Stewart." He chuckled.

"She was my friend."

I turned to see a tiny middle-aged woman standing with one shoulder pressed against the wall opposite us. Her standard-issue scrubs indicated she was forensic, though it was hard to imagine what she might have done to get here.

"Hello," I said.

The woman raised her chin, trying to see past us into Mary's room. Now I saw that she had ragged burn scars up and down her neck. "Is she back? Is Mary here? I need to see Mary if she's here. It's important. It's very important to me."

"No, Lucy. I'm sorry, she's not back," Dr. Blaisdale told her.

Lucy looked crestfallen. She quickly turned and walked away from us, disconsolately trailing one hand along the concrete-block wall as she went.

"Lucy's one of our few really long-term patients here, as was Mary. It was hard for her when Mary disappeared."

"About that," I said. "What happened that day?"

Dr. Blaisdale nodded slowly and bit into his lower lip.

"Why don't we finish this in my office."

# Chapter 111

I FOLLOWED BLAISDALE through the locked door at the end of the ward and down to the ground floor. We entered his office, which was high-end generic, with brass in boxes and pastel-colored mini-blinds. A poster for Banjo Dan and the Midnite Plowboys was framed on one wall and definitely caught my attention.

I sat down and noticed that everything on my side of his desk was several inches from the edge, just out of reach.

Blaisdale looked at me and sighed. I knew right away that he was going to soft-sell what had happened with Mary Constantine.

"All right, here goes, Dr. Cross. Everyone on the ward can earn day-trip privileges. Forensic patients used to be prohibited, but we've found it therapeutically unconstructive to divide the population in that way. As a consequence, Mary went out several times. That day was just like any other."

"And what happened on that day?" I asked.

"It was six patients with two staff, which is our standard procedure. The group went to the lake that day. Unfortunately, one of the patients had a meltdown of some sort."

*Of some sort?* I wondered if he knew the exact details, even now. Blaisdale seemed like a hands-off administrator if I'd ever seen one.

"In the middle of the hysterics, Mary insisted she had to go to the rest room. The outhouse building was right there, so the counselors let her go. Mistake, but it happens. No one knew at the time that there were entrances on both sides of the building."

"Obviously, Mary knew," I said.

Dr. Blaisdale drummed a pen on his desktop several times. "At any rate, she disappeared into nearby woods."

I stared at him, just listening, trying not to judge, but it was hard not to.

"She was a model patient, had been for years. It took everyone very much by surprise."

"Just like when she killed her kids," I said.

Blaisdale appraised me with his eyes. He wasn't sure if I had just insulted him, and I certainly hadn't meant to.

"The police did a major search — one of the biggest I've seen. We left that job to them. Of course, we were eager to have Mary back, and to make sure she was all right. But it's not the kind of story we go out of our way to publicize. She wasn't —" He stopped.

"Wasn't what?"

"Well, at the time, we didn't consider her any danger to anyone, other than herself perhaps."

I didn't say what I was thinking. All of Los Angeles had a somewhat different opinion of Mary — that she was the most vicious homicidal maniac who ever lived.

"Did she leave anything behind?" I finally asked.

"She did, actually. You'll definitely want to see her journals. She wrote almost every day. Filled dozens of volumes while she was here."

# Chapter 112

A PORTER, MAC, who looked as though he lived in the basement of the hospital, brought me two archive boxes filled with tape-bound composition notebooks, the kind a child raised in the fifties might have used in school. Mary Constantine had written far more in her years here than I would ever have time to read today. I could requisition the whole collection later, I was informed.

"Thanks for your help," I told Mac the porter.

"No problem," he said, and I wondered when it was, and how, the response "you're welcome" seemed to have disappeared from the language, even up here in rural Vermont.

For now, I just wanted to get a sense of who Mary Constantine was, particularly in relationship to the Mary I already knew. Two archive boxes would be enough for a start.

Her cursive was tidy and precise. Every page was neatly arranged, with even, empty margins. Not a doodle in sight.

Words were her medium, and she had no shortage of
them. They slanted to the right on the page as if they were in
a hurry to get where they were going.

The voice, too, was eerily familiar.

The writing had Mary Smith's short, choppy sentences,
and that same palpable sense of isolation. It was evident
everywhere I looked in the notebook.

Sometimes it just seeped through; other times, it was
right on the surface.

> *I'm like a ghost here. I don't know if anyone would care
> whether I stayed or left. Or if they even know I'm here at all.*
>
> *Except for Lucy. Lucy is so kind to me. I don't know that I
> could ever be as good a friend to her as she is to me. I hope she
> doesn't go anywhere. It wouldn't be the same without her.*
>
> *Sometimes I think she's the only one who really cares about
> me. Or knows me. Or can see me.*
>
> *Am I invisible to everyone else? I truly wonder — am I
> invisible?*

Reading through and picking out entries at random, I also
got a picture of someone who stayed busy while she was kept
in the mental hospital. There was always one project or another going on for Mary. She'd never given up hope, had she?
She seemed to be the resident homemaker, as much as a person could be in this environment.

> *We're making paper chains for the dayroom. A little
> babyish, but they're pretty. It will be nice for Christmas.*

*I showed all the girls how to make them. Almost everyone participated. I love to teach them things. Most of them, anyway.*

*That Roseanne girl from Burlington, she tries my patience sometimes. She truly does. She looked right at me today and asked me what my name is. As if I haven't already told her a thousand times. I don't know what kind of somebody she thinks she is. She's just as much a nobody as the rest of us.*

*I didn't know what to say to her, so I just didn't answer. Let her make her own decorations. Serves her right. I'd like to smack Roseanne. But I won't, will I?*

*Somebodies* and *nobodies*. Those words, and that idea, had shown up more than once in the e-mails out in California. The inclusion of it here jumped out at me like an identification tag. Mary Smith had been obsessed with *somebodies* — high-profile, perfect mothers who stood out so clearly against the negative space of her own nobody-ness. Something told me that if I kept looking, I'd find it as a long-running theme for Mary Constantine as well.

What *was* missing was any mention of her children. In context, the journals read like a chronicle of denial. The Mary who lived here at the hospital seemed to have recorded no memory or awareness of them at all.

And the woman who lived as Mary Wagner — the woman Mary Constantine had become — could think of nothing but those children.

The common thread as she had evolved was a lack of consciousness around Brendan's, Ashley's, and Adam's murder.

The *A*'s and *B*'s.

I could only hypothesize at this point, but it seemed to me that Mary was on a crash course toward a fuller realization, and wreaking havoc along the way. Now that she was in custody again, the only person she could harm was herself.

Still, if she was in fact moving toward the truth, I hated to think what might happen to her when she got there.

# Chapter 113

IT WAS HARD TO TEAR MYSELF AWAY from Mary's journals — her words, her ideas, and her anger.

For the first time, it seemed possible to me, even probable, that she had actually committed the series of murders in L.A.

When I looked at my watch, I was already half an hour late for a meeting with her lead therapist, Debra Shapiro. *Shit. I need to hustle over there.*

Dr. Shapiro was actually on her way out when I got to her office; I was full of apology. Shapiro stayed to speak with me but was perched on the edge of a couch with her briefcase on her lap.

"Mary was my patient for eight years," she told me before I even asked.

"How would you characterize her?"

"Not as a killer — interestingly. I view the incident with

her children as an aberration to the larger arena, if you will, of her mental illness. She's a very sick woman, but any violent impulses were subjugated a long time ago. That's part of what kept her here; she never moved through anything."

"How can you be sure?" I asked Dr. Shapiro. "Especially given what's happened." Maybe Mary wasn't the only person in denial around here.

"If I were testifying in court, I'd have to say I can't. Beyond that, though, I think eight years of interaction is worth something, Dr. Cross. Don't you?"

I did think so, of course. But only if the therapist showed me some insight.

"What about her children?" I asked. "I didn't find any mention of them in her journals. But for the short time I've known Mary, they've been all she can think about. They're very much alive in her mind now. She's obsessed with them."

Dr. Shapiro nodded while she looked at her watch. "That's more difficult for me to reconcile. I could offer a theory, which is that maybe Mary's therapy was finally actualizing. The memory of those children was slowly, slowly bubbling up.

"As the children came into her consciousness, one way to avoid processing twenty years of repressed guilt all at once would be to keep the children alive, as you put it. It could explain what drove her to escape when she did — to get back to her life with them. Which, to Mary's experience, is exactly what happened."

"And these murders in California?" I was going very quickly on purpose; Dr. Shapiro fidgeted as though she might jump up and leave at any moment.

She shrugged, clearly impatient with the interview. I wondered if her therapy sessions felt like this to her patients. "I just don't see it. It's hard to know what might have happened to Mary once she left here, but as for the woman that I knew?" She shook her head back and forth several times. "The only part of the story that makes sense is Los Angeles."

"How so?" I asked.

"There was some interest in her story a few years ago. Some movie people came and went. Mary permitted the interviews, but as a state's ward, she didn't have the autonomy to grant any farther-reaching permission. Eventually they lost interest and went away. During her last couple of years here, I think they were the only visitors she had."

"Who?" I took out my notebook, folded it open. "I need to know more about this. Are there records of the visits? Anything?"

"I don't actually recall any names," she said. "And beyond that, I'm a bit uncomfortable with the level of disclosure here. I might refer you back to Dr. Blaisdale if you want more specific information. He'd be the one to release it."

I wondered if she was feeling protective of her patient, or maybe just late for something on her social calendar. The clock said 5:46.

I realized I might do better elsewhere, in which case, I had to get going as well. I thanked Dr. Shapiro for her time, and help, and headed back to the administration building.

I was running.

# Chapter 114

STILL AND ALL, I was feeling like a real cop again, and it didn't seem half bad to me. The wall clock in the administrative office said 5:52 when I slipped in.

I smiled across the counter at a young woman with pink-streaked blond hair and a lot of costume jewelry. She was draping a plastic cover over her typewriter.

"Hi, I've got a really quick request for you. Really quick. I need it, though."

"Can it wait until tomorrow?" the woman asked, eyeing me up and down. "It can wait, right?"

"Actually, no. I just spoke with Doctor Shapiro, and she asked me to run down here and catch you. I need to see the women's forensic ward visitor's log for the last few years. Specifically for Mary Constantine. It's really important. I wouldn't bother you otherwise."

The woman picked up her phone. "Doctor Shapiro sent you?"

"That's right. She just left for the day, but she told me this wouldn't be a problem." I held up my ID. "I'm with the FBI, Dr. Alex Cross. This is part of an ongoing murder investigation."

She didn't hide her displeasure. "I just shut down the computer, and I have to pick up my daughter. I suppose I can get you the hard copy if you want."

Without waiting for an answer, she disappeared into another room and came back with a small stack of three-ring binders.

"You can only stay as long as Beadsie's here." She waved to a woman in a goldfish-bowl office at the back. Then she left, without another word — to me, or to Beadsie.

The pages of the visitor's log were divided into columns. I worked from the back of the most recent book, looking for Mary's name under *Who Are You Here to See?*

For two years' worth of entries, there was nothing at all. It was obvious how alone Mary Constantine had been in this place.

Then, suddenly, a rash of names cropped up on the log. Here was the flurry of interest that Dr. Shapiro mentioned. It lasted over the course of about a month and a half.

I slowed down and perused the visitors' names. Most were unfamiliar to me.

One of them, I recognized.

# Chapter 115

MY CELL PHONE and Vermont seemed to hate each other. Apparently, this was the Land of No Signal.

I found a pay phone instead, called Agent Page in Los Angeles, and had him patch in LAPD. A minute later we had Maddux Fielding's office on the line, but no Fielding. What a surprise.

"You know what?" I said to the nameless lieutenant on the line. "Screw it. Transfer us over to Detective Jeanne Galletta."

"What's going on?" Page asked me again, while we were on hold with LAPD.

Then I heard another voice on the line. "Jeanne Galletta. Is this Alex?"

"Jeanne, it's Alex all right. Karl Page from the L.A. Bureau office is on the line, too. I'm in Vermont. I think I have important news on the Mary Smith case."

"I think I may have another connection for you — a murder in Vancouver," Jeanne said. "What are you doing all the way up in Vermont?"

"Hold that thought about Vancouver. Please find Fielding. Or do whatever you have to do, but someone needs to pick up Michael Bell for questioning. Michael Bell. *Marti Lowenstein-Bell's husband.*"

"What?" Jeanne sounded incredulous. Then Page swore, obviously muffling the receiver.

I gave them a very quick rundown of my last two days up here, then finally the names on the visitor log at the state hospital.

"He knows Mary Constantine. He's visited her here in Vermont before. Several times, actually."

"And what? He's been setting her up? How would he even know she was in L.A.?"

"I don't know everything yet. Maybe she looked him up when she got there; maybe they corresponded. If he wanted her story, it would have been worth something. I think he *did* want it, just not for a movie."

"You think it was a cover, maybe to kill his own wife? That's a big-ass coverup, Alex."

"Sure is. It's an incredible story, too. Page, are you getting this?"

"Got it. And I like it. Finally, something makes some sense to me."

"Good. Then do a direct cross-reference — Michael Bell and anyone else connected to this case. I wonder if he had a bigger agenda than just his wife. Find out anything you can, surfer boy. All we need for now is enough to justify holding him once LAPD gets him into custody.

"Jeanne, listen, please. If I'm wrong, I'm wrong. I say figure it out later and get a cruiser over to Michael Bell's house. Now. And, Jeanne."

"What?"

"Don't go over there by yourself. I'm pretty sure that Bell is our killer."

# Chapter 116

SUDDENLY THE WHOLE CASE was on fire again.

About ten miles from the hospital, I pulled over at the first gas station I saw, an ancient Texaco with a flying *A* over the roof. A Ford F-150 pulled in after me, but the only other building in sight was a darkened sugarhouse in a field directly across the road. I could see a couple of Holsteins grazing in the field.

I called Karl Page again from another pay phone. I needed to hear what he'd found out about Michael Bell.

At this late hour, catching a flight out of Burlington seemed unlikely; I wanted to stay updated all the same, and was concerned for Page and Jeanne Galletta. Who knew what Bell was up to in L.A.

"What have you got so far?" I asked him.

"Amazing what you find when you look in the right place," he said. "Before she died, Marti Lowenstein-Bell had just sold her own show to HBO. She was hotter than a fifty-dollar pistol. On the other hand, Michael Bell's last three solo projects went nowhere. His only big successes had been with her, and it looked like she was checking out. She was divorcing him, Alex. They hadn't yet filed, but a friend of hers knew it was coming."

"What did you say to me once? Cha-ching?"

"Yeah, and the hits keep coming. LAPD checked Bell's alibis all right, but they all revolved around his being seen at work, or occasionally at home. Alex, the alibis aren't going to hold up. And listen to this, Arnold Griner seriously trashed more than one of Bell's movies when he wrote for *Variety*. Griner actually called him 'Michael Bomb' in one column, that kind of thing. Of course, in Griner's case it might be justifiable homicide. Antonia Schifman? She backed out of a project that Bell was financing himself last year. Apparently *after* she gave him a verbal promise, which seems to mean next to nothing out here. The whole thing fell apart, and he lost a half million in development."

I could hear the adrenaline in Page's voice. He was like a greyhound at the gate. "I'll bet anything there's more," he said. "Bell's career was headed down the crapper, and he was going to bring everyone down with him."

"Keep digging," I said. "Great work, too. Any more word from LAPD? Jeanne?"

"A cruiser went by the Bell house. No answer."

"Did they go inside?"

"No. But they were pretty sure nobody was home. The house is under surveillance."

"All right. I'll call when I stop again. Probably out near

the airport. Unfortunately, I think I'm stuck here for the night."

I didn't want to spend the night in Vermont, especially now, but it didn't look as though I had much of a choice. I thought about stopping into the small store at the gas station, buying something awful like chocolate cupcakes, or M&M's with peanuts, but I mustered all of my willpower against it. *God, I am impressive occasionally.*

I turned toward the rented car and started to walk with my head down against the wind. It was getting nippy up here. A few feet away from the car, I looked up and stopped dead in my tracks.

I had company.

James Truscott was sitting in the car's passenger seat.

# Chapter 117

THIS MADE NO SENSE TO ME, not at first anyway. What the hell was Truscott doing here? Obviously, he'd followed me again. But why?

I was seeing red as I yanked open the car door on his side. My mouth was open to start to yell, but nothing came out, not a word.

Truscott wasn't here to cause me any trouble — at least not now. The writer was dead, propped up in the front seat like a statue.

"Just get in the car," said a voice from behind me.

"Don't cause a scene out here. Because then I'll have to go in and shoot the nice old biddy who runs the country store, too. I really wouldn't mind, y'know."

I turned and saw Michael Bell.

Bell appeared haggard and disturbed, and he'd lost a lot of weight since I'd last seen him at his house. He looked like hell, actually. His light-blue eyes were badly bloodshot; with his ragged, bushy beard, he looked like a local woodsman.

"How long have you been following me?" I asked, trying to engage him if I could, feel him out, gain some kind of leverage.

"Just get in the car and drive, will you? Don't talk to me. I see through you."

We both got in, Bell in the back, and he pointed out to the road, the direction heading away from the interstate. I started the car and drove where he wanted me to, my mind racing backward and forward. My gun was in the trunk. How could I get to the trunk? Or how could I get inside his head in a hurry?

"What's the plan, Michael?"

"The plan was for you to go back to Washington, and for everyone to go on with their pitiful lives. But that didn't work out so well, did it? You should thank me for taking out the reporter, no? He begged and sobbed for his life, by the way. Great performance. I believed him. What a wimp he turned out to be."

I was surprised he knew I was from D.C., and also about Truscott. But then, he was a watcher, a plotter. There was probably a lot that Bell knew.

"So what now?" I asked.

"What do you think? You're supposed to be the expert, right? So, what happens now?"

"It doesn't have to go like this." I was just talking; saying anything that came into my mind.

"You gotta be kidding. What other way do you think it can go? Let me hear all of the choices. I can't wait."

377

Meantime, he had burrowed the barrel of his pistol into my neck. I leaned away, but only so far. I thought it was best if I knew exactly where his gun was. I wondered if he was executing a plan now, or if he was improvising at this point. Mary Smith had been known to do both.

And this was Mary Smith, wasn't it? I'd finally met the real killer.

We drove for a few miles on an unlit secondary highway. "This looks good here," he said suddenly. "Go that way. Make a left. Do it."

I turned off the pavement onto a bumpy dirt road. It sloped upward, winding away into the woods. Eventually, the fir trees closed around the car like a tunnel. I was running out of time, and it didn't look as if there was any way for me to escape. Mary Smith had me, just the way she'd gotten all the others and killed them without fail.

"Where are we going, Bell?"

"Somewhere they won't find you right away. Or your pen pal, either."

"You know, they're already looking for you in L.A. I made a call."

"Yeah, well, good luck to them. I'm not exactly in L.A., am I?"

"What about your girls, Michael? What about them?"

He pushed the gun barrel harder into my neck. "Not *my* fucking girls. Marti was a cheap little whore before I married her. Before I made her into something. I was a good father to those ungrateful kids, all for Marti. She was a runaround when I met her, and she stayed a runaround. Okay, pull over. This is good."

This was definitely not good. The car headlights showed where the road dropped off to a wooded slope on the right. I had to be real careful not to go over the edge.

Then all at once, I thought the opposite. *If* I could force myself to do it — but I knew I had to. So I mashed the accelerator down and spun the steering wheel as sharply to the right as I could.

Bell screeched. "What the fuck are you doing? Stop the car. *Stop!*"

Three things happened, all at about the same time. Michael Bell's gun went off; I felt a universe of pain explode in my right shoulder; and the car started to plummet — almost straight downhill.

# Chapter 118

SUDDENLY THE PAIN SEEMED TO BE EVERYWHERE in my body, and it was nothing if not extreme. I was only semi-conscious of thick fir trees and underbrush giving way to the car as it rocked and rolled and caromed out of control, threatening to flip.

We probably fell for only four or five seconds. Still, the eventual impact was enough to jam my chest with incredible force against the steering wheel. The seat belt probably saved me from going through the windshield. I knew Bell hadn't been wearing his, and could only hope that he was badly hurt. If I was lucky, maybe he was unconscious, or dead, in the backseat.

I already had my hand on the door handle, and I rolled out of the car as best and fast as I could manage.

My whole body throbbed with a numbing ache that made it hard to move quickly. My right arm hung useless at my side.

I saw James Truscott's body, facedown and spread-eagle in the dirt. Apparently he'd been thrown loose in the crash.

Then Michael Bell moaned in the backseat. He was alive inside. Too bad. With a great mustering of resources, I managed to get up on one knee. Suddenly my shoulder screamed with pain; I knew it had to be broken.

I took a halting step forward, expecting flat ground — but there was an almost invisible bank of tangled brush.

I went down, landing in half a foot of water. I'd been totally unaware of the stream until now.

It was shallow here, but the water stretched out farther across than I could see in the dark. The icy water sent an electric current of shock right through me.

I hadn't thought the pain could get worse, but I saw a wash of white before my sight partially returned.

Again, I started to push myself up, only to be knocked back down. This time, it was Bell. He pushed down on my neck and head, and he was strong as hell. Then I felt his foot pressing down on my back. Water rushed up into my nose and mouth.

"*Where the fuck do you think —*" he was yelling.

I didn't give him a chance to finish. I scissored my legs hard against his ankle, and it took most of the rest of my strength just to do that. It caught him off guard though, and he fell backward off of me. I heard *two* splashes, and hoped one was his gun.

Half in, half out of the water, leaning hard on my good left hand, I raised myself up enough to launch at him. I managed a ground tackle, and then a left hook before he could respond.

He reached up and laid a heavy grip on my face, digging in with his fingers. Michael Bell was about my height, but a super heavyweight; despite his weight loss in the past few weeks, he had at least thirty pounds on me.

I got a hand on his throat, dug in, and pushed as hard as I could. He gagged some, but didn't let go.

Leverage was the only thing I might be able to increase, but when I moved my foot, it hit a slick of algae.

The sudden shift of weight sent me lurching with an agonizing twist of my body, and I landed back in the freezing cold water.

God, it was cold — but I almost didn't care.

Michael Bell stood up faster than I did this time. Not a good sign. He had a second wind. The dead weight of my aching right arm slowed me down.

I saw him in vague silhouette, picking up what looked like a flat rock about the size of an encyclopedia. He raised the rock high in both hands as he came toward me again.

"You stupid fuck!" he yelled. "I'll kill you! *That's* my plan, all right. That's how the story ends. This is how it ends!"

I scrabbled back and away from Bell as best I could, but I knew it wasn't enough. My hand landed on something hard in the shallow water. Not rock, at least I didn't think so. *Metal*?

"You die!" Bell yelled at me. "How's that for a plan? How's that for an ending?"

*The metal object. I knew what it had to be.* I yanked Bell's gun out of the water and fumbled with the trigger. "Bell, no!" I screamed.

He kept on coming with the enormous rock held over his head. "Die!"

So I fired.

I couldn't tell exactly what happened in the moonlit woods. I had no idea where he was hit, but he grunted noisily and stopped for a second.

Then he charged forward again. I fired a second time. And a third. Both upper-chest shots, at least I thought so.

The heavy rock he was holding fell back into the water. Suspended for a moment by some invisible force, Bell staggered away two or three drunken steps. Then he fell over face first into the water, making a loud splash.

Then nothing. Silence in the woods.

Trembling badly, uncontrollably, I kept the gun trained on Bell with my good hand. It took incredible effort just to get over the slick rocks to where he lay.

By the time I reached him, there was no movement. I took his arm, held it up. I checked, but he had no pulse. I checked it again — nothing, nothing but the silence of the woods, and the awful cold.

Michael Bell was dead, and so was Mary Smith. And very soon, in these freezing wet clothes, I would be, too.

# Chapter 119

MY SLOW CLIMB UP and out of the gully from the crash site was hellish, nothing but excruciating pain, dizziness, and nausea. The only blessing was that I barely remembered any of it.

Somehow, I managed to get out to the main road — where an alarmed college student in a Subaru picked me up. I never even got his name. I guess I passed out in the back-seat of his car.

By the next morning, Michael Bell's body had been recovered from the stream, and I was resting in a bed at Fletcher Allen Hospital in Burlington. *Resting* is probably the wrong word, though. Local police came and went from my room continually. I spent hours on the phone with my office in Washington, the L.A. Bureau office, and Jeanne Galletta, trying to piece together everything that had happened from the start of the murder spree.

Bell's plan had been a feat of convolution and madness, but his cover was ultimately simple — diversion. And he'd succeeded until the very end. As Jeanne pointed out to me, Michael Bell wrote and produced stories for a living. Plot was his thing. I wouldn't be surprised if this one ended up as a screenplay, written by someone else. The writer would probably change everything, though, until the movie carried the fishy title "based on a true story."

"Who's going to play you?" Jeanne kidded me over the phone.

"I don't know. I don't much care. Pee-wee Herman."

As for Mary Constantine, I wasn't sure how to feel about her. The cop in me had one response, but the shrink had another. I was glad she'd be getting back into the kind of treatment and care she needed. If Dr. Shapiro was right, maybe Mary was ultimately headed toward some kind of recovery. That was how I wanted to think about it for right now.

Around four o'clock, the door to my room creaked open, and none other than Nana Mama poked her head inside.

"There's a sight for bed-sore eyes," I said, and started to grin. "Hello, Nana. What brings you to Vermont?"

"Maple syrup," she cracked.

She came in timidly, especially for her, and winced when she saw the truss around my shoulder.

"Oh, Alex, Alex."

"Looks worse than it is. Well, maybe not," I said. "Did you have any trouble getting a flight?"

"No trouble at all. You go to the airport. You pay money."

She reached out to put a cool hand on my cheek. It felt

familiar and so comforting. *What would I do without this ornery old woman?* I couldn't help thinking. *What will I do?*

"They said you're going to be fine, Alex. I suppose that's a relative concept, though, isn't it?"

I'd been shot before. It's traumatic — there's no way around that — but not irreversible, at least not so far.

"I'll be fine," I told Nana. "Body and soul."

"I told the children to wait outside. I want to say something to you, and then put it behind us."

"Uh-oh. I'm in trouble again, aren't I? Back in the doghouse."

She didn't return my smile, but she did take my hand in both of hers.

"I thank God for you every single day of my life, Alex, and I thank him for letting me raise you, and see you turn into the man you did. But I want you to think about why you came to me in the first place, what was going on between your poor parents before they died. Simply put, Jannie and Damon and Ali deserve better than you had."

Nana stopped to make room for what was coming next. "Don't make them orphans, Alex."

# Chapter 120

I STARTED TO SPEAK my piece, but Nana Mama went on, gently raising her voice. "I'm the *first* of us to go. Don't you dare argue with me."

Finally, I just shrugged, which hurt my shoulder and neck.

"What can I say?"

"Nothing. You say nothing. You just listen to my wisdom, wisdom of the ages. You listen, and maybe one day you'll finally learn something."

We shared a long look into each other's eyes. A lump rose in my throat, although what I felt wasn't sadness. It was more like gratitude, and the most incredible love for this small, amazingly powerful woman — who was, indeed, wise beyond her years, and certainly mine.

"Believe it or not, I always listen to you," I said.

"Yes, and then you go and do whatever you were going to do in the first place."

Sounds from the hospital corridor came into the room as the door opened halfway. I looked over to see Damon's eager face, and my heart did a little hop.

"Look who it is!" I wiped my eyes. "The man of the house has arrived."

"They told us Jannie can't come in 'cause she's under twelve," he said.

I sat up in bed. "Where is she?"

"I'm right here." Jannie's indignant tone came through clearly from behind the door.

"Well, then get in here before anyone sees you. C'mon. Nobody's gonna arrest you. Except me, if you stay outside for one minute longer."

The two of them came in and rushed over to the bed, stopping short at the sight of my collection of bandages. I reached out with my free arm and took them both in at the same time.

"How long do you have to be here?" Jannie asked into my good side.

"Should be going home in a couple of days," I told her.

"Looks worse than it is," said Nana.

Damon stood up again and looked at the truss. "Did it hurt really bad?"

"Badly," Nana muttered.

"I've had worse," I said. They both looked at me with the same neutral, almost reproachful expression. Who was the parent here, anyway? Somehow they seemed older than the last time I'd seen them. I felt a little older myself.

These two were going to grow and change, whether or not I was around to watch. Such an obvious thing, but the truth of it — the reality of it — suddenly inhabited me.

I finally gave in. "Yeah," I said. "It did. It hurt a lot."

And then, that terrible thought again — *don't make them orphans, Alex* — and I held my kids so tight, even as my shoulder ached, but I couldn't let them go, and I couldn't let them know what I was thinking, either.

# Chapter 121

I STAYED AT THE FLETCHER ALLEN HOSPITAL in Vermont for nearly a week, which was my longest hospital stay to date, and maybe another warning to me. *How many warnings did I get?*

Around 6:00 in the evening on Friday, I received a call from Detective Jeanne Galletta out in L.A. "Alex, has anyone told you the news yet?" she asked. "I assume they have."

"What news, Jeanne? That I'm being released from the hospital tomorrow?"

"I don't know anything about that. But yesterday, Mary Wagner confessed to the murders here in L.A."

"She didn't commit those murders. Michael Bell did."

"I know that. Even Maddux Fielding knows it. Nobody believed her, but she confessed. Then, sometime last night, poor Mary Wagner hung herself in her cell. She's dead, Alex."

I sighed and shook my head a couple of times. "I'm really sorry to hear that. It's just another death Bell is responsible for. Another murder."

The following morning, and much to my surprise, I was released from the hospital. I called home with the news, and I even managed to get on a flight to Boston. From Boston I caught the hourly shuttle to D.C. Never been so happy to get on a crowded commuter plane in my life.

It was easiest to get a cab at the airport, and as I rode into Southeast around 7:00 that night, I felt a soft, warm glow spreading inside my body. *There's no place like home, there's no place like home.* I know that isn't true for everybody, but it is for me, and I also know how lucky it makes me.

The cab pulled up in front of the house on Fifth, and suddenly I was running across the small front lawn, then taking two long strides up the paint-faded front steps.

I grabbed Little Alex up in my arms, and I spun him up high in the air. It hurt, but it was worth it. I called back at the cabbie, who was leaning out his side window, a little befuddled, but even he was smiling some, in his slightly jaded D.C.-cabbie way. "I'll be right there!" I told him. "Be right with you."

"No problem. Take your time, buddy. The meter's running anyway."

I looked at Nana Mama, who had come out on the porch with my young son.

"What?" I whispered. "Tell me what happened."

"Ali is home," she said in a quiet voice. "Christine brought him here, Alex. She changed her mind again. She's not staying in the east either. Ali is home for good. Can you believe it? Now how about you? Are you home?"

"I'm home, Nana," I said. Then I looked into the beautiful eyes of my small son. "I'm home, Ali. I promise you."

*And I always keep my promises.*

# About the Author

James Patterson is the author of the two bestselling new detective series of the past decade: the Alex Cross novels, including the #1 *New York Times* bestsellers *London Bridges, The Big Bad Wolf,* and *Four Blind Mice,* and the Women's Murder Club series, including the #1 bestsellers *1st to Die, 2nd Chance, 3rd Degree,* and *4th of July.* He is also the author of the bestselling love stories *Suzanne's Diary for Nicholas* and *Sam's Letters to Jennifer.* He lives in Florida.